CROSSROADS

By

Riley Hart

Special thanks to Riley's Rebels members: Hope, Abbey, Georgina, Erin, Michelle, Karrie, Mona, Christi, and Rod for letting me use your names.

Dedication

To Mirjana for all your help. I appreciate it more than words can say.

Also, to Rod for letting me talk your ear off and ask you millions of questions.

CHAPTER ONE

"This is fucking strange." Nick Fuller stood in the middle of the empty duplex, his eyes casing the room. It wasn't a small place by any means, but it wasn't a large one, either. It had two bedrooms, and two bathrooms. The front door opened into the living room. To the right of the living room was a decent sized dining room, and behind that a nice, large open kitchen, which had been the only thing he insisted on when getting a place.

He needed a lot of room when he cooked, and a great deal of counter space. The duplex had come with both, and even a little garage off to the left. It was only the second home he'd seen, and after one quick look, he'd known it was the one. The last thing Nick wanted was to be picky about where he moved. Now was the time for low-key, easy and convenient. It was Nick's new motto. Or at least he wanted it to be.

Still, it was fucking strange to be standing in the first and only place that he'd gotten for himself, and by himself. He'd never even lived alone until the divorce, and then Jillian had moved out, leaving him in the house they'd picked together. Scratch that, the house Jillian had picked after months of searching. He'd been done with looking after about a week and had just gone with what she wanted.

Nick groaned and rubbed a hand over his face. He really fucking needed to stop thinking about his ex-wife in context to everything he did. It was an adjustment to only think of himself and what he wanted. His whole adult life had been about the two of them.

He and Jill had started dating when they were seventeen years old. It didn't take him long to realize he was in love with her. It didn't matter that they were young; Nick had known what he felt, and he wasn't the kind of man to run from that. When you loved someone you did what it took to make it work, and they had.

That all shattered when she came home, divorce papers in hand, and admitted to multiple affairs. That's what led him here.

Fuck. Why was he still thinking about his ex-wife?

Nick walked into the kitchen, going through the cabinets and mentally figuring things out as though they'd changed since he signed the lease a few days ago. Hell, he probably wouldn't be spending too much time here anyway. Not with the hours he kept at his restaurant.

Deciding his kitchen hadn't magically rearranged itself since he last saw it, Nick went to the sliding glass door, unlocked and opened it. The only downfall in the new place was the fact that he shared a backyard with whoever moved in next door. Yeah, technically they could divide it in halves, but really, they shared a yard.

The house next door was currently empty.

Knock, knock, knock. Nick turned just as the front door opened.

"Nick? It's Mom."

"Fuck," he groaned. He should have known she'd stop by. If she had it her way he would have moved home after the divorce. It had been hell living at home while he was in culinary school and dating Jill. There's no way he could go back as a single, thirty-year-old man. "Back here, Mom."

She was a small woman, with Nick's brown hair and the same dark green eyes. Nick had gotten his height from his dad, who'd passed away a couple years ago. Everything else was all his mom.

"It's a nice place. I like it." She smiled at him, but he could tell she wasn't fond of his new home. He was her only son. It was Nick and three sisters, and as ridiculous as it was, she very much believed *nothing or no one is good enough for my son.* She'd never liked Jill, for the same reasons Jill's parents hadn't liked him.

"I still don't know why you insisted on rushing to get a place. I'm in that house all by myself. I would love to have you back home. Plus, it would have given you time to put some money away for a house of your own."

A small stab of guilt hit him. It was almost a reflex to tell her he'd stay there, but then, he'd promised himself to make this time about him, and he needed to do that. He knew part of it was the fact that she didn't want to be alone. He was the youngest, the *oops* child, so his parents were a little older than most his age. When his sisters moved out, she had Nick and his father. Now, she had no one. "You know you don't have to keep the house, Mom. It's a lot of space for you alone.

Karrie already told you she and Eric would love to have you at their place." Karrie was his oldest sister.

She waved him off and shook her head. "I raised my kids in that house. I'm not leaving it until I die, and when I do, my kids will get it. Considering I'm fit as a fiddle, it'll be a while before anyone drags me out of my home."

He chuckled. She was a strong woman, he had to give her that. And the thought of losing the home made Nick's gut ache as well. "You're right. I don't know why I said that."

"Thank you. And I still think you should come home. Who's going to take care of you?"

Nick tried not to roll his eyes. His family was extremely old fashion, his mom the worst of them all. "I'm a grown man. I can take care of myself."

"That's not what I mean and you know it. You work a lot. You'll have the house to take care of. I can help out. The girls don't need me much. I can help you decorate, too. The shape of the living room is awkward. You'll have to put your couch there on the far wall for the layout to be smooth." She pointed toward a wall and Nick had to bite his tongue. She meant well, there wasn't a doubt in his mind about that, but that didn't mean she was easy to handle.

"I'll be fine, Mom. I can figure it all out. It's good for me. I went straight from living at home to getting a place with Jill. It'll be good to live by myself."

He could tell she bit her tongue, only it didn't work to keep her quiet. "And look what she did to you! It wasn't as though she was very good at being a wife, anyway."

That had been a big topic of conflict for them. She always had something to say about Jill because Jill didn't do for Nick the things she'd done for his dad. That wasn't what he wanted, though. He liked that Jill was strong; he just wished she hadn't also thought it was okay to fuck other people.

"Let's not do this, okay? Want to check out the rest of the place with me?" Nick nodded toward the hallway, slipped his arm around his mom and led her through the rest of his new home.

Things were going to be different now. His whole life had changed, but maybe this fresh start would be good for him. And this time, he vowed to have a whole hell of a lot more fun than he'd had the past few years.

***

"You share a backyard with your next-door neighbor."

Bryce Tanner shook his head as he looked at his older brother, who stood at the sliding glass door. "Good observation."

"But you share a fucking backyard with a neighbor you don't know." Jamie turned to face him, and then snapped his head back toward the yard as though it changed.

"No shit. I realize that."

"But—"

"Would you shut the fuck up? Yes, I share a backyard. I get it. I doubt I'll be spending much time out there anyway. The price was good, it's a decent size, and it's a duplex that comes with a garage. That's all I care about. I share a wall with them, too."

Jamie's brow rose. "Don't put your bed against that wall."

Bryce chuckled. "Wrong side, asshole. You're such a fucking knucklehead. I don't know how your wife deals with you."

"Cuz I know how to make her scream my name every night." Jamie winked at him.

"I'm telling Hope you said that. She's going to kick your ass and you won't get laid for a month." He nodded toward the sliding glass door. "Close that up, would ya? When is Mitch supposed to be here?"

"Right now." Their other brother stepped through the front door. Mitch was the oldest, Jamie the middle and Bryce the youngest. Mitch was one hundred percent responsible, Jamie ninety percent, and Bryce around twenty-five, if you asked their parents. It had always been that way.

"Did you know he shares a backyard with his neighbor?" Jamie asked.

"Oh, fuck," Bryce rolled his eyes as Mitch said, "So?"

"Exactly. I don't know why he's losing his shit over that. Come on, let's go empty the truck before I kick his ass. He's driving me bat-shit crazy."

The three of them walked out of Bryce's new place. His brothers were idiots, but he loved them. They'd always been close, and never let each other down even though they annoyed the hell out of each other half the time.

"Was Hope at your place when you left? She said she was picking Abbey up and they were going shopping or something," Jamie said as they made it to the U-Haul packed with all of Bryce's things.

"Pulled up when I left," Mitch replied. "FYI...Mom wants all the girls to get together soon for a spa day or something like that. Including Christi."

Bryce dropped his head back against the rental, not sure why he was surprised. Both his brothers were married, while Bryce preferred to fuck his way through life. Well, that and work on motorcycles—but the motorcycles were a new love.

He enjoyed his lifestyle too much to want to settle down. He was able to get his dick sucked when he wanted, but he also had his freedom. That wasn't such a bad gig to him. His mom wanted nothing more than for him to tie himself down like his brothers. It had been like that even before things between Bryce and his closest friend Christi, had changed.

They'd been fucked in the head to think they ever belonged together. Both Bryce and Christi knew that, which was why they'd broken up a couple months ago. The shitty part was he hadn't had the balls to tell his folks yet. It just meant they'd get on his back again about settling down and taking life seriously. Apparently Bryce was the only person in their family who sucked at that.

It didn't help that his mom wanted grandbabies, but Mitch and Abbey didn't want kids, and Jamie and Hope weren't able to have them. Adoption was a possibility, but it wasn't something they'd pursued yet, and his mom was getting restless. That meant she put all her energy into Bryce. He tried to play the youngest brother card, but being thirty-two, that didn't work anymore.

Mitch continued, "Abbey tried to put her off, saying how busy everyone was. You're lucky she loves you."

"Your wife is the best. See? There's no need for me to settle down since you two got the best ones out there. Think Mom will go for that?" Not that Christi wasn't great. She was. He loved her with all his heart. He just wasn't *in* love with her. If there was anyone who could make him settle down, it would be her.

Both his brothers laughed and basically told him he was fucked. When their mom got something into her head, she didn't let it go. She became obsessed and was as determined as they came, much like Bryce. It would be a hell of a battle, which was why he put off telling her about the break up.

"She already loves Christi like a daughter. This is going to kill her. Especially because your lame ass has kept it going for so long," Jamie added.

Fuck. What the hell had he and Christi been thinking? The thing was, for a while there, he'd thought he might die—an aneurysm that could burst. Knowing he could die did funny things to him, freaked him out and made him wonder if his mom was right and he was missing out on what the rest of his family had. But being with Christi had just been wrong, and now he had to deal with the consequences of his decision.

"Come on, let's get this stuff unloaded." An idea popped into Bryce's head and he grinned. "Maybe I'll go out tonight. You know…if I'm ever going to find the right one, I need to get out there and experience what they have to offer."

Mitch shook his head. "Christ, you're ridiculous. You know, one of these days you're going to meet a woman, and she'll end up knocking you on your ass. You'll fall head over heels for her without realizing what's happening, and by the time you do, you'll be a goner. That's what happened to me."

Yeah, somehow Bryce didn't see that coming. Not fucking likely. While Bryce's diagnosis made his Mom want him to hurry up and settle down, it just made him want to hurry up and live. He was healthy, and wanted to grab life by the balls. He'd take whatever he wanted, when he wanted. He didn't see falling in love as one of those things.

CHAPTER TWO

It had been a long night at the restaurant. It was close to midnight when Nick pulled into the driveway in front of his duplex. He'd been here two weeks, but hadn't had time to do much of anything. He was basically at *Nick's*—his restaurant—from open to close, even when he had another chef working. What the hell else did he have to do? Come home to an empty place that he was still working on furnishing?

As shitty as it sounded, that was pretty much all Nick had. He hadn't had many friends when he and Jill were married. His only friends were her friends' husbands, which made things too awkward now. Before he was either with her, them, or work, so now he was either at work or at home. So much for all that fun he was supposed to be having.

Nick stepped out of his car and closed the door. He happened to glance at the home attached to his. Someone had moved in a few days after he had. He'd seen a woman come and go a couple of times, but no one else. He didn't know if it was a family, single person or what. The garage was open now, light spilling out, so he thought, *what the hell,* and headed that way to introduce himself.

When he got closer he saw a motorcycle on a stand, tools, and a man leaning over the bike. He didn't know much about motorcycles, but he could tell this was an older one, a classic, maybe. She was a beauty.

"Hobby or profession?" Nick asked, before noticing a second bike in the garage. The other looked newer. It must be the one he rode while he worked on the other.

The dark-haired man looked up at him, a grease smudge on his forehead and a face full of dark stubble. He wore faded jeans and no shirt, more grease on his chest as well.

"Both." The man grinned at him, stood, held out his hand and then said, "Second thought, you probably don't want to shake my hand. I'm Bryce, nice to meet you."

Nick didn't give a shit about the grease. He was probably covered in food so he reached for Bryce's hand and said, "Nick. I moved in next door a few days before you did. She's pretty." He nodded toward the bike.

"Thanks. She's a 1974 Harley Davidson Shovelhead. Prettiest girl I've ever had. So pretty no one lays a hand on her except me." He winked at Nick. "You ride?" Bryce leaned against the wall of his garage and crossed his arms. His hair was a little longer on the top than the sides. He was maybe two inches shorter than Nick, but stockier.

"Hell no." Nick laughed. "I can appreciate a nice bike when I see one, but, if I'm being honest, they scare the shit out of me. You wouldn't catch me on one."

"No! Don't say that." Bryce chuckled. "It's only because you haven't been on one before. There's nothing like the freedom of cruising on a bike, wind all around you and just fucking going." His voice was all passion, and it almost made Nick want to ride. Almost.

"I'll have to take your word for it. So, do you work at a shop around here?"

"Yeah, I rent a space downtown and have a shop. I also buy old bikes, fix them up and resell them. What about you?" Bryce's deep-set eyes took him in as though he was trying to figure out what Nick did by his clothes. He'd changed before leaving work, though.

"I'm a chef. I own *Nick's.* We make comfort food, home-cooked-meal kind of stuff, with my own little twist."

"I haven't heard of it, but it sounds great. I'll have to check it out sometime. Do you want a beer?" Bryce walked over to a mini-fridge in his garage.

"No, I'm okay. Thanks. It was a long day and I have to be up early again tomorrow. I just wanted to stop in and introduce myself." Jesus, he sounded like he was eighty years old. It was a Friday night. There was no reason he couldn't have a beer with his neighbor. The urge was there to say yes, even though he'd given an automatic no. He'd only spent a minute talking to the guy, but Nick liked him already. He liked the passion in which he spoke about his bike. He could tell this man would be fun to be around, which was what he was looking for, right? Fun.

Just as he opened his mouth to change his mind, Bryce spoke. "Yeah, okay. It was great to meet you." He twisted the lid off his Corona.

"Stop by anytime."

Nick nodded, and again considered changing his mind about the drink, but he didn't. "Same to you, man. Have a good one."

Nick walked away, unlocked his place, went straight for the shower, jacked off, and then fell into bed.

Maybe he'd take Bryce's advice and give riding a motorcycle a try. He'd been given a second chance, and he didn't want to let any opportunities pass him by this time. Who the hell knew, maybe he'd fall in love with it. He could use something else in his life to be passionate about.

***

Bryce kept busy over the next week working at the shop, going out, or just screwing around in his garage. It was a Sunday, and he sat in his living room watching sports highlights on the TV when there was a knock at the door.

"Hold on." It made him an asshole, but he hoped like hell it wasn't his mom. Every time she spoke to him she either grilled him on how he felt—*do you have headaches*—or Christi, neither of which he particularly wanted to talk to her about.

He looked through the peephole to see it was his neighbor—Nate...no, Nick, he thought his name was. Bryce pulled open the door just as the man rubbed a hand over his shortly cropped brown hair. He looked a little flustered, with wide eyes and a frown that seemed pretty comfortable on his longish face.

"Hey, how's it going?" Bryce asked him.

"Not too bad. I actually came over to ask you a favor. If you're busy, no worries. I don't want to take up too much of your time, but I stopped by this little furniture discount store up the road. They're having a going-out-of-business sale and there's a furniture set I'd like for my living room. They can't deliver it until tomorrow and, hell, this is embarrassing." Nick shook his head. "But I'm having my mother over for dinner tonight and—"

"Say no more." Bryce held up a hand. "I get the mother thing. They mean well, but can be a hassle. Let me grab some shoes and my keys and we'll head out. Come in." Bryce nodded inside and Nick followed him. He liked to ride his bikes as much as possible, but he also had a truck for hauling or bad weather.

"Jesus, now I'm feeling even more behind. You moved in after me and you're already finished."

"Have a lot to do?" Bryce asked him as he pulled on his shoes and grabbed the keys to his truck off the kitchen table.

"Not too much. Mom's had a hard time the past few years, though. Since my Dad passed away and my sisters are all settled down, she's put all her energy into me. If I don't have a fully furnished house, it'll be one more thing for her to try and do for me."

Yeah, Bryce could understand that one. "I get it. We'll get'cha set up." They stepped out and Bryce locked the door behind them. "So, no family for you? Wife or anything?" He assumed not because of what Nick said, and the fact that he hadn't seen anyone other than him, but figured he'd keep conversation going by asking.

"No." Nick didn't finish speaking until they got into the truck, and when he did, Bryce could tell it wasn't a conversation he wanted to continue. "I've been separated for a while, but just finalized the divorce."

Nick pointed in which direction Bryce needed to go. "I'm sure that's not helping things with the family. I'm the youngest out of my brothers, and my mom's feeling restless. She wants grandkids, and neither of my brothers will be giving them to her, so she's harassing me about it. Apparently thirty-two is too old not to be married, but not too old to have your mother try to dictate your life."

He knew it only came out of love (and her crazy need to hold babies), but it still drove Bryce crazy. It was worse because of their scare with his health, and then the Christi thing, but Bryce didn't usually offer that information to most people. Especially the aneurysm.

"My dad just lets her run the show," Bryce finished, and Nick laughed.

It didn't take long for them to get to the furniture store. Nick purchased his couch, chair and end tables, and the two of them loaded everything into his truck and headed back.

"I appreciate the help. Do you want a beer or something? I have a few hours before I get into a time machine and become a sixteen-year-old again."

Bryce laughed at Nick's attempted joke, and then shrugged.

"Sure." What the hell? He liked the guy, and he had nothing else planned this afternoon anyway. Might as well hang out with his new neighbor for a little while.

CHAPTER THREE

They'd been talking and drinking beer for a good hour before Nick headed into the kitchen. He needed to get some vegetables chopped for dinner tonight. Bryce leaned against the counter, beer in hand, watching him. "Christ, you're going to chop a fucking finger off or something. How in the hell do you do that so fast?" Bryce interrupted their previous conversation.

"I guess I'm just good." Nick winked at him and then felt like a fucking idiot. He sounded like he was flirting with the man or something. It was strange; usually it took him a while to warm up to people, but he felt comfortable with Bryce from the start. The guy had that kind of personality, he guessed. Bryce was the kind of man to draw people in. "Or it could be the fact that I spent a few years in culinary school. That's probably a more logical explanation."

Bryce barked out a husky laugh. He liked to laugh, Nick thought. His laugh was contagious. It made Nick want to do it too.

"Okay, let's get back to what you were saying before. I didn't mean to interrupt. So you were really with your ex-wife ever since you were seventeen?"

Shit. Nick was hoping the conversation would stay changed. Even though it shouldn't be, it was almost embarrassing to him. He guessed if Bryce knew the whole story, the embarrassment would make more sense. He'd given everything to Jill since he was a kid, and it had all been for nothing. Bryce didn't know that, though. "Yep, seventeen. So nothing serious for you?" he asked.

"No, not really. I guess there was a possibility. I have a good friend, Christi. We gave it a try for a while, but it wasn't meant to be." Nick could tell there was more to the story than that, and briefly he wondered if Christi was the woman he'd seen here. He didn't ask and Bryce continued, "Now let's get back to you, because you're tripping me the fuck out."

This time it was Nick's turn to laugh. Really, it wasn't funny. Six months ago he would have been miserable, but for some reason, hearing Bryce talk about his life made him smile. He was a walking fucking cliché—the nice guy who got screwed over.

"She was your first girlfriend, too?"

"Yep. And my first fuck."

"Whoa." Bryce set his bottle down. "You married the first woman you had sex with?"

Nick tossed the vegetables into a bowl before grabbing an onion. They really needed to change the conversation, and do it quickly. "I was a kid. I loved her. I took that seriously." When Nick cared about someone, he cared one hundred percent. He didn't play games.

The look in Bryce's deep brown eyes changed. His forehead wrinkled, and before the man could say anything, Nick spoke. "Shut the fuck up. Don't feel sorry for me or I'll have to kick your ass. The fact that she was the only woman I'd been with never bothered me while we were married. Now, can we stop talking about my love life, or lack thereof?"

"No, because as fucked as it is to be talking to my male neighbor about his sex life, I'm trying to make sense of it all. I can't figure you out. Are you still in love with her?"

Onion in the bowl, Nick pushed it away. He'd thought he would always love Jill, but after seeing her callously walk away from him and into the arms of the man she'd been fucking for over a year, no, he didn't love her anymore. "No. Shouldn't you be taking notes, since you're so intent on figuring me out? Maybe I'm not even human." Nick cocked a brow at him.

"I'm starting to question whether you are." Bryce picked up his bottle, which was empty, grabbed Nick's as well, and then walked over to the recycling bin and tossed them. "Well, hell. I *am* sorry about the divorce, but if you don't love her anymore, sounds like it was for the best. And hey, you're still young, at least you can go out and make up for your serious lack of female experience."

Fuck. Nick turned away from Bryce and began wiping down the counter.

"Noooo." Bryce sounded shocked. "No, no, no, no. Don't tell me you haven't gone out and gotten a piece of ass since you've been divorced."

"Do you kiss your mama with that mouth?" Nick teased him.

"The women I'm with want to be with me just as much as I want to be with them. They're not looking for anything serious, just like I'm not. It's a win-win for both of us."

"I was giving you shit." Nick walked over to the fridge to get a few things out. He felt like he should be annoyed, but for some reason, he wasn't. Bryce had this passionate energy about him that Nick enjoyed. It made him feel electric, like he could and should go out and do all the things Bryce spoke about. It was like Bryce knew how to live, and he was teaching Nick with his words.

"You didn't answer the question."

"Do you always talk to your friends about their love lives?"

"We often talk about getting laid, yes, and I'm definitely talking about it with you. We need to take you out and get you laid, man. What are you doing next Saturday night?"

"Working," Nick told him, though he really didn't have to be.

"Can you get the night off?"

Nick sighed, closed the fridge and then leaned against it. "I don't need help getting laid."

"I beg to differ. Going off your experience, I'm thinking you do."

A laugh jumped out of Nick's mouth. Jesus, he hadn't laughed this much in a while, but he could see what Bryce was saying. It was pretty fucking ridiculous when he thought about it. Why in the hell hadn't he gone out and gotten laid? Dated? *Something*?

Shaking his head, Nick said, "I can get the night off."

Bryce clapped his hands together. "Fuck yeah. I'm taking you out to show you what you've been missing all these years."

Nick was looking forward to it.

***

Bryce left not long after they made their plans for the next weekend. He knew Nick had a few things to get taken care of before his mom showed up for dinner. His cell rang as soon as he got comfortable in his chair. He pulled it out to see Christi's name on the screen. "Hey you. Did you see the game today?" Christi asked when he picked up.

"I didn't. About to watch some highlights. I was helping my neighbor move a few things."

"Sexy, tall guy with the short, brown hair?" she asked. "He's hot. I've seen him a few times."

Bryce laughed at her. "I can't tell you if he's good-looking or not, but yeah, tall with brown hair. You're not hitting on my neighbor, though."

"Aww, you're no fun, Bry. Why not?"

"I don't know…it's just weird. I have to live next door to the guy." Though he still wasn't sure why that mattered. "He's a good guy. You'd like him. I'm taking him out next weekend. He just got out of a bad marriage." Bryce was looking forward to it. He enjoyed Nick's company.

"So of course you have to show him a good time."

Bryce cocked a brow as though Christi could see him. "Of course."

They talked for a little while longer before getting off the phone. Bryce went to the kitchen, opened a can of ravioli and thought about the food Nick had made next door. It sure as hell sounded better than fake meat and pasta in a can, but this worked for him.

His mind went back to his neighbor. Nick was different. He seemed a bit tight-assed in some ways, but not in others. Like he wanted to let loose and not give a shit about things, but wasn't sure exactly how.

Bryce was good at that. He'd show Nick how it was done.

CHAPTER FOUR

"I'll get the dishes." Nick's mom headed into the kitchen after they finished their meal.

"No, you don't need to do that. It's my house. I had you over for dinner. I'll do my own dishes."

She waved her hand at him. "Hogwash. I'll get it. It's what a good guest does."

Nick sighed. "No, a good host doesn't put the guest to work. They're dishes. I can handle them."

"I guess you're right." She smiled at him. "You know... Karrie has this friend she thinks would be perfect for you—nice and dependable. She's just what you need, a traditional, down-to-earth, family woman."

Nick groaned. Here they went again. "You know what I need?"

His mom studied him.

"To have fun. To not have a plan and to just see what happens. To live my own life." Whatever it was. Nick wasn't even sure, but he wanted to figure it out.

He could tell she didn't like his answer. "Fine, but Rachel is a nice woman. You'd like her, Nick, I know it. A mom knows her son. You'd be happy settled down and married again with the right woman…"

Nick sighed and let her finish. It was the only thing he could do when she got like this—just ride it out until she was done. It was a lot easier than arguing, because if he did, the fight would only turn into tears and how all she wanted was for her kids to be happy. And he knew that, he did, but he wished she would let him figure out how to do that on his own.

***

Bryce sat next to Nick in the busy bar. There was a live band, people dancing and hardly enough space to move. They each had a beer sitting in front of them, their first of the night.

"It feels weird not being at the restaurant," Nick told him, leaning close so Bryce could hear.

"You work every weekend?" he asked. That was the good thing about his job, he worked during the day.

"I work almost every day. Too much, from what I've been told." Nick tilted the bottle and swallowed a mouthful of beer. "Feels good, though…taking a night off."

"Good." Bryce clapped a hand down on his shoulder and then pulled it back. At the same time he saw a woman sit at the end of the bar and glance their way. She had thick, blond hair and red lips. A nice, curvy body. She cocked her brow at him, knowing he was looking.

28

"What about her?" Bryce nodded her way without trying to hide it.

Nick turned on his stool and looked over. She smiled at him; yeah, she was interested in talking to him.

"Go buy her a drink," Bryce told Nick, who'd turned back his way.

"What? No. Not yet."

Bryce rolled his eyes and tried not to laugh. "She's gorgeous, right?"

"Hell yeah," Nick replied.

"Then go buy her a drink, asshole."

"You forget I haven't done this before. Hell, I've never dated outside of my wife. I've never bought a woman a drink in a bar, or asked a woman out."

Bryce couldn't help but laugh this time. "You're not trying to date her. I think she knows that. You're trying to fuck her. Go buy her a drink. If she's not interested, she'll let you know."

Nick looked down the bar again at the woman. She gave him another smile, and then nodded as if to say come here, confirming exactly what Bryce thought. She was most likely looking for a hook-up as well.

"Go buy her a drink. If it works out, great. If not, you're out six bucks. It's not a big deal."

He watched Nick, who ran his hands down his shirt as if to make sure the damn thing wasn't wrinkled or something. Bryce fought to hold in another laugh. As simple as he was, Nick was fun to him. He liked how new things seemed to Nick, and how nervous he was, but also that he wouldn't let that hold him back.

"You're right. I don't know what the hell is wrong with me." Nick downed the rest of his beer, looked at Bryce and grinned. "What do I say?"

Bryce could feel his own eyes stretching wide. He didn't even know what to say?

"I'm kidding. I'm not that clueless. I thought your eyes were going to pop out."

"I thought my eyes were going to pop out, too."

Nick patted his shoulder. "Keep your eyes in your head. I'll be back."

"Hopefully not," Bryce said, but then felt a little stab of disappointment. He enjoyed chatting with Nick. And now he almost wished the reason they'd come out hadn't been for Nick to meet someone, but for them to hang out instead.

They could visit any time though. That wasn't the point of the night. Bryce raised his bottle at Nick, who walked toward the blonde. Bryce saw him speak to her. The man beside her moved, so Nick took the spot and then waved the bartender over.

Nick was a riot. Totally naïve in a way Bryce wasn't sure he'd ever been. Maybe naïve wasn't the right word; almost innocent, but also eager, if that made sense. Like he wanted to soak up all these experiences as though he was a child, seeing everything for the first time. Bryce had never known someone like that. He wasn't sure why he got a kick out of it. He didn't think he'd ever been that innocent.

Bryce tried not to stare at them like a weirdo, but his eyes were drawn to the duo. Nick had gotten them both a drink. They were speaking to each other. She kept touching him—his arm, his leg, his shoulder. Nick didn't return any of them, but he did keep talking. She'd laugh and then he'd laugh.

It was a good thirty minutes later when he wondered why in the fuck he was sitting here watching his neighbor get picked up by a woman, but wasn't trying to pick anyone up himself.

It was time to change that.

Before he had the chance, the woman stood, leaned forward, mouth close to Nick's ear. "There ya go," Bryce whispered to himself. What the hell was this? He was treating Nick like his project or something.

But then Nick backed up. The woman looked confused, rolled her eyes and walked away.

"What the hell was that?" Bryce asked when Nick made it back to him.

"She wanted to fuck me in my car."

Bryce waited for the punch line. Waited for him to continue. Waited for *something* and then… "Umm…and that's a bad thing?"

Nick looked at him like Bryce had suddenly grown a second head.

"Yes. I don't want to sleep with someone in my car who I've known for thirty minutes. Hell, at least say we can go to a hotel room."

Well, when he said it like that, it made Bryce feel like a dickhead.

But still...this was sex they were talking about. Bryce couldn't find words. This was going to be harder than he thought.

CHAPTER FIVE

"The night's still young. We have plenty of time." Bryce scratched his arm as he spoke.

Nick knew he was being ridiculous. He found something wrong with every woman he'd talked to tonight. In his defense, he had gotten one phone number. The woman had been beautiful and nice. Plus, she hadn't wanted to go home for a quick fuck. Yeah, he knew that had been the theme for tonight, but once here, it was just too weird for him. As much as his dick didn't agree with him, sleeping with a random woman he knew nothing about just didn't work for him. He wanted a connection, to actually know someone he was with. He couldn't get that in short conversations at a bar.

He knew Bryce thought he was crazy, and maybe most people would, but that's just who Nick was. "Three brothers, huh?" he asked Bryce, trying to make conversation. He was done making attempts to get laid tonight. He'd rather sit here and just enjoy himself.

The bartender set an order of potato skins down for Bryce. "This is the only place I order these. They're my favorite. And yeah. Mitch is the oldest. His wife is Abbey. She's a real sweetheart. She's a doctor and he's an accountant. Jamie is the middle. He's a dumbass, but I love him. He thinks he's a comedian, but really he's a veterinarian. His wife is Hope. They're both these fun-loving, adventurous people."

Sounded like Bryce to Nick. He was fun-loving. It made him wonder, though… "Your parents are happily married?"

Bryce nodded. "They are."

"Yet you've never had the urge? You have happily married people all around you, but you've never wanted to settle down?" Nick hadn't planned on falling for the first woman he dated, but he also always knew he would settle down and get married. He was okay with being that guy. Then he remembered something else Bryce had said. He *had* come close to something serious with his friend. "What happened with the friend you told me about?"

He wasn't sure why he really wanted to know.

"She didn't break my heart or anything, if that's what you're thinking. We were together for all the wrong reasons. At first, we didn't realize it. Some things had happened, and Christi and I clung to each other, then neither wanted to tell the other when we realized what we were doing. She's a special woman, just not the one for me. The shitty part is, I haven't told my parents yet. They think we're still together." Bryce leaned forward, resting his arms on the bar. "So, the cooking thing… Tell me about that." Again, Nick could tell Bryce didn't want to go into too much information about his friend, and he let it go, even though he really fucking wanted to know why he would let his family believe they were together.

"I've always loved cooking. It makes me feel good to give someone a meal. The initial program was only two years. Jill and I were serious by then, and I wanted to settle into a career so we could begin our lives. I've never enjoyed anything the way I enjoy cooking."

He didn't want it to sound like he'd gone into culinary because of Jill. He did, and always would love it, but he'd also made that decision in part because it was the most logical one for them.

"What about you and bikes?"

"It wasn't like that for me." Bryce shrugged. "I didn't know what the hell I wanted right away. When I first got out of high school, I wanted nothing to do with college. I decided to follow in my dad's footsteps and work for his carpet business. I was young and thought it would be easy. My parents loved the idea, because neither of my brothers followed his path, and honestly, I think they were scared if I didn't do that, I wouldn't do anything. I didn't realize how much I would hate it, though. It wasn't for me. I did odd jobs and then decided to try college. I knew my family thought I should go. I'm the only Tanner kid who hadn't. I tried a computer program, a business program. Then came bartending, another school program unfinished, and a very pissed off, confused family. They thought I should pick something and stick with it. But I need to feel passionate about what I'm doing, and I hadn't found that yet. They saw it as indecisiveness."

Nick looked over at him, and he wondered if Bryce could tell he didn't understand it, either. Not that he was looking down at Bryce, because he wasn't. Nick just sort of followed in the path he'd taken

35

without much thought.

"A few years ago Christi started dating this guy who rode a bike. He wanted in her pants, so he let me drive it. And that was it. I was in love. I knew it was what I wanted. Bought a cheap bike, and taught myself some things about it. Got it put together enough to drive and I rode her all the time. I got my certificate later, and worked as an apprentice at a motorcycle repair shop at the same time. It was automatic for me, though. I love the freedom of riding. It's like there's nothing in the world but me and my bike. I think about all those other programs I tried, and working with my dad. They never would have made me feel like this. I'm glad I held out to find my passion, ya know? To find what I love and can't live without."

"Good for you. It takes balls to do that." Nick wouldn't have been able to.

Still, the way he talked...yeah Nick could hear the passion about bikes, but it sounded like he didn't quite feel that passion in the rest of his life. Not really. In a lot of ways, that didn't make sense. Bryce obviously lived his life the way he wanted, and had a good time doing it, but there was something there that Nick couldn't put his finger on. Something familiar.

Bryce laughed and added, "Jesus, I feel like I'm getting sentimental for no good reason."

"Yeah, that's probably my fault. Wanna shoot some pool?" Nick asked and Bryce said yes. They shot two games, each winning one. They found a booth afterward and sat back, talking again. They were both football fans, and both ex-smokers. They'd already discovered they were both the youngest out of their siblings, both grew up in a similar middle-class kind of family, only Nick's more traditional than Bryce's. Both of them were the only ones not married out of their siblings, and both had secret addictions to the TV show *Gold Rush*.

It wasn't until the bartender called last round that Nick realized how late it was. That they'd sat here talking for hours, thoughts of anything other than their conversation long gone. He couldn't remember when he'd last been so comfortable, and had such a good time.

***

Bryce felt like an ass. He'd promised to take Nick out and help him have a good time, yet he'd sat around and talked to the man all night. They'd agreed to go out and try again the next Saturday night, but it had gone down much like the first. The only difference was Nick didn't talk to anyone except Bryce and the bartender all night. He didn't approach a single woman.

There was something infectious about the guy that Bryce liked. He had this easy charm about him. He wasn't trying to be anyone or anything other than who he was. Nick didn't have a problem laughing at himself, or laughing at Bryce, either. They did a lot of that together, laughing. Bryce enjoyed becoming friends with him.

The third Saturday, Nick told him he'd officially changed his schedule so he would be off each week. He hadn't given himself time off on the weekends in years so he figured he was due a little weekend fun.

That third Saturday they'd worked together in the backyard for a few hours and then went out and had beer and pizza.

Bryce forced him to play videos games in the arcade and spent half of the night laughing at Nick, who really fucking sucked at games.

"You're like a sixteen-year-old trapped in a thirty-two-year-old's body," Nick said when they headed home that night. "Video games, beer, and pizza and you're happy."

"So?" Bryce replied, and Nick shrugged.

"Just making sure you know." And then Nick smiled and Bryce wasn't sure why. The grin made him smile, too, and he wasn't sure the why of that, either.

What he did know was that much the way it had been when he met Christi, he felt an immediate closeness with Nick. From the start he knew Christi would be an important part of his life, and as fucked up as it sounded, he knew that was true of Nick as well.

CHAPTER SIX

Nick was exhausted.

It hadn't been a particularly busy night at work, but it still had felt long. Maybe because it had been a little slower than usual it made the hours drag by. His body felt like weights had been added to it as he dragged himself into the gas station on his way home.

His tank was full. He hadn't wanted to stop, but he knew if he didn't, he'd just drive himself crazy.

"Can I help you?" the cashier asked as he stepped up to the counter.

"I was in here around noon to get gas. I didn't realize it until I was already at work, but two tens were stuck together, so I got an extra one with my change."

The guy stared at Nick as though he'd sprouted another head. "You're bringing back ten dollars from twelve hours ago?"

Was that a trick question? "Well, yeah, it's not mine. I was only supposed to get ten, but I was given twenty." Was it really that rare that a person would return something that didn't belong to them?

"The drawer from earlier has already been counted down. They'll already have considered it short…"

That didn't matter to Nick. They could put the ten back. He knew that. He still wouldn't keep something that wasn't his. "Leave them a note that you're ten over because the drawer earlier was ten under."

He reached out and took the bill from Nick's hand. "Oh…yeah…okay. Thanks, man."

Nick headed out, and made it back to his truck before looking at the bar that sat across the street. He really needed to get home, but then he thought about how shitty Bryce ate. He often tried to bring him home food from the restaurant. Since he spaced it today, Nick slammed the door to his car and jogged across the street.

No, potato skins from a bar still weren't the best food, but Bryce liked them, and the guy had been really great to Nick. He appreciated the friendship, and the fact that Bryce had taken him out every week for the past three weeks. The least he could do was grab the guy some food. Half of the time he was still working on the bike he loved so much when Nick got home from work.

He laughed when he thought about the time they'd spent there the other night. How Bryce said it would be easier to work on it at the shop, but that he was scared someone would touch it there. He was really fucking serious about no one touching his bike.

It didn't take them long to make the potato skins and then Nick was on the road again. He was late. Bryce could very well be inside by now. He felt a slight disappointment at that. They'd fallen into a pattern together that Nick realized he kind of counted on. He'd miss not being able to at least shoot the shit with Bryce for a few minutes at the end of the day.

Which might actually be weird of him to feel, so he decided not to think about it.

He passed Bryce's house to pull into his own driveway. The light was still on, Bryce sitting on a bench as he looked at the bike in front of him. When Nick pulled in, he looked over, nodded and smiled.

It was automatic, the smile he gave back, even though he wasn't sure Bryce could see it in his dark vehicle. It was a ridiculous thing to think about, but he wasn't sure he ever smiled as much as he did with Bryce.

Nick grabbed the food and got out of the car. A few minutes before, he'd been exhausted, but the tiredness seemed to have disappeared.

"You're late. Busy day?" Bryce asked as Nick stepped into the garage. He pulled up a chair that Bryce had brought out there for him.

"No, not really. We were slow, actually. It made me tired as hell. I wanted to go home and crash, but I had to stop by the gas station on my way. They gave me an extra ten bucks earlier so I wanted to return it."

Bryce's dark brows pulled together. "Really?"

"Yes. Damn, why does everybody act shocked by that? You would have done the same."

Bryce shrugged. "I'd like to think so. I definitely would have if I'd only made it to my car, but a whole twelve hours later… You're like a saint. Oh, check that out, Saint Nick. I didn't even do that on purpose."

Laughing, Nick shook his head. "You're such a fucking idiot."

"Listen to that language coming out of your mouth, Saint Nick."

He winked and Nick shifted in his seat, his skin warmed though he wasn't quite sure why. "Oh, hey, I almost forgot, I stopped by the bar and got you some potato skins."

He held the box out toward Bryce, but Bryce didn't grab it. He looked at Nick confused, almost the same way the cashier had earlier.

"You stopped by a bar at midnight to get me food?" he asked. Well, when he said it like that, it made Nick feel weird.

"Yeah, is there something wrong with that?" When Bryce didn't reply right away, he added, "You eat like shit. Even this is better than canned food. I just thought it would be a nice thing to do."

The quiet between them stretched way too fucking long for Nick's comfort.

"You're a nice guy, Saint Nick."

"Don't call me that."

"You're still a nice guy."

"That's a good thing."

"I know," Bryce replied. "You're a different kind of nice than most people, though. Kind. There's a different between being nice and kind.

Me? I'm a sarcastic asshole. You? You're kind. It's refreshing." And then he pushed to his feet, and for some reason, Nick's pulse sped up. That was important to him, being kind. He wasn't sure he realized how much until this second.

"I'll go wash my hands. You want a beer?"

Nick nodded, and then Bryce went inside. Nick didn't move, just sat there thinking about what Bryce said.

***

Bryce washed his hands and dried them with a towel. The mini-fridge in his garage was empty so he grabbed two beers from the kitchen.

He'd been thinking about turning in for the night when Nick got home. He probably wouldn't have. It was almost like they had a nightly routine to talk for a few minutes. He would have missed giving Nick shit if he'd gone in before Nick pulled up.

Jesus, the man really was a good guy. Like he'd said, kind, not just nice.

When Bryce got back to the garage, Nick was where he'd left him sitting in the chair. He had his feet up on the stand where Bryce had the Shovelhead. "Hey, watch those feet around my girl. You accidentally kick her and we're going to have words, you and me."

"Have words, huh?" Nick raised a brow at him, mockingly.

"Don't give me shit. That's my job, not yours." Bryce pulled the bench closer to Nick, grabbed the food, sat down, and put his feet up beside Nick's.

After opening the container, he held it out toward Nick. "Have one. They're fucking heaven."

Nick picked a potato skin from the box. Bryce waited until he took a bite and then asked, "was I right?"

Nick shrugged. "They're okay. I could make them better."

"Look at you. Who would have thought you'd have a cocky bone in your body?"

The right side of Nick's mouth rose and Bryce could tell he was holding in a laugh. *Cocky bone.* Yeah...he could see how what he'd just said sounded wrong. "Pervert. No more *cocky bone* talk."

Rolling his eyes, Nick took another bite. Bryce popped one into his mouth as well. He'd been fucking starved. He hadn't eaten dinner tonight.

"So have you always been such a do-gooder?" Bryce asked. "Going back to the gas station. Getting me potato skins."

"I'm not a *do-gooder.* It's important for me to do the right thing. There's nothing wrong with that."

No, there wasn't. That was one of the things Bryce liked about him the most. He was genuine in a world where not a lot of people were. "Never said there was anything wrong with who you are." Which was true, but he wasn't sure he'd meant to really say it.

Neither of them spoke for a minute after that. They sat there and shared the rest of Bryce's potato skins. He almost teased Nick about it—

they were obviously better than Nick originally said—but he didn't.

When they finished, Bryce threw the trash away, and then there they were again, just sitting there. It was late. He had no reason not to head inside and hit the sack, but still he didn't move.

"What's so special about her?" Nick asked after a few minutes.

"Who?"

"The bike."

Hmm… Bryce wasn't sure he knew how to put it into words. He'd never had someone ask him that before, but for some reason, he was glad that Nick did. "Other than the fact that she's a pretty bike? That she's a good bike? I don't know…I guess it's just that she's mine. It wasn't running when I got it. It was old and hadn't been taken care of. I'm tearing it apart and rebuilding her. When something's not perfect, I start over. There's no rush, no one telling me what they want me to do, and when it's done, I'll be able to say that I did that, that I made this bike exactly what I want, by myself. No one but me." Bryce didn't know why that mattered to him, but it did. "I'll tell you a secret. Sometimes when I'm out here working on her, I'm really not. I'll fuck around, check things out, but not really work on her. When she's done, she's done. Not sure why I want to make it last."

"Because you're in love… you don't want to say goodbye."

Even though he wouldn't be saying goodbye to the bike, what Nick said somehow made sense to him. And yeah, he was in love with what he was doing to this bike. It took Nick voicing it for Bryce to realize why he wanted this to last. "Yeah, I guess you're right."

"I think my dad was disappointed that I wasn't as much into things like this as I was cooking. He never said anything, and it wasn't that we weren't close or anything. I loved being outdoors, playing sports, he went to all my games as a kid; but as much as I loved that stuff, I always loved cooking more." Bryce didn't turn, but out of the corner of his eye, he saw Nick look at him. "I've never said that aloud before. That I think part of me was a disappointment to him."

Bryce was honored Nick said it to him. "You know what you love, that's all that matters. Don't ever feel bad about that. It takes most people a lot longer to figure out what makes them happy. You always knew and you went for it. I respect the hell out of you for it." This time Bryce did turn to Nick. "Wanna help me?" He couldn't believe he'd just asked that, but he had, and he was okay with it.

"Do I want to help you with what?"

"The bike." His Shovelhead. His baby. The bike that he wanted to do by himself. What in the fuck made him ask Nick that? Still, he added, "I'll teach you a few things."

"No." Nick shook his head. "I can't do that. This is your project."

"I wouldn't have asked if I didn't want you to." And that was the truth. Bryce didn't play games. He said what he meant. "We won't work on her too long. We won't do much, but you can help me do a few things tonight."

There was a pause, and then Nick smiled. "Yeah, sure, that'd be great."

CHAPTER SEVEN

They worked on the bike for a little over an hour. Bryce was more serious than he usually was when he spoke about the Shovelhead. His eyes never left Nick as he'd instruct him what to do, like he was afraid Nick would screw up.

He didn't. It wasn't that he was completely ignorant when it came to these things. He understood how mechanics worked. He'd fixed plenty of things that had gone wrong on his cars in the past, but this felt different. Partly because the motorcycle was Bryce's baby. Because Bryce kept the bike here so no one else could touch it, yet he let Nick now. And he seemed to enjoy that they were working on it together. Also because tonight, working on this bike right now, felt like something he was doing for his dad. Something Bryce gave him to do for his father, and Nick hadn't realized it, but he might have needed that.

When they finished working on the bike, he figured they'd make their way to their separate houses for the night...but they didn't. It was nearly two in the morning, but Bryce grabbed them another beer and they sat there drinking them.

They didn't talk about anything important—crazy shit they'd done when they were kids, trips they'd taken, things like that. Time kept passing and they kept thinking of things to talk about.

He enjoyed talking to Bryce, enjoyed hearing how Bryce saw the world, because in some ways it was so incredibly different than Nick, while in others it was the same.

"It's five, you have to be at work in a few hours," Nick told Bryce. It was Wednesday morning and they both had to work today.

"Yeah…I know."

Nick reached out, stretching his arms. When he did, his arm brushed hot skin, rough hair, and he pulled back, realizing it was Bryce's arm and they'd stretched at the same time. "Sorry."

"I forgive you." Bryce winked at him. "Guess we should go in." He stood and his knee popped when he did.

"How old are you again? Your bones are cracking." Nick teased, and Bryce shook his head, smiling.

"Who's the one who couldn't hang? I could have sat out here all night, old man," Bryce teased him back.

He could have sat out here all night as well, but still, he stood. "Thanks…for letting me work on the bike with you. I enjoyed it. You didn't have to do that. I appreciate that you did." More than he thought he would.

"No problem. I was scared the world might end, but looks like it didn't." Bryce winked. "I was glad to do it. We're still on Saturday night, right?"

Nick was counting on it.

***

It was the fourth Saturday in a row he'd spend with Nick when he got a phone call from Christi. The summer was just starting, and the Virginia air warming around them. "Is there a reason I haven't seen you in a month?" she asked.

He'd been so busy working or with Nick, he hadn't even realized it had been so long. Saturdays weren't the only day he and Nick spent together. Nick would visit after work while Bryce messed with the motorcycle in the garage, or they'd hang out earlier in the day or the mornings sometimes, too.

"Miss me?"

"Nope. I just know your life is boring without me in it. I just figured you were due a little bit of fun. You're seriously a downer without me, Bry."

He shook his head and laughed at her. "You're funny, and you have a big head."

"See? Who could handle life without their funny, big-headed friend in it every day. What's up? Where ya been?"

Bryce still lay in bed, not wanting to get up, but he knew he had to make a trip to the store and stop by the shop for an hour or two, so he pushed up. "Nowhere. Work and hanging out with Nick, really."

"Hot neighbor Nick?"

Bryce groaned. "Would you stop calling my neighbor hot? It's weird."

"No…it's really not."

Jesus, leave it to Christi to push things. "Well, it is to me. You're my ex-girlfriend and he's my friend."

"I was your friend before I was your girlfriend, and your friend again after. I think you're weird. And I miss you. You broke my heart a few months ago, and now you can't even hang out with me." Bryce froze, a small ache forming in his chest. Was that what she thought? Was that what he was doing? It had been mutual, their break-up.

"Christi?" And then there was loud laughter through the line. Bryce almost hung up the phone as he made it to the bathroom to turn the shower on. "Fuck you."

"Do you know how many times a week I wake up crying at night because I miss you?"

"Shut up," he said, fully aware that he sounded like he was pouting.

"Bryce, my heart will never be the same without you! How can I live without *your* big head and magic penis!?"

Right now he really, really hated his friend. "I'm hanging up on you now. Good-bye."

"No! Wait. I'm giving you shit."

"I really have to go," he told her. "I have some shit to do, and then we're going to barbeque this afternoon."

"You and hot neighbor Nick? What time should I be there?"

He rolled his eyes at her, but then said, "three." He realized he wanted his best friend to meet Nick. Wanted them to get along, since Christi had and would always be a big part of his life...and Nick was quickly becoming a part of his life, too.

CHAPTER EIGHT

Nick made his way next door as soon as he heard Bryce's motorcycle rev in the driveway. "You have to let me marinate the meat."

He pulled off his helmet as he sat on his bike in the garage, and then turned it off. "Oh, I do, huh?" He pulled his leg around the bike and stood. "And that sounds kinky. Be careful who you're saying shit like that to." Bryce winked at him and Nick rolled his eyes.

"I'm telling you, you won't regret it. It'll be the best steak you ever put in your mouth." He'd kick Bryce's ass if he tried to make his last statement sound like something it shouldn't. Bryce opened his mouth and Nick held up a hand. "Shut up and give me the meat." It was surprising to him how comfortable he felt around the guy. They'd fallen easily into a friendship, when Nick hadn't done that in years.

Bryce slid the backpack off, opened it and handed two bags to Nick. "I need to clean up a bit while you go play with the meat. I'll be out soon. Oh, and Christi called. She's feeling left out so I invited her over to hang out with us. Is that cool?"

"Your ex-girlfriend Christi?" he asked on reflex. He wasn't sure why it mattered who it was. "Or I guess I should say, your current girlfriend, depending on who's around?"

"Ex works. Better yet, just call her a friend. That's all she ever should have been, anyway. She's great. You'll love her. See ya in a few." Bryce walked over to the door that led into his house, but for some reason, Nick didn't move. It was a strange concept to him—the fact that they were so close, had been together, broke it off, but were still close. Oh, and add in the fact that they kept their break-up from Bryce's parents. It was none of his business one way or another, but...he didn't know. It was just weird to him. Probably because his only relationship experience was Jill, and she'd screwed him over so royally.

Still, he was used to it just being the two of them, and now they'd have someone else with them. *And, I sound like a fucking weirdo. What the hell is wrong with me?*

"You plannin' on marinating your meat in my garage, or what?"

Yeah. He guessed that probably wouldn't work too well. Nick wasn't sure what the hell was wrong with him. "You're a riot. See you in a bit." He walked out of the garage, around the house and back to his place.

As Nick tenderized their steaks, and added all his favorite ingredients to the marinade, his mind went back to his neighbor. There was something he wasn't telling Nick when it came to Christi. He had a feeling it was something pretty personal to Bryce, and considering he had no obligation to tell Nick jack-shit, he needed to quit worrying about it.

It didn't take Nick long to get everything put together before he wrapped the meat in saran wrap so it could soak in the mixture he'd created.

He changed into a pair of blue jeans and a black T-shirt, the whole time wondering what Christi would be like. Since she was so close with Bryce, he had a feeling they would be similar, which meant Nick was in a whole hell of a lot of trouble. He could hardly keep up with Bryce sometimes, so he had no idea how he was supposed to keep up with Bryce and the female version of him.

A few minutes later there was a knock on his sliding glass door. The only possibility was Bryce so he called out, "It's open." He heard the door sliding in its track and then Bryce spoke.

"We need to get some outdoor furniture for back here. I brought a couple chairs from my kitchen since my shit's not as nice as yours."

"Yeah, I thought about that. I was actually thinking of going and picking some up soon. It's pretty barren back there. Though it looks a whole lot better since we cleaned it up."

Nick looked over to see Bryce standing in the doorway, his hands above his head, grabbing onto the ledge. His T-shirt pulled up, showing dark hair and taut skin on his lower stomach. *What the fuck?* Nick jerked his eyes upward and they landed on muscled biceps as Bryce gripped the upper part of the door.

Nick shook his head, quickly turning around. *What the fuck was that? Why did I just notice Bryce's body?* He shook his head again, as though that would make the thoughts fall out.

"You okay over there, buddy? You're shaking your head like you're a dog and have something in your ear."

That comment kicked all the strange thoughts right out of Nick's head and he let out a loud laugh. "You're an asshole."

"So I've been told." Bryce shrugged and walked inside. As he did, Nick heard a car idling outside.

"Sounds like your girlfriend is here."

"My friend, and you're an asshole, too."

Bryce stepped around him and opened the door. "Over here," he called. Nick leaned against the back of the couch as he waited for Bryce's friend to come in.

As soon as she did, she gave Bryce a kiss on the cheek and then Nick a big-ass smile. She was beautiful—thick red hair, curvy, a few freckles on her nose and cheeks. She was tiny, more than a foot shorter than him, but one grin from her and he could tell her personality was the biggest in the room.

"Well, if it isn't hot neighbor Nick. I'm Christi. It's great to finally meet you."

Oh yeah. He was definitely in for it with these two.

***

How was he surprised that Christi went there? She was just as big a flirt as he was, and the fact that Bryce told her he didn't want her to flirt with Nick would make her do it even more. "You'll have to excuse her. She has no filter and enjoys pissing me off." Bryce wrapped an arm around her shoulders and ruffled her hair like she was ten.

"Bry! Stop it before I embarrass you in front of your friend." She pushed away and Nick laughed at them. It was a husky laugh, and one Bryce was quickly becoming accustomed to. The man laughed nearly as much as he did.

"As I was saying." Christi straightened her shirt and held out her hand. "It's nice to meet you hot neighbor—"

"Yes. He's hot. We get it. Jesus." When two sets of wide eyes whipped his way he realized what he said. "We get that *you* think he's hot. You know what I meant. Be good or I'm kicking you out." Bryce put both hands on Christi's shoulders and led her toward the back door. Nick followed behind them and the trio went outside.

"Want a beer? We'll get you a beer," Bryce told Nick, who waited in the backyard as he and Christi went inside his house.

"You really don't want me to have a crush on your friend. What's up with that? You change your mind and realize you're madly in love with me?" she asked as Bryce pulled three bottles of beer out of the fridge.

"Yes. Please, marry me. Make me the happiest man in the world. I don't know what I'd do without you," Bryce said with a straight face. Christi punched him, almost making him drop the bottles.

"Shut up."

She turned for the door but Bryce called out, "hey," and she stopped. "Don't mention the aneurysm thing, okay?"

Christi's brows pulled together. "I wasn't planning on it, but okay. Why?"

He shrugged. People got weird when they realized someone had recently been sick, or nearly died. He'd had major surgery on his brain, and he didn't want anyone to look at him differently because of it. He didn't want Nick to.

"You're being weird. You okay?" She was nothing but serious now. He really did love her. Not the romantic kind, but he didn't know what he would do without this woman in his life.

And he *was* being a little weird, only he couldn't put his finger on exactly why. "I'm fine. Let's go. I wouldn't want you to waste any of your time with hot neighbor Nick."

CHAPTER NINE

"So, we're in this bar and I notice a woman checking Bryce out," Christi said as the three of them sat in chairs outside with their feet up on the porch.

"Which honestly, is an everyday occurrence for me—the women wanting me, not the bar." Bryce shrugged and Christi rolled her eyes.

"Probably because they've never seen a head as big as yours," she replied.

"They don't realize that until they get my pants off."

Nick laughed. Christi hit him and then Bryce rubbed his arm. "She's violent. Stop trying to beat me up and tell the story."

Nick felt a strange pang in his chest watching the two of them together. He could understand why they'd gone from friends to lovers; he just didn't get the going from lovers back to friends. They finished each other's sentences and obviously had a lot of love for one another. Had he ever had that with anyone? Looking at them, he couldn't remember he and Jill being that way. And there was a quiet part of him, buried deep inside, that was jealous that Christi had it with Bryce.

It made sense, he guessed. Bryce was the first person he'd really met and hung out with in years because it was who he wanted to be friends with and not a friend of his wife. He was the first person he had besides his family who wasn't attached to Jill, and obviously Nick was becoming a territorial bastard over friends he had no right to be territorial over.

"So anyway," Christi continued. "I pretended to have an argument with him."

"I was confused as fuck," Bryce cut her off. "Here we are having a drink and then she's suddenly mad at me because I don't want her!"

"I can see how that would be confusing," Nick told them and then waited for the friends to finish their story.

"Then she just walks away," Bryce says.

Christi cuts him off. "Shh. This is my story. So then I just walk away." Both Nick and Bryce laughed at how she said the same thing Bryce had, but she just continued. "I walk over to the girl, looking sad, start talking about how sexy he is, how I just want one night with him, but he's not the type to just hook up."

Nick almost choked on his food. That was exactly the type Bryce was.

"I see you know him well. So, this woman, it was obvious she was the competitive type. I finish my sob story and then walk away. Bryce is confused out of his mind. Ten minutes later I peek back inside and guess who's sitting next to Bryce? That was the first time I helped him get laid."

"Now wait a minute. I didn't need your help. I could have done it on my own."

"Of course you could, sweetie." Christi pat his leg but then winked at Nick.

The stories kept coming after that—high school, and afterward. She spoke about Bryce's family like they were her own. The whole time Nick wondered why they had broken up. Why they were still pretending to be together for Bryce's parents and why they weren't just really together.

He wanted that—a close relationship with someone. Wanted it so fucking much it made his chest ache. He'd always known he wasn't the kind of man for a string of random hook-ups. It's part of the reason why what happened with Jill devastated him so much. Part of the reason he'd stayed and tried to tough things out when in hindsight he should have seen them pulling apart.

He wanted to be with someone he felt comfortable with, someone who knew him, who laughed with him. Unfortunately for him, the only person he'd ever had that with was the ex-wife, who left him for another man.

***

"Go long!" Bryce called out as Nick jogged backward. Bryce pulled back his arm and threw the football to the other man. Christi went after him, and then the two of them stumbled on each other, falling to the

61

ground.

Christi had a hand on Nick's bare chest. Bryce and Nick had both taken their shirts off not long into the game. It was fairly dark, the porch lights and the moon making it so they could see. She dropped her head back and laughed, Nick doing the same, when Bryce felt it—the cramp in his gut at the sight of the two of them together.

His oldest friend and his newest one. It was great that they got along, but...well, he guessed he'd never really played well when he wasn't the center of attention. Some might call it a character flaw, but all Bryce knew was it was just who he was.

"Okay, the two of you. That's enough. You suck, Nick. You weren't supposed to let her get the ball. Throw it back to me and I'll show you how it's done."

Christi used the hand Nick offered her to stand, and Bryce stood around watching them like an idiot. He walked over and downed the rest of the beer in his bottle.

"I'm done. I'm going to puke if I play anymore. You two finish." Christi walked over to the porch, sat on it and leaned her head against the house. "I'm drunk."

Bryce was feeling it as well. Still he wasn't ready to go in yet. "Toss it back," he nodded at Nick, who threw him the football.

They kept that up for a few minutes, random comments from Christi here or there about hot, sweaty men playing with balls.

When Nick threw the ball to him again, Bryce caught it and cocked a brow at his friend. "Betcha I can score on you."

"You can try, but I don't think you'll get very far," Nick countered.

Game on.

Bryce hugged the football close to his body as Nick moved toward him. He flexed his arm muscles as he did and Bryce couldn't help but laugh. "Not sure what you think you're gonna do with those little things." Really, the guy had a nice body. That was okay to think, wasn't it? He didn't mean nice like he wanted him, but he obviously kept in shape, with defined muscles and a six-pack.

"We'll see about that." Nick ran toward him. Bryce faked left, then went right, but Nick didn't fall for it the way he'd hoped so he hung back. "Giving up already?" Nick asked.

Not fucking likely. Bryce made a quick move, ran right and slipped past Nick. It didn't last long before the other man's arms were around him—sweaty skin against sweaty skin, and then they were both on the ground, a tangle of limbs.

"Oh, fuck. I'm too old and drunk for this shit." Bryce dropped his head back and looked up at the sky. His chest heaved in and out. Nick was touching him, and not moving, their arms entwined and Nick's leg over his.

Umm...he wasn't sure this was normal. But they were both drunk. For all he knew Nick didn't even realize he was half lying on Bryce.

"Yeah, me, too." And then he was gone. No, not really gone, but he'd pulled away. Stopped touching Bryce the way he knew the man should. The air on his skin where Nick had touched suddenly felt like too much.

He'd definitely had too much to drink.

They lay side by side, both of them looking up, their breaths mingling, for what felt like an eternity.

It was Nick who spoke first. "Thanks for letting me hang out with you guys tonight. I had fun."

Yeah...Bryce had, too. They always had fun together, though. They'd been having fun together for weeks. "Nothing to thank me for. Glad you were here, and really, Christi is the one who crashed our night."

"No...I see it. Why your mom wants the two of you together. It fits. I'm a little jealous, if I'm being honest. I'm trying to remember if Jill and I ever had that...if it wasn't with her, there's no one else I could have ever had it with."

Those words found their way to Bryce's chest. Nick was a good guy. He deserved to have whatever he wanted. "You'll get it. Until then, you're stuck with me. I'm not a woman, but I can be a good friend."

It took Nick a few minutes to respond, making Bryce suddenly feel stupid. It wasn't something he typically felt. Normally he didn't give a shit what people thought.

"Yeah...yeah, you are a good friend."

Bryce's lungs deflated with the heavy breath he released. "It's late." He pushed off the ground and stood, then held his hand out for

Nick. Nick paused a second, and then let Bryce help him up. His hand was strong, sweaty, the same size as Bryce's.

He pulled back, glanced at the porch to see Christi had her eyes closed. He nodded her way. "I should get her inside. She doesn't need to drive tonight."

Nick nodded and then the two of them walked to their side-by-side porches.

Bryce kneeled and said, "Come here, sweetheart." He lifted Christi into his arms and she wrapped hers around his neck.

Then...nothing. He just stood there watching Nick, who stood on his own porch watching them. Their eyes didn't leave each other as the minutes ticked by, yet he had no idea why.

"Good night," Bryce finally said.

"Good night."

He waited until Nick went inside before Bryce went into his own place. He left the slider open since he couldn't close it with Christi in his arms. He took her to the spare bedroom and laid her on the bed. It wasn't until he got to the door that she spoke in a quiet, sleepy voice. "I like him a lot."

Bryce crossed his arms. Damn it. He could tell she liked him. It made him feel raw. "Don't hurt him. He wants something that will last." He felt foolish for taking Nick out to get laid. It was obvious anonymous sex wasn't his thing. He respected Nick for that even if he did give him a hard time.

"No...not like that." Christi didn't open her eyes as she continued. "As a friend. I'm not going to try and sleep with him. I get it now."

Bryce had no idea what she meant by *I get it now,* but he had to admit, he was glad Christi didn't want to get together with Nick. "You're drunk. Get some sleep. I'll see ya in the morning." Bryce closed the door behind him, went to the slider and closed it as well.

After a shower, Bryce climbed into bed, but he couldn't make his eyes close. Tonight had been...the most fun he'd had in a long time, and that was saying a lot. Bryce was pretty fond of a good time, and made sure to have it often—riding, going out, fucking—yet just hanging out at home tonight had been a million times better than that. He felt content...settled, in a way he never had. In a way he had never thought he wanted.

He rolled over, hoping that Nick enjoyed himself as much as Bryce had.

Still...his eyes didn't close.

***

Nick couldn't sleep. He lay in bed thinking about the two people next door. Did they still fuck each other? Did they do the whole friends with benefits thing people talked about? They were likely next door getting off while Nick lay here thinking about them like a pervert.

"I'm losing my fucking mind," he mumbled to himself as he continued to lie there, looking up at the dark ceiling, for the rest of the night.

CHAPTER TEN

The next couple of weeks went on like the last few had. Nick kept busy at work and spent most of his spare time with Bryce. He made them food often, always cooking extra to take next door for Bryce. When he wasn't home to cook, he'd still bring food back from the restaurant and Bryce would stock his fridge.

It was a few weeks after their barbeque with Christi that Nick's cell rang, Bryce's number on the screen. He knew Bryce was at the shop, so it surprised him that the man was calling in the middle of the day.

"Hello?"

"Hey. Do you have plans this Saturday?" Bryce asked him.

"Do I ever have plans other than work?" Well that made him feel like a piece of shit. He really needed a life. Actually, that wasn't true; he had plans with Bryce every weekend.

"Jamie just stopped by. He reminded me we're getting together at my parents' house this weekend for Mitch's birthday. You wanna come hang out with us? Christi will be there. I know she'd like to see you again."

Umm, Nick wasn't sure that was such a good idea. He would feel too awkward. "I have no place at your family's house for your brother's birthday. I haven't even met them. I appreciate the offer, but I have to pass."

"Ah, come on. What else do you have going on?"

The comment hit Nick in the gut. No, he didn't have friends other than Bryce, but that didn't mean they had to hang out all the time. "You don't have to take pity on me. I think I'll survive on my own for a night. Hell, maybe I'll even go out. I have the ability to meet other friends." Even to his own ears he sounded like an ass, but he didn't want to be a charity case. He didn't need a babysitter.

"What the fuck are you talking about? I'm not taking pity on you. We hang out all the time. My family's the *more the merrier* type. They'll want to meet the friend I've been spending so much time with."

It was then Nick realized he wanted this—really fucking wanted this—to be around a big group of people—friends and family. Yeah, he had that himself, but it was different. They all had something to say, whether it was about Nick, his life, or Jill. He couldn't just relax around them and try to enjoy the present instead of focusing on the past.

"Come on, man. Plus, I might need backup. You forget I'm going to have to pretend to be in a relationship with Christi while I'm there."

Nick shook his head. Why the hell was Bryce doing this? "Why don't you just tell them?" He really didn't understand the reasoning behind the whole lie. Especially since Bryce's brothers and their wives knew.

There was a pause, and then, "It's hard to explain. Listen, I need a yes or no, so I can let Jamie know. He's taking care of the food."

Nick sighed. "Let me. I can cater from the restaurant." That would be the only way Nick could let himself go. He needed to contribute. He didn't want to just be Bryce's lonely friend, hanging out during their family time.

"I can't ask you to do that. My clan can eat. That's a lot of food."

And Nick understood that need of Bryce's. He would be the same way. "Then how about we do it at cost? That way you're paying, but it'll be a whole hell of a good deal for your family. Deal?" He hoped so. He wanted to do this for them. Wanted to cook for them.

Bryce paused a second before saying, "Let me talk to Jamie. That sounds like a good deal to me. I gotta go. See ya at home." Bryce hung up and Nick held the phone in his hand. *See ya at home.* Obviously Bryce said it because they were neighbors, but it felt so natural that for just a second, he'd almost forgotten that was the reason.

***

As soon as Bryce hung up with Nick, he dialed his brother Jamie.

"You're not canceling," Jamie said instead of hello.

"What? No shit. Why would you think that?"

"Because this will be the first family gathering we've had since you and your girlfriend broke up, but considering you haven't told our parents, you're going to have to pretend you're still together. I'm assuming the reality of that has hit you since we last got off the phone."

"Fuck you." Jamie knew him too well. That's exactly what had happened, but as soon as he'd realized it, the first thing he'd done was call Nick and invite him. Talk about reacting in a way that made no sense. But maybe with a new face there, his mom would find more to talk about other than Bryce and Christi.

"Sensitive today, aren't we? Why don't you be a big boy and tell Mommy the truth?"

Because I don't want to let her down...

He felt like he was always doing that—with the carpet business, the schooling, lack of relationships, and hell, even when he'd gotten sick, because he knew it had killed his mom to see him that way. "I'm not talking to you about Christi right now. I was talking with Nick and I invited him over—"

"You invited your neighbor we've never met to Mitch's birthday?"

"Yes. Christ. Why do you care? Anyway, he's a chef and owns a restaurant. It's called Nick's. The food is incredible. I can't get enough of it. He was saying he could make food for everyone and we'd get it at cost."

"Good thinking, little brother. Now I see where you're going with the neighbor thing. That'd be fantastic."

Well, wait. He didn't want Jamie to think that was the only reason he'd invited Nick. Hell, Bryce hadn't even thought about it himself. That had been all Nick. He'd invited his friend because he wanted him there.

Deciding he didn't want to go into detail with Jamie about it right now, Bryce let it go. He found out the time of the party, head count and all of that. He'd need to get an idea about food from Nick—what their options were and all that stuff—but this would give him a place to start.

He felt better knowing he'd have Nick there as backup, someone for him to talk to during what would no doubt be a crazy day. Though, he had no one to blame for that craziness other than himself.

CHAPTER ELEVEN

The day of the party, Nick was at the restaurant early to prepare. They'd decided on baked ziti and an Italian sausage bake he made. Once he had everything set up, he raced back home to shower and get ready. He was nervous, which was a fucking joke. What in the hell he had to be nervous about he didn't know, but he was.

Just as he got ready, there was a knock. "Come in," Nick called and Bryce walked in.

"Where'd you go this morning?" Bryce asked as he stood by the door waiting.

Um...was that a trick question. "To cook?"

"You had to get up early and go to work to make the food for us? You should have told me. I didn't want you to go to so much trouble."

"Did you think it would cook itself?" Nick shoved his wallet into his back pocket and grabbed his cell. He wore a casual, button-up, short sleeve shirt and jeans. Bryce was in jeans and a T-shirt, casual as well, so he figured he'd worn the right thing.

"Well, no. I'm not an idiot. I just figured whoever was working would take care of it or something like that. Not that I want to cause your employees extra work, either but, again, I didn't want it to cause trouble. I shouldn't have let you do it."

Nick shrugged him off. It wasn't a big deal at all. "I like to cook. I could have had someone else do it, but I wanted to. The other chefs are great, but...well, I guess we all trust ourselves more than anyone else. I wanted to make sure it was a perfect meal, so to do that, I needed to take care of it myself."

Nick went into the kitchen to get one of the chafing dishes. Before he had the chance, Bryce reached out and grabbed his arm. His fingers were rough, Nick noticed, probably from working on bikes.

"Thank you. I appreciate you going to so much trouble for us."

Nick didn't move and Bryce didn't let go. *You're welcome,* danced on the edge of his tongue, but he had yet to make the words come out. Finally, he settled on, "No worries. What are friends for?"

Still, they both stayed in the same place, and goddamned if he didn't think he felt Bryce's thumb brush back and forth against his arm. *What the fuck, Fuller? What's going on here?*

Finally, Bryce broke the silence. "Well, you know...if you ever need work done on a bike, I'm your guy."

Nick knew he should laugh, but for some reason, he couldn't make it happen. Instead he said, "We better go before we're late. We still have to pick up your girlfriend." Nick was in on the truth so he had no idea why he'd called her that.

It was then that Bryce finally let go of his arm. "She's not my girlfriend."

It shouldn't matter either way. Whatever Bryce had going on had nothing to do with him. Still, Nick said, "She is today."

Bryce's dark brows pulled together. There were creases in his forehead as though he made the same facial expression often, and then it was just gone.

They loaded the food into the trunk of Nick's car, and Bryce gave him directions to Christi's. The car ride was awkward as hell for some reason.

When they pulled up to Christi's apartment, Bryce got out as she jogged over. She kissed him on the cheek. "Hey, hot stuff. I'll get in the back."

"Yeah right. You're not sitting in the back. Even if that wouldn't make me feel like an asshole, Ma would kick my ass when we got there." Bryce climbed into the back, and Christi in the front.

She surprised Nick by leaning over and kissing his cheek the same as she had with Bryce. "Hi, hot neighbor Nick."

"Hey." Bryce leaned forward and playfully separated them. "You're my girlfriend, remember. No kissing my friends."

Bryce obviously had feelings for her, even if he didn't realize it. Maybe it was his fear of settling down or his need to have fun, but Nick had no doubt the two of them would be exactly what Bryce's parents still thought they were: a couple.

"Boo, you're no fun." She crossed her arms, and Nick found himself glancing back at Bryce in the rearview mirror.

Bryce caught his eyes, returning the look as he said, "I need to tell my parents the truth. Soon."

"I've been saying that for a while," Christi replied, and Nick turned away. His head was all fucked up. He didn't get what he was thinking so he tried to clear his head, pulled onto the road, and asked for directions to Bryce's parents' house.

***

"The party can start now. We're here!" Bryce called out as they went into the house. He heard Nick chuckle behind him and Christi mumble something about him being an idiot.

There was something about today that had him on edge. He never felt that way coming home, even though he was being an asshole by lying to his parents about Christi. He knew his parents always worried about him, saying he was never as settled or responsible as Mitch or Jamie. They'd celebrated as though he'd become a doctor when he got his certificate as a motorcycle mechanic.

Then he'd found out about the aneurysm and his mom went a little crazy, worried about all the things she thought he would miss out on in life, love, marriage and a family being on the top of that list.

It had helped her when Bryce and Christi tried to date. He could remember back to high school when she told him she knew they'd end up together one day. As he got older, she'd ask when he'd stop playing

75

around and officially make Christi her daughter.

The truth was, that would never happen, and he didn't know how to tell her that.

When they stepped into the living room, Mitch said, "Considering it's my birthday, the party starts with me."

"Hey, what about me?" Jamie added.

His mom stood and shook her head. "See what I have to deal with in this house full of boys? Thank God for Abbey and Hope. They saved me, and pretty soon we'll be able to add Christi to the mix."

Bryce held in his groan.

Christi squeezed his hand.

Nick was silent.

"Subtle, Ma."

"Are you kidding me?" she asked. "I'm a Tanner. We don't do subtle." She hugged him and then moved to Christi, giving her the same treatment. "Hey, you."

"Hi. Thanks for having us." Christi let go and then nodded to Nick, who sort of hung out behind her. "This is Bryce's good friend, Nick. I swear these two are attached at the hip lately. Fit right in together, though—like it was meant to be. They're both a handful, though Nick's a little less of one than your son. I like him."

Bryce stared at her for a second, trying to figure out why it sounded like Christi was trying to sell Nick to his family. Then he wondered why she had to go and add *I like him* at the end. She was supposed to be *his* girlfriend. Then he felt like a fucking idiot because his thoughts were doing all sorts of crazy shit lately, and he needed to:

A)   chill the fuck out.

B)   introduce Nick to his mom himself.

"Nick, this is my mom, Georgina. If you're not careful she'll try to find a nice girl to marry you off to." As he finished, the rest of his family stood and made their way over.

"It's very nice to meet you, Nick. We don't get to see a lot of Bryce's friends, except Christi, of course."

"Thanks. I appreciate you having me today." Nick smiled at her and shook her hand.

Bryce continued introductions. "This is my dad, William. The tall, dorky looking guy behind him is my oldest brother, Mitch."

"Hey! Nerds are sexy!" Abbey shook her finger at him.

"Are you calling me a nerd, too?" Mitch asked her, before smiling and turning back to Nick. "Nice to meet you. Excuse my boneheaded brother." Mitch shook his hand. "The woman defending my honor is my wife, Abbey, and this knucklehead is our middle brother, Jamie, and his wife, Hope."

They all shook Nick's hand and started in on the questions. Bryce could tell Nick felt a little awkward so he walked over, put his hands on Nick's shoulders and said. "Alright, that's enough. You guys act like you've never met someone new before. We're going to get the food.

77

We'll be right back."

He kept one hand on Nick's shoulder as they turned for the door. His family went on arguing, laughing and doing all the things Tanners did together as he led Nick outside.

"They're a rowdy bunch," he said as they got outside. When he realized he still had his hand on Nick, he pulled it back.

"I can see that. I'm used to it in some ways. I have three sisters and they're all married, except they all have kids as well. My family's a little different, though. We're a little more…."

"Normal?" Bryce supplied, and Nick laughed.

"I was going to go with subdued."

"You'll get used to them. They're a great bunch. Mom definitely runs the family. She likes to have a hand in everything, but she does it out of love. Dad's quieter…a hard worker, but never at the expense of his family. Jamie and Mitch are great brothers, and I love their wives."

"And Christi. She's like family."

"She is," Bryce replied as they got to the car. He felt like he needed to say something, only he didn't know what. Just as Bryce opened his mouth to make something come out, Jamie was jogging up to them. "You guys need help? I tried to send Mitch, but Mom said that makes me an asshole since it's his birthday."

Nick's head whipped toward Jamie. "She really said that?"

"Yeah. What? Your mom doesn't call you an asshole if you're being one?"

Nick's green eyes darted back and forth between Bryce and Jamie, as though he was trying to figure out if Jamie was giving him shit or not. He wasn't.

"Okay, give him some space, asshole," Bryce winked at Jamie. "Help us get this food into the house. Nick made it this morning. He's an incredible cook. You guys are going to love it."

Suddenly, Bryce felt like this might not be such a strange day after all.

RILEY HART

CHAPTER TWELVE

"Hey. You doing okay in here?" Christi stepped into the kitchen with Nick. He'd disappeared a few minutes ago with the excuse that he needed to check on the food. Each course was heating in the chafing dishes.

"Yeah, I'm fine. They're great people." And they were. Nick liked all of them a great deal. Everyone was friendly to him and included him, but he still felt slightly like an interloper. It was Bryce's parents, his brothers and their wives, Bryce and Christi, and then him.

"They are. I've always felt completely comfortable with Bryce's family. They're extremely welcoming people. Georgina loves her family something fierce. It can be a little overwhelming sometimes." Christi leaned against the counter behind him. "She's kind of like those exaggerated TV moms that are always in their kids' business, but not usually in the same annoying way they make it for television. She loves them, worries about them, sometimes goes overboard or pushes the wrong thing, but I know she'll always come around. She just wants her boys happy."

Nick nodded, not sure why Christi was telling him all of that. He did appreciate it, though. He liked having more insight into Bryce's family and was glad to hear she'd come around and not be too upset when she learned about Bryce's split with Christi.

"How long have you known them?"

"Since I was fourteen. That's when I met Bryce."

Holy shit. That was a lot of history.

"That's kind of why I'm just as nervous as Bry to tell his parents the truth. I know they had their hopes up…but it just never would have worked. I was worried about Bryce when…"

"When what? And why worried?" he asked when she didn't finish.

She shrugged and gave him a smile. "When am I not worried about him? But yeah, it felt right at the time to give the relationship a try, but I think even then I knew it wouldn't work. I'll always love him, but I'll never be in love with him. I just want him happy."

Nick wasn't so sure about that. Not that he didn't think she wanted Bryce happy, he knew she did, but that she wasn't in love with him.

"I'm glad he met you." Christi nudged Nick's arm. "You're good for him."

"Not sure what I really do for him, but thanks. He's a good friend. He's made this whole new transition in my life a little easier." Less lonely as well. "The food is warm. We should tell them we can eat at any time." He felt the need to change the subject. Christi nodded and stepped away.

"Let's go."

As soon as they made it to the living room, Nick saw Bryce walking their way. "I was just coming to check on you. Is everything okay?" He stood in front of Nick, looking at him as he spoke. When Nick glanced up, he saw Jamie and Hope watching them.

"Yep. Your girlfriend was just helping me check on the food. We can eat whenever everyone is ready."

He watched as Christi stepped forward, wrapped an arm around Bryce and then patted his stomach. "What are we going to do with you, Bryce?"

Georgina walked over, squeezed Christi in a hug. "This is a perfect day. I love having all my kids together, and it's nice to have a good friend of Bryce's here to enjoy it with us as well."

***

"Wow, this is very good, Nick. You made this?" Bryce's mom asked as they all sat around the large table eating.

"Thank you. I did. I'm glad you like it. I love to cook."

Bryce sat between Nick and Christi, with his father at the head, his mom next to his dad. Mitch was at the other end, with Abbey at his side. Jamie sat across from Bryce like he always did, with Hope. "I'm going to get fat. He feeds me something good almost every day, and my fridge is kept stocked because of Nick. Beats the hell out of what I usually eat."

Nick shrugged. "I'm used to making a lot of food. I always have leftovers or can bring things home from the restaurant. Makes it easy."

"Are you married?" his mom asked, and Bryce held back a groan. He was pretty sure Nick didn't want to talk about his ex-wife. Bryce didn't know all the details, but he did know it hadn't ended well.

"No, I'm divorced."

"Oh, I'm sorry about that. Do you have any kids?" she questioned.

"Okay, Ma. Stop grilling him, please," Bryce interrupted.

"I wasn't aware I was grilling him. I thought I was making polite conversation."

"It's fine." Nick nudged him and then turned toward his mom again. "No, we didn't have any children."

"If your mom is like me, I bet she's dying for grandbabies."

He fucking *knew* they would end up on this discussion.

"I have three sisters, and they all have kids. My mom spoils them rotten."

"Lucky her." His mom cocked a brow at Bryce, but he pretended not to notice.

Jamie saved them all by changing the subject. Once they finished eating, Bryce told his family he would take care of the dishes. Both Nick and Christi offered to help, but Bryce told them no. "Don't let them torture him too bad, okay?" Bryce whispered in Christi's ear before he went the opposite direction to the kitchen. It was a few minutes later that he heard someone behind him. His first thought was Nick. He wasn't sure how comfortable the man was here, but when he turned, he saw that it was Jamie.

"How ya doing?" he asked.

"Um...fine?" Bryce replied. "Just doing dishes."

Jamie started loading the dishwasher. "So...how does it feel to be in your first real relationship?"

Bryce turned to his brother. What the fuck was he talking about? "You know Christi and I broke up. Don't you start in on me about settling down with her, too."

Jamie chuckled and Bryce had the sudden urge to punch him.

"Let's try this again... How does it feel to spend the day with your ex-girlfriend/best friend/woman your mother thinks you're dating while pretending your current boyfriend is just a friend?"

The plate in Bryce's hand dropped, clattering against the counter the same way his heart suddenly beat against his chest. "What the fuck are you talking about?"

"It's okay. It's surprising, but okay. It'll take Mom and Dad some getting used to, but they'll come around."

Bryce almost choked on his tongue. His heart wouldn't stop pounding. "What the fuck are you talking about, Jamie? I'm not *gay*. Nick isn't my boyfriend. Christ, where in the hell did you get that idea?"

Jamie took a step back and studied him. It felt like a week before his brother spoke again. "You're serious, aren't you? I thought you were hiding it for some reason, but you really don't see it, do you?"

Bryce went off reflex and shoved his brother. "What that fuck are you talking about?" he asked again.

"First of all, if you ever push me again, I'll beat your ass. Second, get a fucking clue. The two of you haven't taken your eyes off each other all day. You constantly watch him, and he does the same with you. You defend him with mom for some reason, and you touch him more than I'm thinking you realize. Every five minutes you're making sure he's okay or checking if he needs a drink, or whatever other excuse you can think of to be near him. I swear you look like you want to bite Christi's head off every time she talks to him, and the kicker is, he's doing the same thing with you. I've never seen you treat anyone else the way you treat him, not even Christi. You're into him, Bryce. I have to admit, it's strange as fuck, but it's there. Now the question is, what the hell are you going to do about it?"

Like he hadn't just dropped an atomic fucking bomb into Bryce's lap, Jamie walked away. Bryce stood back, trying to process what his brother said. He couldn't be right...could he?

CHAPTER THIRTEEN

Bryce had been quiet the rest of the day. He'd speak when spoken to and tease his brothers when they teased him, but Nick could tell something was on his mind. Something was different, but he didn't know what.

They had cake and Mitch opened gifts, but Bryce's sullen attitude stayed the same.

Afterward, they said goodbye to his family. Nick watched as Bryce's mom hugged Christi, whispering something in her ear, and then the three of them left.

"You're being quiet back there, what gives?" Christi asked as they drove away.

"Nothing. Just tired." Bryce told her. She sighed but didn't bring it up again.

When they got to Christi's house, Bryce got out of the car to tell her goodbye. Nick watched as Christi pushed up onto her toes, kissed his cheek and told him to call her later.

Then, it was just the two of them. The tension in the car got thicker with each mile they drove, with Bryce just staring out the window. Nick felt it in his chest, and all around him. He hadn't spoken a word to Nick the whole time, and he knew that somehow the tension was related to him.

"Are you sure everything is okay?" he asked when they were almost home.

"Yep. Just thinking," was the only reply he got. He wasn't sure why he thought Bryce would tell him if he hadn't been willing to tell Christi, but it didn't feel right not to ask. Plus, Bryce was his friend. They'd talked about a lot over the weeks they'd gotten to know each other. If he'd done something wrong, he wanted to know.

"Did I screw up somehow?"

"What?" Bryce turned to him for the first time. "No, not at all. I'm fine. I don't know what's wrong with me. Just a strange day, I guess."

"Okay." It felt like more than that, and it bothered Nick more than it should.

They continued the rest of their car ride in silence. When they got home, Bryce tried to help him carry the dishes inside, but Nick refused. He needed to bring them back to the restaurant anyway.

They were at their own doors, about to go inside when Bryce's voice stopped him. "Hey."

Nick turned to him, could see stress or confusion in every one of Bryce's features—his dark, brown eyes, the muscles in his body, the way he stood, everything. "Yeah?"

"Thanks for coming today. I'm glad you were there."

Nick let out a relieved breath. "Thanks for having me. I was glad to be there."

When Bryce turned around and walked into his house, Nick had no choice but to do the same.

Bryce sat alone in his house, unable to sleep. Glancing at the clock he saw it was after midnight—not too late, but considering he'd been lying in bed since nine on a Saturday night, it was late enough.

His brother thought he was into Nick...into another man. What a fucking idiot.

Yeah, he felt close to Nick, felt like he'd known him a whole lot longer than six or so weeks. There was a bond there, a connection he didn't really understand, but Jamie thinking Nick was his boyfriend? There was no possible way Bryce would even want that—a boyfriend.

Rolling over, Bryce grabbed his cell phone off the bedside table. He dialed without second thought, and a few rings later, Christi picked up. "Can't sleep?" she asked.

"Nope...here's a laugh for you. Jamie thinks I'm attracted to Nick. He thought we were a couple and trying to hide it."

Bryce waited for Christi to tell him how fucking cracked in the head his brother was. Waited for her to laugh, but he got nothing except silence. "You're being quiet. Why in the hell are you being so quiet, Christi?"

"Are you going to freak out if I answer honestly?"

"I don't know. I guess it depends on what your answer is. We're talking about me being into a dude, here."

"When's the last time you got laid?" she asked.

Yeah. That's what this had to be about. He wasn't sure why he didn't consider it himself. It had been too long since he had sex. "It's the longest dry spell I've had in I can't remember how long."

"Exactly. That's not like you. And you didn't even realize it, did you?" When Bryce ignored her question, she continued. "When's the last time you hung out with anyone other than Nick?"

"I hung out with you not too long ago!" Christ, what the fuck was wrong with everyone? Why did they think Bryce had it for his neighbor?

"Yes, me and Nick. I was an afterthought. I was the third wheel. I've never been a third wheel with you, not even when you were out looking to get laid."

Bryce shook his head. She was wrong. They both were. It wasn't that he was homophobic or anything. He just identified as straight and liked women.

"How many drinks did you get me today? Zero. How many did you get him?"

"That's because you're just as comfortable at my parents' house as I am! It was his first fucking time there."

"Why'd you invite him to your brother's birthday? Why do you freak out every time I call him hot? Why did you tell me not to flirt with him or hook up with him?"

Bryce pushed up into the bed, his body tense. His pulse drummed the same way it did in his parents' kitchen while talking to Jamie earlier. "Because it'd be weird if you hooked up with my neighbor when my family thinks you and I are together? Because you're both my friends? Jesus, what's wrong with everyone? I've never been into a man in my whole life." Everything he said sounded like excuses, even to his own ears. The truth was, the more Christi spoke, the more he started to hear what she was saying. Bryce wasn't sure what to think about that.

"If it helps, I think he feels the same way you do…I also think he's as stubborn and in denial as you are. Or maybe you're both boneheads and really don't see it."

"No, that doesn't help. You don't know what you're talking about, Christi. I gotta go." He tossed the phone on his bed.

His best friend and his brother were both fucking crazy. Nick was his friend, nothing more, nothing less. Bryce would prove it. After pushing to his feet, Bryce grabbed a pair of basketball shorts and jerked them on.

He'd go next door, probably be a total asshole by waking Nick up, but he'd tell the guy what his brother and Christi had said. They'd have a laugh over the fact that Christi thought they were both into each other, and they'd confirm the lines the crazy people in his life thought he'd crossed.

Bryce didn't grab shoes, a shirt or anything else, just made his way next door. He felt like an ass, but that didn't stop his fist from pounding on Nick's door.

He waited a minute, heart in his throat, before he banged on it again.

His pulse sped up even faster when he heard the locks clicking and then the door opening. Nick's eyes were wrinkled around the edges. They looked small, tired. He had a frown on his face, as he cocked his head and looked at Bryce.

He wore sweatpants that hung low on his hips, the top of his underwear peeking out, tight against his flat, muscular stomach. There was a trail of hair that led under his sweats, and Bryce's eyes followed it down. He saw the outline of his erection through his sweats before ripping his eyes away.

Holy shit.

"I couldn't sleep," Bryce managed to say over the screaming in his head. He noticed Nick's body. He wanted to look at it again.

"I can see that." Nick rubbed a hand against his abs, then ran it through his short hair. He stepped back, and Bryce noticed the stubble on his face and the curve of his lips. The way he moved, smooth, yet unsure. The concern for Bryce in his eyes.

"Bryce...what's wrong? I know it's something. Come in. You can talk to me."

It was then that Bryce realized they were right. Christi and Jamie were fucking right. He wanted Nick. *Wanted* the man. He was attracted to him, liked spending time with him, and wanted to be closer to him.

91

He cared about him. Bryce didn't know how much or what that meant, but it was fucking there, and now the only question was...what did he plan to do about it?

"Bryce?" Nick asked and then licked his lips. Every logical thought fled from Bryce's brain. All he did was react.

He took a step inside, then another. With a slow hand, he touched Nick's cheek, fingers shaking as they rubbed against the growth of hair on his jaw.

Then, he slowly leaned in and pressed his lips to Nick's.

CHAPTER FOURTEEN

Nick didn't move. It was like his brain shut off. There was nothing there except Bryce. Bryce, who was pressing his lips to Nick's—once, twice, three times, each time a little harder. Bryce's tongue that snuck out of his mouth, licking at Nick's lips, trying to get in.

Holy fucking shit, the man was *kissing him.* Instinct took over. Nick jerked away, and swung his arm. His fist connected with Bryce's mouth, *the same mouth that had just been kissing him,* and the other man stumbled back.

"You fucking hit me!" Bryce's hand was shaking as he wiped the blood from his bottom lip.

"You fucking kissed me!" And then Nick was pacing the room. Just a minute before his brain had shut off, and now it wouldn't stop going. Bryce had kissed him. Bryce was a man...his friend...and part of him hadn't wanted to stop it.

"Shit." Bryce shoved the door closed and went into the kitchen. "I shouldn't have gone for it like that. I don't know what I was thinking. Actually, I wasn't fucking thinking. Jamie and Christi thought I had a thing for you, and I didn't know what to believe. I came over here to prove them wrong and then, Jesus, you looked so fucking sexy when you opened the door all tired, and bare-chested with those fucking abs of yours. I realized they were right, so I just acted." He wet a paper towel and wiped his mouth as though he hadn't admitted...a whole hell of a lot of shit that Nick was still processing.

"Wait. Slow down...your brother and Christi think you have..." The word "feelings" got stuck. Or hell, maybe that wasn't even what Bryce meant, so Nick just said, "*something* for me." Bryce's sullen attitude this afternoon made a whole hell of a lot more sense now.

Bryce held the towel to his face, guilt slamming into Nick. He couldn't believe he'd fucking hit him. Nick had never hit someone in his life. He grabbed a baggie from the drawer, filled it with ice and then handed it to him. "Here." Nick jerked his hand back so they didn't touch, and he could have sworn he saw Bryce flinch.

That just made the guilt thicken, turning to mud in his veins.

"Yeah... Jamie mentioned it when I was doing dishes. He thought we were together and hiding it. It tripped me the fuck out at first."

"Welcome to the club," slipped past Nick's lips and he couldn't help but chuckle. Logically, he knew there was nothing about this situation that should make him want to laugh.

"I didn't see it. Or maybe I did and I was in denial. I called Christi to have her tell me Jamie was crazy, only she said the same thing. I came over to prove they didn't know what they were talking about and you opened the door," he waved a hand at Nick. "Like that. Christ, put a shirt on, would you? And I just reacted. I'm sorry. I don't know what I was thinking."

Nick backed up until he ran into the fridge and couldn't move anymore. His head swam with a thousand different thoughts—Bryce, Jill, his family, Bryce's family, the kiss, the feel of Bryce's lips on his and his rough hand on Nick's face. The pain, and fear, and fucking bravery in Bryce's voice and actions. Yet the thing he landed on was… "You said I'm sexy." It had been in his first rambling explanation, but the words were only sinking in now.

Heat lit Bryce's steel eyes as he took Nick in. "You are. Jesus, you so fucking are. I kept noticing shit like that before, but I ignored it."

Nick couldn't believe this. He didn't know what to think or feel. His gut twisted and he felt the need to run, but he didn't. Couldn't. He needed to understand. Needed to know more. "Have you ever…?"

"No. Fuck no. Not with any other guy except you. Have you? Wait. I guess you haven't said if you're feeling whatever the fuck I am about you. And there's the fact that you've only been with one person. Fuck." He shook his head.

Nick squeezed his eyes closed. Locked his hands behind his head. The thing was, he did feel…whatever it was that Bryce felt. He did, and he didn't know what that meant. But he couldn't lie, either. "I do… I don't understand it, but I do. I think I'm fucking jealous over Christi."

"I swear I wanted to tape her mouth closed and keep her as far away from you as possible every time she calls you hot neighbor Nick. Or touches you. I hate that, too." Nick's eyes popped open at Bryce's words. He still leaned against the counter, holding a bag of ice to his mouth.

"I'm sorry I hit you."

"I'm sorry I kissed you…I think. Maybe not. No, I think I'm just sorry you hit me, too."

A loud laugh fell from Nick's lips. He couldn't stop it, and soon Bryce was laughing with him. It was a crazy, ridiculous, fucked up response to whatever was happening here, but it was all he seemed to be able to do.

When they finally calmed down, Nick said the only truth he could. "I don't know what to do with this. What I *can* do with it. I don't understand it."

He froze up when Bryce took a step toward him, then another…and another one. He stopped when their toes touched. "I can't believe how fucking much I want you." His breath whispered across Nick's skin, and damn if his dick didn't start to go hard. "Maybe it's because we're both so fucking horny. I haven't gotten laid in months, and I know it's been even longer for you."

"Yeah, maybe," Nick said, even though there wasn't any part of him that believed that was true.

His heart seized up when Bryce's hand raised and touched his face again.

"It feels weird…good, but weird to have rough hair against my hand. Do you want to touch me, too, Nick?" he asked.

Yes, yes, I fucking do.

But he couldn't. How in the hell did he process all of this? They were both straight men. Nick had been married and in love with his wife for years. "I can't. Not yet. I need a couple of days to sort through this...to figure out what the hell is going on. Can you do that? Give me a couple of days?"

Bryce's hand dropped away and Nick immediately wanted it back. "Yeah, yeah, I can do that. Whatever you need. That's probably smart. I tend to leap before thinking. We both need to figure out what the fuck is going on here. Just don't hit me again."

Bryce winked at him and Nick smiled. "I'm sorry."

"I know. I'm gonna..." Bryce took a step back and another before pointing behind him. "Go next door. Maybe get drunk or something. We'll...yeah, we'll talk later."

Nick didn't turn away, didn't take his eyes off Bryce's back and the way his muscles moved, the masculinity of his body as the man walked out of his house, closing the door behind him.

His first instinct was to call him back.

***

Bryce hadn't been lying when he said he was going to get drunk. He did. Thank God he was off the next day, because he spent the whole night in his house, slamming beers.

And watching straight porn.

It didn't change a damn thing.

Yeah he got hard, jacked off and came like nobody's business as he watched men fuck women on the computer all night...but he suddenly wondered if it was just the women who were getting him off, or maybe the men, too. It wasn't something he ever thought about before this whole business with Nick—and he didn't know if this was *just* a Nick thing or if he was an equal opportunity lover and just hadn't realized it before.

He came all over his hand more than once that night, and if he was being honest, it wasn't just the porn doing it for him, either. He thought about the kiss, as innocent as it had been. But he'd definitely liked the feel of Nick's lips under his. Nick's solid body against his, and the roughness of him. Another dose of honestly? The fact that Nick was strong enough and big enough to have hit Bryce the way he did got him hard as well. Not that he was into pain...but yeah, that strength in the other man made his dick ache, which probably said Bryce was a little more fucked up than most, but hey, he'd always been a kinky bastard who enjoyed sex. That was fine by him.

He'd drank and came so much that his body was worn out, and he'd slept half of the next day.

It was one o'clock in the afternoon when he woke up. He knew without looking that Nick would be gone, but Bryce went out and checked the driveway, anyway. Sure enough, Nick's car was gone. Bryce had a feeling Nick would find quite a few excuses to stay away from home as much as possible until he figured out whatever was going on inside his head.

Bryce got that. He did…but he also knew what he wanted. That kiss hadn't been enough for him. All it did was make his desire pump through his veins with even more force. He'd always been the kind of guy to go after what he wanted, and he didn't think that would change now.

But he also knew he had to chill the fuck out, because if he pushed, Nick would freak.

He took a quick shower, and then headed to Jamie's work.

"Hey, Bryce. How's it going?" Jamie's receptionist smiled at him.

"Good. Is he in his office or in a room?" He nodded toward the door. Jamie was a veterinarian and owned his own small practice.

"Office. He just finished lunch."

Bryce knew that if Jamie were too busy to see him, Lydia would have said something, so he went straight to the door and opened it. Jamie looked up from behind his desk. "Jesus, what happened to your lip?"

It was slightly swollen and bruised. "Oh, this?" Bryce pointed to his mouth. "I kissed Nick last night and he hit me. Thanks a lot, asshole."

Jamie let out a loud laugh. "First of all, why am I an asshole? I didn't make you kiss him, and I didn't hit you. Second, did you warn the guy before you did it? I have to say, I'd hit a man if he kissed me, too."

Bryce fell into the chair across from his brother, slightly surprised that neither of them were freaking out more about this. It wasn't every day he told his brother he'd kissed a dude.

"It's your fault because you made me realize I wanted to kiss him. And no...if I would have told him, I probably wouldn't have had the balls to do it."

Jamie was quiet for a minute, which didn't happen often. "Sorry he hit you. Are you guys okay?"

Bryce shrugged. "I think so. After he hit me he calmed down. We talked a bit. He said he needed a few days. What the fuck is going on here?" Bryce ran a hand through his hair before leaning forward, resting his elbows on his knees. "I swear I've never been into a guy before. Why aren't you freaking out about this more?" Why wasn't Bryce?

Jamie shrugged, stood up and walked to the other side of his desk and leaned on it. "I'm not sure why I would be freaking out. Yeah, I admit, it's strange. Not because I have a problem with being gay, but because you're my brother and you've never been into men before. It'll take some getting used to. The real question is...are you freaking out? Are you okay with it? Is it something you can accept? That's what matters. Everyone else will accept it or they won't, and honestly, fuck anyone's opinion except yours and Nick's. You gotta be okay with it, though. You and him. If you are, go for it. All that matters is how you guys feel, man."

He had no idea when in the hell his middle brother had gotten so smart. That wasn't true; both his brothers were smart. Jamie just wasn't serious most of the time. He was dead fucking serious now. "I want him more than I'm freaking out. That's all I know."

"Then there's your answer. He seems like a good guy. I'm happy for you." Jamie pushed off of the desk and stood. "I need to head back out there. You going to be okay?"

He nodded. He would be; he just hoped Nick would, too. "Thanks, man." Bryce stood and gave his brother a hug. "Don't...don't say anything to Mitch, and ask Hope not to mention it to Abbey." Because he knew Jamie would tell his wife. Jamie told her everything, and he was okay with that. "When I figure out what's going on, I'll make the decision if anyone else needs to know."

He hoped like hell Nick would let him know soon what was going on. He'd go crazy waiting.

CHAPTER FIFTEEN

It was Monday evening and Nick hadn't seen Bryce since Saturday night. He sure as hell hadn't stopped thinking about the man the whole time—the kiss, the fact that he wanted to do it again, the fact that it scared the fuck out of him for two reasons. The first was the obvious: he'd never wanted a man before. He'd always considered himself straight. The second being the people in the house in front of him. None of them would likely understand.

He'd been raised in a very traditional family, and this, *Bryce,* would be extremely hard for them to comprehend. He didn't even understand it himself. His sisters would probably come around, he thought. They loved him. That's all that would matter (he hoped), but his mom finding out terrified him. Disappointed wasn't a strong enough word for how she would feel.

And now wasn't the time to really think about it, either. Hell, so far they'd only admitted to wanting each other. Maybe families wouldn't even need to be involved.

Nick got out of the car and walked up to his sister Karrie's house. From the outside, the house was perfectly manicured like it always was.

He had no doubt the inside would be as well. That's just the way his sister was. Karrie stayed home with her kids. Her husband was a lawyer. He knew she worked hard to keep their home in order, and always made sure of that when they had company. She was a good sister. They all were, but he was closest with Karrie.

Nick knocked on the door before pushing it open. "Hello?"

"In here!" Karrie replied, and then all sorts of little voices chanted, "Uncle Nick, Uncle Nick, Uncle Nick." Besides Karrie's two kids, his second sister, Erin, had two, and Michelle, the youngest girl, had two with one on the way.

"Hey, guys!" He kneeled as a group of kids jumped all over him. For living in the same city, they didn't get together enough.

Once he said his hellos, Nick followed his nieces and nephews into the family room where his three sisters, their husbands and his mother sat. The first thing that popped into his head was...*how would it feel walking in here with Bryce?* Which was crazy and ridiculous. They were attracted to each other, not getting married.

"About time we see our baby brother. I almost forgot what you look like." Karrie hugged him, followed by Erin and Michelle.

"You leave him alone," his mom scolded. "Nicholas works hard, the way a good man should. His *wife* didn't appreciate that. He doesn't deserve to get it from his family as well."

Erin rolled her eyes and Karrie stifled a laugh. Nick was annoyed as hell. "Thanks, Mom, but you don't need to defend me to my own sisters. I appreciate the concern, though." He walked over and gave her a kiss on the cheek before sitting down next to his brothers-in-law.

They chatted for a minute and then Nick went upstairs to play with the kids. He loved his nieces and nephews. He'd always thought he and Jill would eventually have kids. It wasn't something he dreamed about or anything, it was just what you did in his family. You got married and had a family. He was the only one who'd gotten divorced, or didn't have kids.

It wasn't long before Erin called up the stairs that dinner was ready. He watched as his sisters made sure the kids had their plates. Michelle's husband, Ken, waited at the table while Michelle made his plate. Karrie and Erin's husbands didn't, but he noticed they didn't offer to help their wives with the kids, either. In a lot of ways, he knew the girls didn't mind. It was how they'd all been raised. But it rubbed Nick wrong at the same time. Why did they have to serve everyone?

That had never been Jill, and he was okay with that. His mother, on the other hand, hated it. She felt Jill wasn't doing her womanly duty, whatever the fuck that was.

"Sit down, dear. I'll make your plate for you." His mom patted his shoulder.

"It's okay. I'm a big boy. I can handle it." She flinched as though his words hurt. He knew she just saw this as taking care of whom she loved, but Nick didn't need anyone to serve him. "Why don't you sit down and I'll make yours?"

She waved her hand at him. "You don't want to make your mama's plate, and you shouldn't have to."

"If I were you, I'd take advantage of that!" Karrie smiled, but his mom just followed him to the food, where they made their plates.

"My son is a good man. He deserves a woman who sees him as such." She smiled proudly and Nick's stomach seized up.

It's not a woman I want right now, Mom. It's a man...

"You spoil him too much, Mom. It wasn't Jill's job to take care of him. It was only her job to be a good wife." Karrie nodded, proud of herself.

"I'm with you on that one," Erin added.

His mom frowned. "All I want is for him to know how he should be treated. He's my only boy, and I just want what's best for him."

Nick knew his mom would never think of Bryce as what was best for him.

***

It was close to ten Monday night when there was a knock at Bryce's door. Without looking, he knew exactly who it was. He shoved off the couch and went for the door. "It took you long enough," he said when he saw Nick standing there.

"What the hell do you mean? It's been forty-eight hours." Nick stepped inside and closed the door. He looked slightly frazzled, his mouth in a frown. But he was here, he was fucking here, and Bryce knew exactly why. "I need to know what you're thinking. What this means and what you want. I mean, what's the plan?" Nick asked as he paced back and forth across Bryce's living room. Bryce felt a smile tug at his lips. He liked this frazzled side of the man.

"Honestly? I don't have a plan. I'm not really a thinking-things-through kind of guy. Unless it's just thinking about the fact that I want you. That's all I know. I don't know what that means, either. As far as I've gone in the planning stage is paying more attention to the men in straight porn on Saturday night, and Googling 'men kissing' Sunday night."

Nick froze at that, before slowly turning to face Bryce. "You looked up men kissing?"

"Yep."

"How was it?"

"Sexy as fuck. Wanna look it up with me? Or do it with me?"

It was then that the frown sort of fell off Nick's face. He stood about ten feet away from Bryce, staring at him. "I was up thinking all night Saturday, didn't sleep for shit. Sunday, I went to work early, tried to forget it, but that didn't work. Today, I thought about you all fucking day while I tried to avoid you...then I went to dinner with my family. It'll be a fucking disaster if they find out. It'll break my mom's heart, but that doesn't change what I want. Maybe that makes me an asshole. Maybe it's too early to even worry about family or anything like that. All I know was the longer I was with them, the more I wished I was with you. The why of it didn't matter anymore." Nick's shoulders rose and then dropped. "So here I am."

That was exactly what Bryce wanted to hear. He felt it, the fear and nerves, but they were just a quiet pulse in the back of his mind. A whisper that spoke softer than the want inside him.

"I guess we just...see what happens." Nick walked to the couch and sat down.

Bryce knew what he wanted to happen. His body already started to overheat and respond at just the thought. "You want a beer?"

"Abso-fucking-lutely."

Bryce laughed and grabbed them each a bottle. He handed Nick his before he sat down next to him on the couch. "We can look up some gay porn...you know...see what we're getting ourselves into. I only went as far as kissing."

Nick shifted on the couch, stretched his long, jean-clad legs before saying, "I'm not sure I'm ready for that yet. I just..." He leaned forward, set his beer on the coffee table, and then reached for Bryce. Bryce let Nick lead, let Nick touch his hair, his face, his bottom lip. "I can't believe I hit you."

"I know how you can make it up to me." Bryce smiled, and kissed Nick's finger.

"How's that?" There was a flirtation in Nick's voice that Bryce didn't often hear from the guy. He hadn't heard it at all the nights he took Nick out to the bars.

"Put your lips on me. Let me taste you."

"I don't know if I can."

"You can," he said.

Nick paused...and then was doing exactly as Bryce asked. Slowly he leaned forward. He pressed his mouth to Bryce's, way more slowly than Bryce had done the other night. The first couple of kisses were soft, gentle other than the feel of Nick's scruffy face against his own. Then there was more power, strength, as Nick moved in closer. His tongue probed Bryce's mouth, and Bryce let him in.

It was totally different than kissing a woman. He felt the difference in the way Nick moved, smelled and felt. In the way he tasted, beer on his tongue, but he somehow tasted masculine as well.

And Bryce wanted more.

There was a clatter, and he realized he'd dropped his beer to the floor.

Nick pulled away. "Oh shit." He reached for the bottle but Bryce grabbed his hand. He pushed it down on the hard dick underneath his shorts.

"You've got me so fucking hard, just from a kiss. Who gives a shit about the beer?"

For a brief second, he thought he pushed too much too fast. That Nick would pull away. But he didn't. He just grinned at Bryce and said, "Not me," before his mouth came down hard on Bryce's again.

CHAPTER SIXTEEN

"Come to bed with me, so we have more room," Bryce said against Nick's mouth between kisses. Logically, Nick knew he should question this. Knew it should be harder for him to say yes. But it wasn't.

"Let's go."

Bryce pulled him up and didn't let go of Nick's hand as they went to the bedroom. He nodded toward the bed, and Nick sat down. Neither of them moved to take off their clothes. That might be a little too much, too early, but he sure as shit hadn't had enough of kissing Bryce yet.

So Nick kissed him again, reveled in the taste of him—mint and beer. He smelled slightly like the engine of a bike, mixed with soap. Bryce's calloused fingers touched Nick's face as he cupped his cheeks, deepening the kiss.

"You taste so fucking good. I could keep my tongue in you all night."

A shiver raced down Nick's spine at Bryce's words. They were sexy as hell and made his cock harden even more. He hurt, he was so stiff.

"I like that...when you talk to me like that."

"You do?" Bryce asked and then said, "Wanna taste your skin, too." And then he licked Nick's neck, briefly sucking the skin into his mouth before letting go again. "I could get used to this...how you taste. It's hot as hell."

Then they were kissing again, frantically, teeth clanking, tongues tangling, hot, heavy kissing. Nick's cock wept. He felt the pre-come wet his underwear and wondered if Bryce's was doing the same. If he had the other man so hard that he couldn't stop leaking.

He grabbed Bryce and pulled the man down as he laid on the bed. Bryce went easily, resting on top of him, and Nick spread his legs. The second their hips touched he felt it, Bryce's erection against his own. "Oh fuck. Do you feel that? Do it again."

Bryce grinded his hips against Nick's. Their cocks rubbed together. Even through both their layers of clothes, he felt the heat of Bryce's dick. A fucking *dick* rubbing against his own.

"My balls hurt. Christ, they're so full. They're gonna explode any second." Bryce thrust against him again. This time Nick started to do the same. They were dry-humping so hard, Bryce's bed kept hitting the wall.

Nick went off instinct, reached around and grabbed Bryce's ass. The muscles flexed under his hands as they continued to thrust against each other—cock against cock, hard thighs against hard thighs. Man against man.

Nick's balls tightened. "Fuck...me, too. I'm gonna come." He couldn't hold it back anymore as he emptied a load into his underwear. Bryce was still moving, and then he stiffened above him and groaned as he no doubt emptied his balls the same way Nick just had.

Together.

Two men.

Nick and Bryce.

There wasn't a single part of him that regretted it.

"Did you just come as hard as I did?" Bryce asked as he still lay on top of him. Nick's dick was soaked in come, seeping through his clothes, but he wasn't ready to move yet.

"Harder, I think. Holy shit, Bryce...We just..." But he couldn't finish the sentence. Not yet, and he wasn't sure why.

"Yeah, we did. I'd do it again, too. Just give me a little rest and I can get it up again."

His cock twitched. His dick definitely wanted exactly what Bryce said, but... "Maybe we should wait. That was sexy as hell, and my cock exploded so hard I thought my head would pop off, but...it's a lot. We have a lot to think about and consider. We're both straight. Your mom thinks a girl she loves like a daughter is your girlfriend. Hell, she's probably already planning the wedding. And my mom...she doesn't think anyone is good enough for me. This will be hard on her." But then, Nick couldn't stop himself from running a hand through Bryce's dark hair. He grabbed onto it, letting the strands fall through his fingers. "This feels good, too."

"Then maybe thinking about it should be the last thing we do. Fuck, maybe we should just enjoy it." Bryce pushed up, hands flat on the bed, holding himself over Nick. He looked down at him. "I can't believe how fucking sexy you are to me."

Nick's pulse sped up. He smiled because he liked that, being sexy to a man like Bryce. "You are, too."

"Stay."

"I'm a mess."

"And I have a bathroom and clothes. Funny how that works. Don't wash off too much, though. You smell like sweat and sex and man. I didn't know that did it for me." Then he leaned forward and took Nick's mouth again. Nick let him. He wanted it. Blood already headed south again, going straight to his dick.

"Okay," he said, even though his brain told him not to.

They took turns cleaning up. Bryce lent him a pair of shorts to wear, and he free-balled it, while Bryce wore a pair of boxer briefs and nothing else.

"This okay with you?" Bryce asked.

Nick's eyes seared a path down his body—his muscular chest and abs, the light hair dusting his body. It was more than okay. "It is."

Bryce hit the light and then climbed into bed with him. Besides Jill, Bryce was the only person he'd ever slept beside.

***

Bryce woke up, not really sure what to do. It was the first time he'd ever been in bed with someone when he didn't know his next move. He didn't often spend the whole night with a woman, but it did happen. It had happened with Christi, and in those situations they either said their goodbyes, or fucked again before saying them.

But then, he hadn't fucked Nick, just rubbed off on him, and now he didn't know how in the hell things would be between them.

"You freaking out a little bit, too?" Nick's husky voice came from the other side of the bed. He had his back to Nick, and he could tell from the sound of Nick's voice that he had his back to Bryce as well.

"I'm going with a yeah on that one. No regrets, just...yeah, what do we do now?"

"I was wondering the same thing. And no regrets over here, either."

"Well, no shit. You were with me."

He got the laugh out of Nick he was hoping for. The sound was comforting, giving Bryce the push he needed to roll over and onto his back. There was a slight lag time, and then Nick did the same. As soon as he turned, Bryce's eyes went straight to the lump in the sheet, Nick's morning wood standing tall. It made his own dick get even harder, giving a little jerk against his stomach.

And it also gave him an idea.

"Jack off for me."

"What?!" Nick's head whipped toward him as he flew into a sitting position.

The reaction made Bryce want to see it even more. He enjoyed a frazzled Nick, enjoyed being the one to do it. "Push your shorts down, wrap your hand around your dick, and jack off for me. I want to see you." Wanted to know how long he was, how thick. How his balls hung, how full they were. How much hair he had. "It'll show me what you like. I know what I like, but I've never tried to please a man before. Show me, Nick. Show me how you get yourself off."

He could almost swear he heard Nick's heart beating. The man looked like he might make a run for it...but then his eyes drifted down Bryce's body, to his very obvious bulge, and said, "Holy shit, I can't believe I'm saying this, but what about you? If you need to see me, I need to see you."

The words made his cock jerk again. Bryce's own heart sped up and he figured Nick could probably hear his as well. He was nervous, fucking nervous, when he'd never been scared about any sexual experience in his life. Every one of them with Nick freaked him out...but he wanted them, too. Wanted them enough to say, "Okay," and rip the top sheet and blanket off the bed. He knew if he didn't just go for it, Nick wouldn't, so Bryce pushed his underwear down his legs and kicked them to the floor. His erection bobbed against his stomach, a thin line of pre-come dropping from the tip and touching his abs.

"Holy shit," Nick whispered, eyes on Bryce's erection. "I've never..."

"I know. Now, you're not being fair. You get to look; I want to look, too. Take off the shorts. Let me see the dick that I rubbed off against last night." He hoped he sounded more confident than he felt. Not that he wasn't secure in what he wanted, because he really fucking was, but there was nothing about being with Nick that felt familiar to him.

"We're not easing our way into this, are we?" For the first time since Bryce stripped, Nick looked somewhere other than Bryce's dick, and held Bryce's eyes.

"We're going slow. How are we not going slow? We haven't even touched each other yet. Not really." He took a deep breath and added, "Let me see you, Nick. For the first time in my life, there's another dick that's just as important as mine. Show me." And then Bryce went for it. He spit in his hand, wrapped a fist around his painful erection, and started to stroke.

"God damn…" Bryce smiled at what sounded like amazement in Nick's voice. "You're leaking."

"I bet you are, too. Is there a wet spot on those shorts? Take them off." Bryce didn't stop working his dick as he spoke. He sucked in a sharp breath when Nick lay down beside him again, held his hips up and pushed down the black shorts. His erection sprang free—thick and full of veins. The head was purple and spilling out pre-come. Again, fucking thick. Did they really make cocks that thick?

Nick's balls were big, full and heavy as they sat below his dick. His pubic hair was darker than the hair on his head, and Bryce had the sudden urge to lean over and inhale. He wanted to know what Nick smelled like down there. If it was all sex, the way he looked. "I don't know what to say. I'm caught between, holy fuck, that's a big-ass dick, and, Christ, you're sexy as hell. Stroke it. Tell me what you like to do."

Bryce had never had a problem with his cock. He was long, had decent girth and he knew how to fuck. He had no problems working his dick and bringing people to orgasm, but Nick was much thicker than he was. Much.

All thoughts fled from his mind when Nick spit in his hand before fisting his erection and pulling on it. With his other hand, he reached for his balls, playing with them.

"Um...my nuts...I like 'em played with. Pulled on a little. I edge myself sometimes and then wrap my fingers around my balls so I can't come too soon." So obviously he was ignoring the big dick thing.

Bryce's whole body shuddered. "Holy fuck, I think that's the sexiest thing I've ever heard."

"What...what about you?" Nick asked, still fucking his own hand and playing with his balls. Bryce wanted to know how hot his cock was, how heavy his sac would be in his hand.

"My head is really sensitive. When I'm getting blown, I like a lot of attention there, a tongue swirling around me, or I get my hand nice and wet and play with the head."

Bryce tightened his hold on his erection as he saw Nick start to jerk himself faster.

"I want you to be the one to touch me next time. Will you do that? Play with the head of my cock? I'll play with your balls the way you like."

Nick let out a loud moan, thick, white semen shooting out of his dick and onto his chest. "Fuck. Oh, fuck, I didn't mean to lose it that quickly." But he kept jerking, kept squirting.

It was enough to send Bryce over the edge with him. He spilled his own load, the first shot going up his chest, the second pooling in his navel as his balls emptied.

They didn't speak...just lay there in Bryce's bed not touching each other, covered in come. Finally, Bryce said, "If I didn't have a Dyna FxdL at the shop waiting on me to work on, I'd stay home."

"I think a little space would do us some good, anyway. And I have to work this afternoon. I won't be home until late."

"Will you come over when you get off?" Bryce asked.

"Yeah...I think so." And then he rolled over and stood up. When Bryce looked at him, Nick's face was slightly pink.

"You're blushing."

"You're naked, and I just jerked off while telling you I like edging myself and playing with my balls. So, yes, I'm blushing."

"I like it."

Nick picked up a pillow and hit him in the face with it. "I know you do."

Nick turned, looking around before a, "hey," slipped out of Bryce's mouth.

"Yeah?"

"I don't know why this is happening. I know it's kind of fucked, and that neither of us really knows what in the hell we're doing here, or what it means for us. We'll figure it out, though. No obligation, okay?"

Nick didn't speak for the longest time. So long that Bryce thought maybe he was going to tell him right then that whatever the hell they were doing was already over. But then he leaned down and pressed a quick kiss to Bryce's lips before grabbing the shorts he'd taken off and wiping his stomach off with them.

"Grab another pair out of the drawer," Bryce told him.

When Nick replied with a "thank you," Bryce knew he wasn't thanking him for the clothes.

CHAPTER SEVENTEEN

Okay, so it was a whole hell of a lot easier not to dwell and overthink things when an orgasm was in the imminent future. With his hand on his dick, or Bryce's tongue in his mouth, the pleasure pushed away most of his logical thought. Now was a totally different story. As Nick showered, brushed his teeth, got dressed, drove to work, the fact that he'd had two orgasms with another man wouldn't leave his mind.

The kicker was that Nick wasn't freaking out over it. That didn't mean he wasn't confused, scared, nervous, stressed out over what it meant, but even though all those thoughts crowded his head, it wasn't enough to make him want to stop...whatever this was.

Because there was something about Bryce. They'd connected quickly, yeah, on a friendship level at first, but it was almost like the transition to something more was inevitable. Like he couldn't have stopped the progression if he wanted to.

He still didn't know what that meant—if he was gay, if they were serious or just fucking around, or a hundred other things he was unsure of—but he did know that he wanted to explore more of whatever this was with Bryce. He couldn't walk away.

He didn't want to tell anyone about it, though. It would mess things up. *My family will never understand.*

"Umm...Nick? You're burning—"

"Oh shit!" Nick jerked the pan off the burner when the waitress snapped him out of his Bryce-related thoughts. He couldn't remember the last time he'd ever burned something.

"Are you okay?" she asked.

"Yeah..." He thought so. Bryce was quickly becoming a constant distraction in his head, something he'd never experienced before. "Just a long day, and I didn't get much sleep last night." *While I was in another man's bed for the first time...*

He really needed to get his shit together. All they'd done was jack off together and Nick was acting like a love-sick kid. "Give me a minute and I'll get this fixed up."

Nick managed to keep his head in the game for the next hour or so. Since it was Tuesday, the dinner rush slowed down early tonight. When he could, he announced he was taking a quick break and started making his way back to his office.

As soon as his ass hit the chair, he pulled out his cell phone to call Bryce, only it started ringing before he got the chance.

Jill.

Well, shit. The last person he wanted to speak to was his ex-wife, but it wasn't as though she called him much anymore, so maybe something was wrong. "Hello?"

120

"Hey, Nick. It's Jill. How are you?"

Did she really think he didn't know who it was considering she hadn't changed her cell phone number when they divorced? "I'm fine. How are you?" There was a large part of him that didn't want to have a conversation with her, but he also wasn't the type of man to be rude to someone like that. Yeah, they had their bad history, but if she called, he figured he should listen.

"I'm doing wonderful, actually. Life is great. I'm happy...I'm working on a few things as well. Do you have a minute?"

I'm happy, too... When he first discovered Jill had affairs, he wasn't sure he'd ever feel happy again—outside of his career, at least. But he was. He enjoyed his quiet life, hanging out with Bryce and coming to his restaurant. "I have a few minutes. I'm at work and need to head back out there. What's going on?"

"Well, the past few years have been really hard on me. I've been going through a lot of changes and reevaluating my life."

No shit. He experienced that with her. And wait, did she say hard on her? She hadn't been the one to find out their spouse was fucking other people, one of them long-term. "Try experiencing it from my side."

She sighed. "I'm trying to do something important here, Nick. This isn't about you, it's about me."

That sounded familiar. Everything was always about her. "You have about three minutes, Jill."

"My therapist says it's a good idea to confront people from my past. To tell them how I feel—how they've hurt me and how I've hurt them."

Wait. "How I hurt you? What did I do to you?" He'd loved her, taken care of her, worked his ass off for their future.

"Are you really asking me that? Were you not there for our marriage?"

There was a spike in his pulse, but not the good kind. Nick squeezed the phone in his hand to keep from throwing it. "Yeah, I was. Were you? You're the one who went out and fucked other men. I was there, not you."

"You weren't really there, Nick. I should have known you'd do this. You won't even try to understand!"

No, he wouldn't. "I have to go, Jill. Have a good night." Nick hung up, but his anger didn't simmer down. His whole body got hot, his jaw tense. Who the fuck did she think she was?

***

It was nine o'clock, and Bryce hadn't left the shop yet. He knew if he did, he'd drive himself crazy. He wouldn't be able to chill out and relax until he spoke to Nick again. Christ, he'd never been like this. It was the not knowing that got to him the most—not knowing what to do, or if they would keep going.

He'd always just sort of let things roll off his back, whatever happened, happened, but as hard as he tried, he couldn't keep that attitude where Nick was concerned.

He wanted to keep the man as a friend, but he wanted to fuck him, too. Every time he thought of that, he got a headache and his dick got hard. Talk about conflicting emotions.

So instead of going home and driving himself crazy, he drove himself crazy at the shop instead. He decided to take apart a motorcycle because that would distract him better than anything else could.

When he heard his phone vibrating against the table, Bryce wiped his hand on his jeans and picked it up to see a text from Jamie. **Tell Mom you're gay and not giving her babies with Christi yet?**

Bryce rolled his eyes. **Shut up, fucker.**

At least tell Mitch. It's killing me.

Not as painfully as I'll kill you if you don't shut your mouth.

There was a pause before Jamie texted again. **I'm giving you shit. Just checking in. Everything good?**

It was better than good. Hell, all he'd done was rub and jerk off with Nick and he'd come harder than ever. Bryce didn't think his brother wanted to hear that, though. He definitely didn't want to hear about Jamie and Hope. **Good. Figuring shit out. Quit being nosy.**

That was the end of the texting. That was Jamie. He'd probably lost interest already and found something else to occupy his brain until Bryce popped into it again.

Bryce's thoughts didn't stop with the end of their texting, though. He knew he needed to talk to his mom. Even if he didn't drag Nick into it—which he probably shouldn't since they didn't even know what they were doing—she deserved to know about Christi. That he'd been lying to her about their relationship.

CHAPTER EIGHTEEN

Nick was fucking exhausted. After he'd gotten off the phone with Jill, they got slammed with two large parties. He'd been running around like crazy, and trying not to be pissed at his ex-wife at the same time. All he wanted to do was climb into bed and pass out. He didn't have the energy to fumble through he and Bryce tonight, but since he told Bryce he'd come, Nick figured he owed him to at least stop by.

Nick's fist came down lightly on the door. Almost instantly he heard, "Come in."

He slid the door open to see Bryce sitting on the couch with his feet on the coffee table. He wore sweats and nothing else. His hair and chest were wet as though he'd just gotten out of the shower.

"You're staring. Like what you see?" Bryce asked, and even though he'd felt like shit for hours, Nick found himself smiling. "You think I'm hot. Hot enough to make the straight man not so straight anymore, huh?" he teased, and Nick's smile widened.

He loved Bryce's humor, the way he said whatever was on his mind. He made Nick feel lighter just by being in the room with him. "I could say the same thing to you."

"I know. Why're you standing in the doorway?" Bryce cocked a brow at him.

"Because I planned on telling you I think I should probably just go home tonight."

"Freaking out?"

"Not really. Just a shitty day."

"Then get your ass in here, Nick. If you're not telling me you need some space, you can recover from a shitty day here just as well as you can twenty feet away at your own house. Or I can go over there if you want. We're friends first and foremost. What's going on?"

It was a reflex to do just as Bryce said. He was right, after all. They were friends first. Bryce had become his best friend over the last couple of months. There wasn't any reason why he couldn't relax on the couch beside Bryce and be in a shitty mood, the same as he would at home.

So, he closed the door, kicked off his shoes and walked toward Bryce. "Want to watch something?" Bryce aimed the remote at the TV.

"No."

The screen went black after that. Without Nick saying anything else, Bryce stood. "Hit the lights, would ya. I'm tired, too. Do you need to shower or anything? Brush your teeth?"

"I have a weird thing with teeth. I brush mine in my office before I leave work." And he always changed there as well.

When they got to Bryce's room, the man fell onto the bed, with his arms bent and hands behind his head. It took Nick less than ten seconds before he pulled his shirt off and let it fall to the floor. "Why do you think this is so easy?" he asked.

"I don't know. If we keep it up, things probably won't stay this easy. They'll get a whole lot tougher."

There was no doubt in Nick's mind about that. When it was just the two of them, it felt like the easiest, most natural thing in the world. It's when he thought about everyone else being in the mix that he worried this was destined to be a big fucking mistake. He didn't want to think about that right now. He didn't want to think about much of anything. If Nick was being honest, he wasn't even sure about getting physical with Bryce tonight. He needed things to settle in his head. He just wanted to relax, but he also wanted to be near Bryce.

As though he could read Nick's mind, Bryce said, "Get in bed, Nick. I'm tired."

He didn't take his eyes off Nick as he unbuttoned and unzipped his jeans. His fingers fumbled, shaking slightly before he shoved the pants down, turned off the light and then lay down in his underwear. He lay on his back, the same as Bryce.

For a moment they only lay there, but then it was Bryce who broke the silence. "It's crazy...the hair on your chest is sexy as fuck to me. Can I touch it? That's all I'll touch."

"Yeah."

Bryce's hand was warm as he slowly ran it up and down Nick's chest. "It's kind of exciting...everything being so new."

Yeah, it was. Though for him, Bryce was only the second person in his life he'd been this intimate with, so it was new for more than one reason. "For me, too. I like your touch." It was as though it centered him. He'd had a fucked up day, but for the first time in hours he felt like he could breathe.

And he wanted to share it with Bryce, so he opened his mouth and said, "She cheated on me. I gave her everything and she couldn't even stay faithful to me."

***

Bryce figured that was the situation with Nick's ex. He'd never asked because it hadn't been his business, but he had suspected. Now, he not only wanted to know, but he wanted it to be his business as well. "What happened?"

"Basically what I told you. We started dating when we were seventeen. She was my first everything. Her family didn't really like me. They never thought I was good enough for her. My mom hated her. I'm her only son, and I remind her of my dad. I don't think there will ever be anyone who she thinks is good enough for me."

Bryce knew that meant him. Nick wasn't saying it to hurt him, but to tell him that if this thing continued, it would be a problem for his mom. "I'm hearing you."

Nick shifted closer. "Put your head on my arm. Is that okay?"

It really fucking was, so Bryce leaned up and rested in the crook of Nick's arm, hand back to his muscular chest and the soft hair there. Nick wrapped his arm around Bryce.

"So yeah…it was tough, but I loved her. I thought she loved me just as much. I was determined to prove her family wrong. That I was good enough for Jill. I worked my ass off and built my career so I could give her whatever she wanted. Worked two jobs sometimes to get as much experience as I could before opening Nick's. I came home one day and she had her bags packed. Apparently she didn't appreciate my hard work and she felt neglected. The new man she was with gave her the attention she deserved."

"Fuck." Bryce leaned forward and kissed Nick's chest. He waited for it to feel strange or awkward, the fact that it was muscled flesh and hair there, not breasts, but it didn't.

Nick tried to sound as though none of it mattered, that it didn't hurt, but Bryce could tell in the sound of his voice, the softness of it, that it did.

"Apparently he wasn't the first, either. He's just the one that lasted. The other was a one-night-stand, she'd said."

"Christ, did she not see what you're packing down there. Hell, your come shot alone was pretty fucking spectacular."

Nick chuckled. "You're funny."

"I try to be…" But then, "I'm not trying to make light of your pain. Just wanted to make you laugh."

"I know," Nick told him. "Anyway, she called me tonight. Apparently her therapist wants her to speak to people who've hurt her in the past. Not quite sure how I made that list, but I did."

Bryce growled. Nick's ex sounded like a bitch. That wasn't the only thing that made him feel violent, though. He heard something in Nick's voice that set off this wild possessive streak he didn't know he had. "You still love her."

"What? No." Nick shifted beneath him but Bryce didn't let him move. "I'm not in love with her. If I was, I wouldn't be here. I don't work that way, Bryce. That's something we're going to have to figure out as well."

He got what Nick was saying—he didn't play games in relationships. He wasn't the kind of man to screw someone and walk away afterward. They had too many things against them, too many things to figure out. It was all adding up. "I hear it. You love her. It's okay. You spent most of your life with her."

Nick sighed and Bryce felt his warm breath in his hair. "There might be a part of me that will always love her. I married her. I planned on spending the rest of my life with her. But I'm not in love with her. I fucking hate her most of the time for what she did, but I guess I care, too. We'd made plans together that I'd counted on, that I wanted to live out with her, and it's almost like realizing a part of my life had been a lie."

That made sense. A piece of Bryce felt rage and possession because he didn't want any fucking part of Nick to belong to a woman who would do that to him. But he got it. It made sense with who Nick was. He was loyal, and dependable. Being kind meant something to Nick. Bryce respected his morals.

He figured it was also time for him to share a few truths with Nick as well. "A while back, my doctor discovered I had an aneurysm. They worried it could burst... My mom and Christi never left my side the whole time. It's how everything started with Christi. It's part of the reason I don't want to let my mom down."

CHAPTER NINETEEN

Nick's muscles tensed, hardened as though they turned to stone. "What? How long ago? Holy shit, how could you not have told me?" He tried to pull away from Bryce but the man held onto him, rolled over and lay on him, one of Bryce's hands on each of his wrists, holding him down.

"This. This reaction right fucking here is the reason you didn't know. I get it, finding out someone you care about had a major medical scare is hard, but I'm fine. I got lucky and I'm fucking *fine.* I swear I'll kick your ass if you start treating me like there's something wrong with me. Or if you start harassing me about doctors and headaches. Not you. I can't handle that shit from you."

Nick had never heard Bryce speak with so much authority. Each word was sharp, a dagger that Bryce threw at him.

"Do you understand what I'm saying?" Bryce asked.

Nick's body started to relax. He understood. It still freaked him out, but he understood. "Yeah. Sorry. You threw me for a fucking loop. I didn't expect that." Nick couldn't imagine anything ever being wrong with Bryce. He was too alive for anything to ever try and bring him down.

"I think I'll stay right here just in case."

Even though Bryce couldn't see him, Nick rolled his eyes. Yeah, Bryce was laying on him only because he thought Nick might freak out again. Horny fucking bastard. "Okay, fine, but you need to start talking."

"There's not a lot to say. I was feeling...I don't know. I just didn't feel right, but I let it all go. Finally, I went to the doctor for an exam, had scans and tests, and they found it."

On reflex, Nick ran a hand through Bryce's hair, needing to touch more of him.

"So yeah...it was toughest on Mom. She loves us so damn much. The thought of something happening was too much. She kept thinking of all the things I would miss—falling in love like Jamie and Mitch, getting married. She would tease me about how I needed to have the surgery, recoup and then go on with my life, so I could have a little Bryce. Apparently the world isn't complete with just one of me."

Nick laughed as Bryce settled more on top of him. The weight was welcoming. His body was solid, firm and comforting.

"I think it rubbed off on me. I started to freak out as well. I had this thing in my head that could fucking burst, but surgery was dangerous, too. There's a high risk of stroke. It scared the fuck out of me. I had this crazy...I don't know, I just clung to Christi."

When he paused, Nick thought he was going to say something else.

That he had a crazy *something* in specific, but he just continued. "I know she was scared to lose me. She doesn't really have anyone. My family is hers. She's family to me. We just sort of fell into it. I had surgery. She was there for recovery, which I obviously fucking rocked." He chuckled. "When I got better, I kissed her one day and she kissed me back."

A low growl formed deep inside Nick. He liked Christi, but the idea of the woman's lips on Bryce's made his gut ache. Bryce thought Nick still loved Jill, and maybe he did in some ways, but that was nothing compared to what Bryce and Christi had. They were close. They both loved each other.

"Anyway, my brothers suck at secrets. Everyone found out and my mom fell in love with the idea. I don't think either of us realized what we were doing at first. We just knew we didn't want to lose each other, so we clung the only way we knew how. Made ourselves believe we were more than friends. Finding out you have anything life-threatening makes you realize how fucking fragile life is. What if I walk down the street and get hit by a car? My house burns down? You just never know what will happen.

"I worried I would miss out on all these things that my family thinks are essential. They all loved so big, but I'd never had that, so Christi and I kept it up, kept trying. It lasted quite a while, but after some time, I think we both realized we were staying with each other more out of fear than being in love. Still, neither of us wanted to say anything. Eventually, I had to, and realized she felt the same, so we called it off."

But they hadn't told Bryce's parents. The parents who loved Christi and who thought Bryce and Christi were in love with each other. Bryce's family would have a hard time with this just like Nick's would, only in different ways. "What are we doing here, Bryce?" They were two straight guys, each screwing around with a man for the first time, when there were so many things standing in their way. They were a fucked up accident waiting to happen.

"I don't know." Bryce's hand was in his hair then. "I just know that I can't imagine not doing it."

Those words were Nick's truth as well. As much as it scared him, and even though there was a part of him that knew this would blow up in their faces, he couldn't imagine not doing it. "Me, either."

Bryce shifted, moved up and then covered Nick's mouth with his. Nick let him in immediately, their tongues tangling as they fucked each other's mouths.

Nick's cock grew, hardened as Bryce thrust against him. "Let me jerk you off, Nick. I want to play with your balls. Get you close to coming, and then hold you off until I'm ready for you to empty your load."

Nick shuddered. How in the fuck could he say no to that?

"Yeah...do it," he groaned. "Touch me."

Then the weight was gone. Bryce rolled off, shoved Nick's underwear down and moved around on the bed as though he was taking off his clothes as well. Nick wished the lights were on. He wanted to see Bryce's long erection, the way it slightly curved. Nick had only seen him once, but he remembered everything about him.

He cupped Bryce's ass when he climbed back on him. He laid the length of Nick, thrust forward, and when he did, his ass-muscles tightened beneath Nick's hands. "Oh fuck. I can't believe how good you feel. Touch my balls."

"My pleasure," Bryce replied. He palmed Nick's sac, tugged on it a little bit before sliding his hand up to Nick's straining erection.

"Spit in your hand. Get it wet."

Bryce did, and then he was stroking Nick's cock. Each pull sent a shot of pleasure through him, making his balls tighten. Bryce's grip was firm, tight as he jacked his hand up and down in quick, smooth strokes. Nick felt his orgasm closing in on him and then Bryce pulled away.

"I'm almost there. Fuck, I'm almost—put your goddamned hand back on me!"

And then Bryce did, only not on his cock. He wrapped a hand around the base of Nick's erection, pulling and keeping him from coming. "You like teasing yourself, you said."

"I like coming, too. Make me come, Bryce."

"I will, when I'm ready." His mouth went down on Nick's again. It was an urgent, hungry kiss. He thrust his cock against Nick, rubbing himself off as he rolled, palmed and played with Nick's balls.

He pulled away to spit again and then they were kissing, Bryce was jacking him off and rutting against him.

It was fucking incredible.

Everything about him—what he did and how he felt, all man against Nick. It made Nick feel like more of a man to have Bryce on top of him.

His balls were full, heavy, needing to explode. "I'm going to come. Fuck," Nick groaned out as he shot. Bryce kept jerking him, his come making it more wet, sliding between Bryce's fingers as he kept working Nick.

He kept rutting against him too until... "Fuck!" Bryce called out, hot, thick fluid landing on Nick's skin, pooling between their bodies.

Bryce's come.

On him.

He wanted more of it.

Bryce didn't move. He lay still, holding Nick's now flaccid cock as the come dried between them. "We'll just keep going. See how things go. Maybe they'll end on their own. If they don't, we'll be sure of what we want and what we're doing before we add our families into the mix."

"Okay." That sounded like a great plan to Nick. Why freak everyone out if they didn't need to?

***

Over the next week, they spent all their free time together. They both stayed at either Nick's or Bryce's house each night. Nick finally jerked Bryce off after a couple days. They got off together as much as they could, dry fucking each other or stroking each other's cocks.

Bryce loved playing with Nick's balls, bringing him close to the edge, before pulling off again. Nick made him feel like his whole fucking world was exploding when he'd tease the head of Bryce's dick—play with the hole at the tip, get him nice and wet as he rubbed his hand over him. It was fucking perfect. He spent his days working on bikes, and his nights getting off with Nick.

Being neighbors made things a whole lot more convenient.

He wanted a blowjob next—both the thought of sucking Nick off or getting blown by Nick made Bryce's dick go hard in about two seconds flat. Everything about the man did it for him. He didn't question it, either. He just knew he enjoyed this more than he'd ever enjoyed anything in his life, and that's all Bryce cared about.

It was a Wednesday afternoon and Bryce's cell rang. He was at work, but he knew it would be Nick. They'd spoken earlier and Nick said he'd call when he got a break. "I'll be back," he called to Tim, the other mechanic who helped him out at the shop.

"I've been doing some research." Bryce walked into his office and closed the door.

"Oh no. That's a scary thought. What kind of research?"

"Sex. Is there any other kind that's more important?"

"You have to research sex?" Nick asked. "I'm sorry, I was under the impression you knew what you were doing when it came to that. How is it I've only been with one person besides you and I don't have to research how to fuck?"

Bryce rolled his eyes. "You're fucking funny. I'll show you just how much I know what I'm doing. And this isn't just about the sex. There's a whole hell of a lot more that goes into it. Did you know that your prostate is supposed to be like orgasm fucking heaven?"

"Shh!" Nick hushed him through the line and then there was a clatter, Nick obviously having dropped the phone. Bryce burst out laughing.

"Did I embarrass you?" he asked when Nick got back on the phone. "Does the thought of me sticking a finger in your ass and rubbing your prostate make you nervous? Don't worry. I've already decided you can do it to me first."

There was a deep gasp on the other end of the line, and then, "Really?"

"Did you not hear what I said? Orgasm heaven. Yes, I'm fucking serious. There's a catch, though. I want a blowjob at the same time. If I'm the guinea pig, I get whatever I want out of the deal."

Nick was quiet and Bryce let him think it through. Finally he got an, "Okay... I think I can try that. I can't make you any promises on how it will go, though."

"That's not all."

"How many demands do you have, Bryce? You just told me I'm putting a finger in your ass and your dick in my mouth in one shot." There was laughter in Nick's voice along with nerves, so Bryce couldn't help but chuckle as well.

"Don't worry. This next part is going to help us work up to it. You have a date with me Saturday night. If we're doing this, we need to know exactly what we're getting into. I bought a subscription to a gay porn website. We're going to watch it together."

He could practically hear Nick swallow his own tongue.

"I think...I think that's probably a good idea. I've never had anal sex. Jill wouldn't—"

"Let's not talk about her. She pisses me off."

"Okay, but that doesn't change the fact that I've never fucked someone in the ass, and I sure as hell never had someone touch mine. Is that going to be a thing that happens between us? Are we eventually going to want to do that?"

Bryce was pretty sure they would. At least he would want to if they kept things up. "I would assume so. Eventually. Which is the reason for the porn. Trust me, it'll be fun."

"I trust you," Nick replied, and it made Bryce's heart race and his palms sweat. Christ, what this man did to him. He didn't understand it. He just knew he liked it and wanted more.

"You've turned my whole fucking world upside down, you know that?"

"Yeah," Nick whispered. "Yeah, you've done the same with mine."

Bryce smiled. "Obviously. I'm going to turn you into my little cocksucker."

"Fuck you. Just for that, my mouth is staying as far away from your," he lowered his voice, "erection as it can."

"Aww, come on. Don't say that. If it makes you feel better, I'm planning on being your very own cocksucker, too."

Bryce got off the phone laughing. His whole life he'd tried to have as much fun as possible. What he didn't realize was, he didn't even know what fun was until he'd met Nick.

CHAPTER TWENTY

The man was going to drive him insane. Nick hadn't realized he wanted to go crazy until he met Bryce. He did, though—at least that meant doing it with Bryce. He kept Nick on his toes, made him laugh more than he thought was possible, and made him feel comfortable at the same time.

He hadn't realized something was missing from his life, but it had been. He felt full in a way that was completely foreign to him.

And now he had even more reasons to be scared to add to the list. Not only how their families would feel, and nerves about the sex, but he couldn't stop thinking about the fact that Bryce had been sick.

While Bryce was apparently researching prostate stimulation and sucking dick, Nick was researching aneurysms, what they entailed, or if people often got another one.

Because the thought of losing Bryce freaked him the hell out.

Nick cared about him. A lot. Still, he tried to push serious thoughts out of his head. Bryce seemed to be good at it, and if he could handle it, Nick should be able to as well.

The next few days went by in a pattern of work and spending time with Bryce, much like the past couple of months, but with the addition of kissing and touching.

Before he knew it, it was Saturday. Bryce was working at the shop, but they both had the evening and night off. His shop was closed Sundays and Mondays, and Nick made sure he was off Saturdays and Mondays (except for paperwork he did from home those days). It gave them some time together that way.

And tonight they were watching porn. Gay porn.

And he was supposed to give his first blowjob.

You know, just a normal Saturday night.

He was scared shitless.

Nick did a little bit of paperwork but couldn't really concentrate, so he got dressed and drove down to Bryce's shop. He figured he'd find out what the man wanted for dinner, which would give him something to do.

He'd only been here once before. Nick walked through the glass doors, but didn't see Bryce or anyone else there. He hadn't noticed anyone in the open garage, either. He pulled out his phone to text Bryce just as another man walked around the corner. "Can I help you?" the guy asked. From talking with Bryce, Nick knew this must be Tim.

"Hi. I'm Nick. I'm looking for Bryce."

"Oh yeah. You're his neighbor, right?"

The word neighbor rubbed him raw when it shouldn't. It's what he was. "Yeah. Is he around?"

"He's in his office with his lady. I'll call back there and let him know you're here."

Well fuck. He'd thought only being called Bryce's neighbor rubbed him wrong; it had *nothing* on being told Bryce was with his lady. Nick's body temperature went up about a hundred degrees as he tried to take a few breaths to settle down.

Logically, he knew who it was. It had to be Christi. But he hadn't realized everyone still thought they were together. He thought it was only Bryce's parents.

Why does it matter? I know the truth...

But it also hadn't been that long ago that he watched them together and knew it was only a matter of time before they got back together.

"Nick?" Bryce's voice pulled him out of his thoughts. He hadn't realized Tim called back for Bryce already. "I said your name three times. Get your ass back here. Are you okay?"

He should be, but he didn't really feel okay. This whole situation was so foreign and fucked up. He hadn't realized until that second that there might be a part of him that didn't trust Bryce. A fear that he would do the same thing to Nick that Jill had, and he wasn't sure how to deal with that.

***

Bryce studied Nick as he moved toward him. There was something off, but Bryce didn't know what it was. "You okay?" he reached for Nick, but pulled his hand back. Christ, he'd almost touched him right out in the open.

"Well if it isn't hot neighbor Nick." Christi smiled as Nick walked into the office. Bryce closed the door behind him.

"Shut it, Christi. I told you no flirting with him." Maybe it was okay before he'd decided he wanted Nick, but not anymore.

"Hey," Nick replied just as Christi said, "You're no fun."

"On the contrary, I've been told I'm a whole hell of a lot of fun." He winked at her and Christi rolled her eyes.

"I'm just here for a minute and then you guys can get back to whatever you're doing. I came to see what you wanted me to make for dinner." Nick looked at Christi, then Bryce, before crossing his arms, a frown on his face. What the hell was his problem?

"Okay, there's enough tension in this room to cut with a knife." Christi stood. "I'm going to go to the bathroom. Knock on the door when you're done and I can pretend it took me a really long time to pee."

Bryce nudged her as she passed, both appreciative and a little annoyed because of the way she'd put it out there. She'd asked about him and Nick, but Bryce didn't tell her anything. It was their business. She made it pretty obvious she knew something was going on, though. Not that Nick hadn't made it pretty fucking obvious by coming in to ask him what he wanted for dinner. That sounded about as domesticated as anything Bryce had ever heard.

"I think Christi has us figured out. Though in all honesty, she realized before I did, but I think she knows it's moved past my secret crush on you to something more."

Half of Nick's mouth kicked up. It was the first time he'd almost smiled since Bryce saw him today. "You had a crush on me?"

"Obviously. And I'm glad you're smiling. You came in here like you wanted to set the place on fire. What's up?"

Bryce walked over to him. He put his hands on Nick's waist just as the man asked, "Why do you think it didn't work out between you and Christi?"

Umm…what? "Because we were better off as friends. It was a mistake. Now come here so I can kiss you." When Nick didn't move, Bryce leaned in. Nick's lips automatically parted for him. He hadn't shaved today, so rough stubble met his skin.

He pushed his tongue into Nick's mouth, thinking this felt pretty fucking amazing. He loved kissing this man. Nick gave as good as he took—rough and eager. Tongue probing, mouth hungry.

"Be careful or you're going to give me a hard-on." Bryce pulled back. "I really should get back out there. I need to get this bike finished so I can get home on time today."

"Okay." Nick pressed his lips to Bryce's one more time before pulling back.

"I don't want Christi. I need to make sure you know that."

Nick nodded. "Okay," he said again. "What do you want me to make for dinner?"

Was that even a question? Bryce shrugged. "Doesn't matter what you make, it'll be good. Honestly, I don't give a shit what we eat. I get to watch porn with a sexy man tonight and get my dick sucked. Nothing else really matters."

When the man smiled at him, he couldn't help but lean forward and take Nick's mouth one more time.

CHAPTER TWENTY-ONE

Nick almost forgot he'd been frustrated until he had to knock on the bathroom door so Christi would come out. But then…if there was anything going on, she wouldn't have hid out in the bathroom to discretely give them time together.

She opened the door and mouthed, *"Finally."*

He liked her. In a lot of ways she would be the perfect woman for Bryce. She could keep up with him, match him sarcastic jab for sarcastic jab. But he didn't want that…because Bryce was his.

"Can I walk out with you?" she asked.

"Yeah, sure. Weren't you waiting to go back in with Bryce, though?"

She shook her head. "I'm done with him. I was waiting for you." Christi fell in step beside him. When they got outside, she walked toward her car and he followed her over to be polite.

"I want you to know you have nothing to worry about with me. Bryce and I…it was a mistake. We were scared to lose each other. We were confused. That's all it was. I'm not in love with him, and he's not in love with me, either."

"I wasn't...I'm not..." But he really was worried.

"I saw your face when you came in. It's okay. I get it. He's happy. I've never seen him like this before. He sure as hell doesn't look at me the way he looks at you."

A warmth spread through Nick's chest. As weak as it made him feel, he needed to hear that. "Thanks. He's..." He's what? Bryce meant something to Nick. He wasn't a hundred percent sure what, but he knew it was big. He knew he'd felt real jealousy thinking of Bryce and Christi together. Nick had wanted a connection with someone, and he got that with Bryce. Got it in a way he never had before. "He's hard to put into words."

She laughed. "That's one way to describe him." Christi reached out, grabbed Nick's hand and squeezed. "He has you just as upside down and backwards as you have him, doesn't he?"

Nick nodded. There was no reason to deny it. "There are a lot of variables involved, though."

"None that should matter besides the way the two of you feel. If anyone else's tune doesn't go with yours, it's just background noise. I know it's easy for me to say that, but it's true. Thanks for giving this...giving him a chance. It feels good seeing him like this. I know he doesn't show it, but Bryce isn't very good at letting people in. It's just not the way he's built. He let you in, though."

"Thank you," Nick told her. No matter what happened, or how

things went with them, this, *Bryce*, was important to him. This was very real to Nick. He wouldn't be here if it wasn't. The thing was, that wasn't a guarantee it would work. If Bryce and Christi, heterosexual best friends, weren't meant to be together, two straight guys who suddenly wanted each other sure as hell wouldn't be.

They said their goodbyes and Nick headed to the grocery store. He got the stuff to make homemade pasta, his secret sauce and rosemary chicken breasts.

When he got home, he took a shower and changed before getting dinner ready. It was a few minutes after five when there was a knock on his door.

Bryce was home...and their night was about to start. In that moment, nothing else mattered. Nick couldn't wait.

***

Bryce was leaning against the house when Nick opened the door. He crossed his arms and looked at the other man with a grin on his face. "You're covered in flour, and I'm covered in oil." Nick wasn't really very messy, but Bryce was. He reached out and wiped the dusting of white powder off Nick's cheek.

"I like it when you're dirty." His eyes darted down. He looked almost shy to have said something like that to Bryce, but he didn't have any reason to be. It was fucking hot.

"It's a shame I have to go shower then. I can still be dirty for you, though—just in a different way. It'll be more fun that way, too."

Nick adjusted himself. "You're going to give me a hard-on before we get started."

Nick's words made him stumble over his thoughts for just a second. He was giving another man an erection.

Yeah, he wanted that.

He was done with overthinking things. "Good. I'm going to go get cleaned up. Hold that thought."

As he went to turn, Nick said, "Okay. I have to finish up the pasta real quick."

"Can you do that after?" He wasn't lying when he told Nick he'd been doing some research. There were things he had to do to get ready for sex—for any kind of penetration— with Nick. He never had to think about this stuff before. Not that they planned to fuck tonight, but Bryce wanted to be ready just in case. This was a whole new ballgame for him. He'd stuck a finger up a woman's ass before, with no problems, but if they went any farther than that, he figured he should be ready. So the plan was: take care of business, shower, sex, then food.

"Eager?" Nick cocked a brow at him, conceit clear in his expression.

Bryce laughed and shook his head. "Look at you, getting all cocky. Yeah, I'm excited. It's a blowjob and porn. What's not to be excited about?" He didn't want Nick to know exactly what he was doing. Bryce turned again to head to his place, but Nick's words stopped him.

"Hey. Are we really doing this?"

Bryce didn't know if Nick meant the porn, the sex, seeing each other or all of the above, so he answered the only way he could. "Unless you tell me we're not, we are. Gimme a little bit and I'll be over." Bryce didn't let anything stop him this time as he made his way to his place.

He grabbed a pair of sweats and a T-shirt so he'd be comfortable before he went into the bathroom. Bryce dumped his bag out on the counter, did what he needed to do, and then climbed into the shower. This was all pretty awkward and would take some getting used to, but hell, he wanted Nick enough that he'd do just about anything. He still didn't get the why of it—why he'd suddenly want a man when he'd never had the feeling before, or why Nick felt the same. Why Bryce couldn't get enough of him, and hell, even why he liked just spending time with the guy so much. But he did, and that was all that mattered to him. He couldn't wait to get back next door.

Oh, and if the websites were correct, he also had orgasm heaven to look forward to.

CHAPTER TWENTY-TWO

Nick felt like an inexperienced virgin. Yeah, in a lot of ways he wasn't incredibly experienced. He'd had a lot of sex in his life, but it had all been with the same woman. Jill wasn't very adventurous...or maybe he'd never tried to be adventurous with her. All he knew was he'd never watched porn with another person in his life, and he'd never sat around and planned out a night of sex and visual stimulation with someone else. He could see where Bryce was coming from, because this was so new to both of them, but it still felt fucking strange.

So was the thought that he'd have a dick in his mouth soon. He knew what he liked when it came to getting head, and he hoped like hell that made it easier for him to give it.

Holy fucking shit, he'd be giving another man head tonight! How did this happen again? And how did he feel about it? There were all sorts of lines getting crossed with him and Bryce that he never saw himself crossing. But then, he never saw himself with anyone other than his ex, either. And the connection between him and Bryce...it was there, in his chest, pulling them together in a way he'd never experienced. Being with Bryce felt much less foreign than the thought of fucking a random woman in his car. Nick needed to feel something for the person he was with, and he did with Bryce. Maybe that's all that mattered.

He jumped when there was a knock at the door. He really needed to calm down. Before he had the chance to say *come in*, the door opened and Bryce walked inside. His hair was wet, messed up from the towel, and he obviously hadn't taken the time to shave, and just like earlier, the blood started heading toward Nick's cock. Bryce was sexy to him. So fucking sexy...and that made some of his nerves calm down. Or maybe that was just Bryce and not even the sexiness. From day one Nick had felt comfortable around him.

"You good?" Bryce's brows pulled together, and Nick silently cursed. Bryce didn't look nervous at all. He didn't want his nervousness to be so obvious.

"Yeah, I'm good."

"It's okay to be nervous. This is a big fucking deal, Nick. Life-changing. If you're having second thoughts—"

"No!" he rushed out. He wasn't. He probably should be, but he wasn't. "I want this. Want you."

Bryce grinned and winked at him. "Then go in your bedroom and get kinky with me."

Nick stood, suddenly feeling a whole lot more at ease. Bryce had that quality about him. "You're getting bossy. Plus, I was sitting here wondering what the hell I get out of this night. You get a blowjob and orgasm heaven. What about me?"

Bryce grabbed his arm as Nick tried to walk by. "I'll taste you, too. I want that. I want to try everything with you."

Everything suddenly sounded like the biggest word in the English language. If he didn't know better, he'd think Bryce meant more than just sex. But he couldn't—not this man who wanted nothing to do with commitment, and definitely not this soon. Still, Nick replied, "I'm counting on it—all of it," and wondered if he meant the same kind of *everything* he thought he'd heard in Bryce's words, and if he could possibly mean it.

"Then let's go."

Nick led Bryce to his bedroom. He hit the light, and headed over to his computer. Bryce was right behind him. "I have a twenty-four inch computer screen. That'll help." He felt the urge to ramble about anything and everything he could think of just to calm himself down.

"Let me log in to the site." Bryce got the computer up and running before he browsed for the website.

"Sexy Man Lovin?" he asked, trying to keep the laughter out of his voice. "How in the hell did you find that?"

"You'd be surprised at some of the shit out there! Believe me, Sexy Man Lovin was the best place to start. Their tagline is, Real Sex for Real Gay Men."

Nick's pulse suddenly went crazy like he was on drugs, while Bryce sort of froze in this place. They were going to watch real sex for real gay men before they went and did some of this stuff with each other. That made them gay—or at least bisexual. Yeah, he knew that going into it, but thinking about it put a different spin on things.

"It's just a label," Bryce said, as though he could read Nick's mind. "It doesn't matter."

And Bryce was right, it shouldn't. But to some people, it would.

Then Bryce was there, standing in front of him, his hands on Nick's face. "Don't think about anything else but us. We want this. I'll even suck you off first, if it helps. I'll admit it's fucking scary and confusing, but I do. I want to taste you. Want to smell your skin and drive you fucking wild. Just know that if I do, at least a finger is going inside you...maybe more. Eventually we'll know each other's bodies inside and out."

Male voices started in the background—two guys telling each other what they wanted to do, to taste, to feel, the same way Bryce was telling him. And yeah, he fucking wanted it. His dick already stood at attention. His balls already getting primed to let loose. This was just them—this man who made Nick feel different than anyone else ever had. His friend. His lover. Just them.

As much as he wanted what Bryce just said, maybe minus the fingering, Nick knew he had to be the one to give it to Bryce first. Bryce deserved that for being patient with him—for having the balls to make all the first moves. "No...I want to do this for you...to you. I want to be the one driving you out of your mind tonight."

Bryce smiled, all cocky fucking grin, leaned forward and kissed him. "Cocksucking 101 is about to start."

CROSSROADS

***

Bryce had never been so hard in his life.

He and Nick lay on Nick's bed, watching the two men on screen make out. They were all muscle, hairy bodies, and rough masculinity, and Bryce had to do everything in his power not to shove his hand down his sweats and jerk off until he came all over Nick's bed. "They're gorgeous together."

He watched as one of the men dropped to his knees, grabbing the other guy's cock and licking the tip. That, right fucking there, was what he wanted. His dick jerked, his sweats suddenly too tight. "I'm going to make you get on your knees for me, Nick."

"Fuck off..." and then... "Not the first time at least."

He wanted it, too. He heard it in the inflection of Nick's husky voice.

They didn't touch each other as they watched. Guy two took the first man, balls deep. The guy fucked his throat before he pulled off and sucked the man's balls into his mouth. They both groaned, and cursed, fucking loving it, and Bryce knew he would love it, too. He and Nick, just like the two men on the screen. "I'm going to come the second your lips are on me."

"Shh. I'm watching," Nick replied from beside him, and Bryce laughed.

Bryce watched as they moved to a couch. The guy who'd been sucked lay down, as the other man licked his finger. He pushed at the man's anus, slowly, breaching it open. Oh...that looked nice. He slid his finger in and out and told the man how tight his hole was as the other man's eyes rolled back and he rode one finger, then two, and three.

Bryce rotated his hips, pushing his rock hard cock against the bed. He needed to be touched, kissed, needed to get off, but he wanted them to watch this, too. Not just because they were doing these things for the first time, but he thought it was important for them both to see how much two men could enjoy each other.

"I'm leaking all over the place."

"Oh, fuck," Bryce shuddered. "Don't say shit like that. You're going to make me blow before we even start."

"Then let's start. I can't wait." Before Bryce realized what was happening, Nick's mouth was on his. He shoved at Bryce, rolling him over, and climbed on top of him. Their pricks rubbed together as their tongues invaded each other's mouths. It was like a war, both of them fighting for possession as they grabbed at each other while their mouths dueled. It was rough, urgent, passionate and everything else he could imagine as his cock begged to shoot the load in his balls.

"Take my clothes off, Nick. I want your mouth. Either that or roll the fuck over and let me taste you."

Nick jerked off of him, more urgent and needy than Bryce had ever seen him. He ripped his shirt over his head and Bryce did the same. The second he got it off, Nick's hands were on the waistband of Bryce's sweats and he pulled them down.

Bryce's cock burst free, bouncing against his stomach. He lay on his back, Nick kneeling over him. "I can't get over what you do to my body." Nick pinched a nipple. "Your flat nipples, the hair on your chest, the muscles, and your rough hands. I think about you all the fucking time. It's like I have to remind myself I should second guess this, us."

"Fuck that. Don't second guess anything. Take what you want, Nick. When's the last time you let yourself do that?"

Bryce could see the wheels turning in Nick's head—see his question hit home.

"What do you want, Nick?"

"Right now? Nothing, but you." And then he kissed Bryce's chest, his right nipple, then down his body. Nick lay between Bryce's legs, his mouth so fucking close to Bryce's cock that he knew if he just changed the angle, he could shove right in. Pre-come dripped from his head.

"Tell me if something I'm doing doesn't feel good or if I'm fucking it up."

"As long as you don't use teeth, there's no way to fuck this up."

Nick leaned in, got closer. "You smell like sex...musk and sex. It makes my dick ache from wanting you."

Bryce had to grab his balls to keep from blowing his load too soon. He had a feeling he was the only person Nick had ever talked to like this. "Gimme your mouth. Taste what you're smelling, and then I'll do it to you."

Nick looked up at him, desire and fear in his eyes. Bryce smiled, hoping that helped, because he didn't know what the fuck else to do. Yeah, he got this was a big deal for both of them, but it was right. He knew it in a way he'd never known anything else.

Bryce touched Nick, ran his hand down the side of Nick's face, and then Nick leaned forward. His tongue slipped between his lips as he swirled it around the swollen head of Bryce's dick. It was all wet, fucking heat, and on reflex, Bryce thrust his hips forward. "Fuck, that feels so good, baby. Do it again."

And Nick did. He licked at the head of Bryce's erection before sucking just the tip into his mouth. Bryce still touched the side of Nick's face, felt the growth of hair there, let it rub his palm as Nick sucked him.

He didn't take Bryce deep, but he didn't have to for Bryce's balls to want to empty into his mouth. He groaned, fought to keep himself still, as Nick explored him. Bryce's legs trembled. The heel of his foot dug into the bed as he fought with his squirming body.

"Your skin is salty, and hot. It's...different...but good, so fucking good, Bryce." Nick's tongue started at the base of Bryce's dick, right above his balls, and then ran up to the head, where he sucked on it again. Nick moaned, and the vibration was like sensory fucking overload.

"Do that again. Moan around me. Fuck, I want to last all night, but this isn't going to go long."

Nick's mouth was suddenly gone and Bryce reached for him, tried to grab him and shove his head back down to his crotch where it belonged. "Push your legs up. I want to see your ass...your hole." He couldn't even let the fact that Nick couldn't just say his asshole bother him right now. Later, he'd think about it. Right now, he just wanted it under Nick's inspection. Wanted to feel a tongue, finger, or hell even just Nick's breath there.

Bryce planted his feet on the bed and spread his legs, and that's when it hit him, too. This man was looking at his asshole. No one had ever done that before. He was kinky and got with kinky women, but none of them went anywhere near his asshole, and he hadn't given it a second thought until Nick.

"It looks so fucking tight. How will I ever fit in there?" Nick's warm breath ghosted across him. Part of Bryce could think of nothing except, *YES, he's eventually going to want to fuck me*, while the other thought, *He's right. How will he ever fit, and do I want him to?*

It was like an electrical jolt went through Bryce when he felt Nick's finger brush over his asshole.

"Get your mouth on me or your finger in me. I'm going fucking crazy here." Bryce could hardly control his own body. The need to come was right there, so fucking strong that he hurt.

Nick moved, and Bryce growled for him to come back, but the man only moved to grab lube from his beside drawer. "We should use this to make it easier on you."

Nick didn't take his eyes off him as Bryce looked down at where the man lay between his legs again. Bryce nodded and Nick smiled. He had no doubt Nick was as nervous as he was, but they both wanted it. There was no doubt in Bryce's mind about that.

Nick squirted his finger and then touched it to Bryce's hole. It was cold, but he needed that to cool him the fuck off.

"Do I just...?"

"Push it in, Nick. Let me feel you inside me."

And then he pushed. Even just a finger was a tight fit. Bryce moved as he felt the tip penetrate him, push past the ring of muscles. At first, his body told him it didn't belong, but then Nick moved in deeper, retreated almost all the way before pushing in again.

"What does it feel like?" Nick asked, breathing against Bryce's nuts.

"Different..." Bryce closed his eyes, his body automatically pushing to fuck itself on Nick's finger. "I'm not sure. Try another one...and go deeper." He sounded needy, when he'd never been needy for anything in his life. But Bryce couldn't find it in himself to care.

There was more cold, more pressure, more stretching, and then, "Oh fuck. Yeah...like that, baby. Let me feel you, Nick."

Nick pushed deeper, faster. "It's so fucking sexy, watching my fingers disappear inside you. Jesus, Bryce. You should see this."

"We'll record it next time."

Nick froze up and Bryce laughed. Then Nick was fingering him again—faster and with more confidence than he was before. Bryce's eyes jerked open when Nick's hot mouth sucked his cock again. Still not deep, but it was enough. The suction, along with the finger-fucking, made Bryce crazy. He shoved down, fucking himself on Nick, gripping Nick's hair as he sucked Bryce's cock—again, not deep, but that didn't matter.

The position of Nick's fingers changed. He pushed and curved them, rubbed and then—"Holy fuck!" His dick erupted. He didn't have enough time to warn Nick as he shot a heavy spurt into Nick's mouth. Nick tensed up, stopped moving and then sucked harder, pushed on Bryce's prostate again, making another long stream of come pulse from his dick and into Nick's mouth. He couldn't have stopped it if he wanted to. Not that he did. Nick's name pulled from the back of his throat, a strangled cry as Bryce filled his lover's mouth.

When Nick pulled off, he dropped his head right on Bryce's spent dick, and Bryce could only mutter three words. "Orgasm fucking heaven."

CHAPTER TWENTY-THREE

"You okay?" Bryce asked as Nick lay on him, his head to the side and staring off. Bryce read him pretty well. He seemed to be able to tell when Nick had a lot on his mind, and Nick loved that Bryce didn't shy away from asking him.

"I am. Just thinking about what I did...that I liked doing it to you." Never in a million years did he see himself here, but it's where he was, and now he just had to figure out how to navigate it. "If I'm being honest, I hadn't planned to swallow. It snuck up on me, and I just did."

Bryce laughed, grabbed Nick and pulled him up his body. He had his head on Bryce's chest. Nick was still hard, the need to come still bearing down on him, but he liked this, too, lying with Bryce.

"It snuck up on me as well. It's like a magic-fucking button or something, and now I want to suck you off, too." Bryce rolled so he lay on top of Nick. "And just so you know, I do plan on swallowing."

Aaaaand, his cock got even harder, stiff and rigid. "I'm clean. I got tested after Jill. I have the results."

"Me, too. I get blood work every three months, and I haven't been with anyone since my last test. Now relax. I want to see what you taste like. I'll suck on your balls. I know how much you like your nuts played with."

Fire shot through Nick's veins, engulfing him even more than he'd already been. It felt like an eternity since he'd been blown. When Bryce slid down his body and buried his face in Nick's crotch, he about lost it. The other man went straight for his sac, sucking as much of it as he could into his mouth, making Nick's eyes roll back in his head. "Oh fuck...Bryce."

"Keep saying my name. I like it. Your balls are already tight. They want to let go, don't they?"

Nick didn't answer because Bryce's face was there again, right between his legs, sucking and licking his balls. He was fucking good at this. Nick would never suspect that it was his first time.

Bryce's thumb brushed over his taint as he went for Nick's cock. Bryce didn't do anything half-assed, so Nick wasn't surprised when he tried to take Nick to the back of his throat. He gagged slightly, but that didn't stop him. He bobbed his head up and down, each time trying to take more of Nick inside his hot, wet mouth.

Nick fisted a hand in Bryce's hair. He didn't dare take his eyes off the man. He wanted to see each muscle in Bryce's back move, his ass in the air. Wanted to see and know exactly who it was that he had between his legs sucking him off.

There was a *pop* when Bryce pulled off. "You're not saying my name. I wanna hear it."

"Bryce," Nick gritted out as Bryce used his hand on him, his mouth going back to Nick's tight balls. "Fuck...right there, Bryce. Jesus, you feel good."

"You did, too. Especially right here." Nick was pulled out of the moment briefly when Bryce touched his asshole. "Not tonight, but I want inside here, too. Will you let me, Nick? Fuck, I want to do everything with you."

"Yes," he hissed out. There wasn't any other possible answer. They were in this together, exploring and figuring out what this was between them.

Bryce sucked him deep again. When he did, he pulled a little on Nick's balls, palmed them and played with them. He used his other hand to jerk Nick off as he sucked him. His orgasm built bigger and bigger until he couldn't' hold it back anymore. He erupted. His balls tightened as he squirted once, twice, three times into Bryce's mouth. The other man didn't hesitate to swallow it all down. And then their mouths were connected. Bryce pushed his tongue into Nick's mouth. He tasted himself there, but the taste of Bryce was even stronger. He knew it already, and so he pulled Bryce closer, deepening their kiss as Bryce rubbed their bodies together.

They kept that going, just made out with each other. Their naked bodies molded together, their crotches, chests and everything else rubbing against each other. Sweat made them stick together. It was messy... and the sexiest fucking thing he'd ever done in his life. When they stopped, Bryce didn't roll off him. It was as though the computer screen called both their names. It was a different couple by now. He had no idea how many scenes had gone by, but the two men now were in the midst of fucking.

Nick would be lying if his stomach didn't drop slightly. The guy's asshole was stretched a whole hell of a lot bigger than Bryce's had with two of his fingers. And he and Bryce were both fairly big men.

"It'll be okay. You can have me first," Bryce again read his mind. "I can't fucking wait for you to take me, Nick."

Yeah, he was nervous about Bryce fucking him, but he was also scared to fuck Bryce. He'd always known he had an above average-sized dick, but now, thinking about how it would stretch Bryce's asshole…he didn't know what to think.

The men on the screen were definitely enjoying it—even the guy on the bottom. He clung onto the top, begging him for more. Nick ran his hand down Bryce's body, clutching his muscular ass. "I want you, too." This whole thing made Nick's heart race and his stomach twist. Not just Bryce being a man, but how much Nick wanted him. He didn't put himself out there that easily. He didn't just fuck anyone. The fact that this was more than sex was the scariest part of all. "I…this is probably the wrong time, and probably the wrong thing to say, but you know this is more than sex to me, right? I don't—"

"Yeah. I know. You're not the only one. I don't know what this is, but it's not just sex."

Some of the knots in Nick's gut started to unwind. Unfortunately, not all of them, because he knew this was only the beginning of what would be a long, confusing road.

"I'm going to talk to my parents."

And, now he was in knots again. "Not yet. I'm not ready to tell people."

Bryce leaned up and stared down at him. "Chill out. You're going to give yourself a heart attack before we even get to the rest of the fun stuff. I'm telling them about Christi, not you. They need to know. I can't keep it from them any longer."

Nick knew what he was saying—because this was the beginning of them. Because it would make things easier when he eventually told his parents they were...what? Dating?

Yeah, this was definitely just the beginning, and Nick knew it would be one hell of a ride—one he hoped didn't wreck them.

***

One day later that week, Bryce left work early. It was a pussy move, but he wanted to be sure he spoke with his mom without the chance of anyone else being there. His dad worked, because the man would probably never retire, and both his brothers and their wives would be busy. Even though Jamie, Mitch and their wives knew about Christi, they'd give him shit about waiting so long to tell his parents.

His dad wouldn't be nearly as affected as his mom. Sure, he wanted Bryce to settle down, and often times lectured him on "growing up," as he put it, and taking things more seriously, but his father let Bryce live his own life. Dad didn't count on Bryce to give him grandkids.

Mom did.

He knew he was too damn old to live his life for other people, but he also felt an obligation to the people he loved.

And now he was about to tell his mom he'd changed his mind about something else—someone else. Someone she loved. This wasn't going to go over well.

He knocked, opened the door, and stuck his head in. "Hey, Ma. It's the best looking Tanner boy. You here?"

"Hey! I'm in the living room. What are you doing off work early?"

He walked into the room to see her sitting on the floor surrounded by photo albums. "Just wanted to come and see you. What are you up to?" He sat down on the floor next to her.

"I'm trying to figure out something to do for Christi. When I had all three of the girls over the other day to help with the scrapbook I'm making for your father, she seemed to really like it."

Christi was over at his parents' house? He hadn't even known.

"I'm sure she talks to you about this, but I think it's hard for her. She's never had much family besides us, so I thought maybe she might enjoy it if I made a scrapbook for her, too. I have a thousand pictures of you kids growing up. Maybe you can grab some more recent ones of the two of you. What do you think? Will she like that?" His mom looked over at him with the same brown eyes that Bryce had, and a smile from ear to ear. She had no idea Bryce's gut dropped. That he'd come over here to disappoint her.

"Yeah...that's a good idea. Listen, Ma—"

"Wait. I want to say something first. I've been thinking about it for a while. I just..." she shrugged. "Your father and I want you to know how proud we are of you. We always worried about you. You've always had your head in the clouds more than your brothers. It took you a little longer to find your way, and if I'm being honest, I worried if you ever would. You have, though—first with how hard you've worked at starting your shop, and now you've settled into a relationship with Christi." She reached over and squeezed his leg. "I'd be lying if I didn't admit that I'm glad it's her. She's a special girl. She's always felt like a part of this family, and now with the two of you together, it feels more official. You waited for the right girl, and she's so lucky to have you, too, Bryce. It was worth all the worry, and the ups and downs, because they brought us here. You're happier than I've ever seen you. A mom knows those things."

She pulled away and winked. "Now we just have to hope for a wedding and babies and everything will be perfect."

Bryce tried to smile at her, but he was pretty sure he probably just looked constipated. He *was* happy, but as much as he loved Christi, it wasn't because of *her*. In a lot of ways, he felt like his life really was coming together. He hadn't realized he wanted that until recently—but with the shop, his new house, and Nick, yeah, he did feel settled. He was about to shake all of that up, though—this situation with Nick made things different. Bryce wanted it, he knew he did, but he also didn't want to hurt his family.

And that's exactly what he would be doing. He fucked up big time with this whole thing with Christi. He'd waited too long and done something he hadn't thought about in the beginning. He'd gotten his mom's hopes up. He made her believe something that wasn't true, and now he had to break her heart by telling her what a fraud he was.

Bryce's gut ached.

"Hey. What's wrong? Are you feeling okay?" she asked.

He tried to snap himself out of it, and waved off her concern. "Yeah, I'm fine. Just tired."

"Regular tired or over-tired? You're not pushing yourself too hard, are you? Maybe you should go to the doctor and—"

"Ma, I'm fine," he cut her off. "I'm tired just like everyone else gets. It's nothing serious."

She gave him a sad smile. He knew how hard him getting sick had been on his family. No parent wanted to see their child suffer that way. "Okay, as long as you're sure. Now, why don't you tell me why you stopped by? I'm not buying that you came just to see me. Then, if you want, you can help me finish this for Christi. I think it'll mean a lot to her."

It would. Bryce knew that, but he really couldn't stay here and do this with his mom right now. "I should get back to work. I just stopped by on my way to pick up a part." Bryce pushed to his feet, guilt making his body feel heavy. "I love you."

"I love you, too."

171

CHAPTER TWENTY-FOUR

Nick was busy in the kitchen when one of the waitresses came back to talk to him. "Hey, there's a group out there having dinner who says they know you. I guess you're a friend of their son's?" she asked. Immediately, he knew it had to be Bryce's family. How sad was it that Bryce was the only possibility it could be? He really needed to get out there and meet more people. "They said not to bother you, but I thought you might want to know."

Nick almost wished she hadn't told him. Bryce went over earlier today to tell his mom that he and Christi weren't dating—that they hadn't been for a while. It was absolutely ridiculous, but his first thought was...*will they know? Somehow, will they know that I'm dating their son instead of Christi?*

"Yeah, okay. Thanks, Liz. I was about to take a break anyway. I'll go say hi." She started to walk away, but Nick asked, "Have they ordered yet?"

"No."

"Their dinner is on the house, okay?"

She looked startled for a second before she said, "Okay. No problem."

It was the first time Nick had ever offered a free meal to anyone. He finished up what he was doing, washed his hands and then made his way into the dining area. He spotted Bryce's family immediately...only it wasn't just his parents. Jamie and Hope were with them—Jamie, the brother who knew something was going on between Nick and Bryce.

Jesus, his life had taken a strange turn since meeting Bryce. He was going out to say hi to the family of...his boyfriend? Is that even what Bryce wanted? Is it what he wanted?

He almost snuck back into the kitchen, but instead he moved forward. What was the big deal? He was just saying hi to his friend's family—and his brother who *knew.*

"Nick! Hi, you didn't have to come out. We didn't want to interrupt you. Jamie and Hope were taking us to dinner, and Jamie thought it might be nice to come here. The food was so wonderful at Mitch's birthday."

Nick couldn't help but glance at Jamie. What? Did he want to check out Nick again since he knew what was happening with Bryce?

Jamie looked almost embarrassed as he shrugged, and Nick returned his attention to Georgina. "It's not a bother at all. It's great to see you guys again. Order whatever you want. It's on the house tonight." He wanted to make a good impression with Bryce's family. Holy shit, he was trying to woo his boyfriend's parents with free food.

"No, we can't let you do that, son. It's a nice offer, though."
William smiled at him and he realized it was the same as Bryce's.

"No, please. I'd be honored to. Bryce has been a really great friend
to me." *I care about him and want you to like me.* "It's the least I can
do."

"We couldn't—"

"Ma," Jamie interrupted her. "He wouldn't have offered if he
didn't want to. Let him."

Nick tried to give the man a silent thank you. Somehow he realized
this was important to Nick.

"If you insist. You'll have to come to dinner one night with Bryce
and Christi, then. I'm not as good of a cook as you, but maybe it'll be
nice to get the night off."

Nick's stomach rolled and his hands tightened. Bryce didn't tell her.
He knew it by the way she said that. *It's none of my business anyway…
It's not like we're going public with our relationship. It's not like we
know if it'll last…*

That didn't change the way he felt, though. It didn't change the
slight pinch of hurt in his chest.

"I'd love that. Thanks for asking."

"Have you gotten to spend much time with her? She's a wonderful
girl and perfect for Bryce. We never thought he'd settle down."

The pinch grew, spread out, intensified…turned into an ache. This
was really fucking bad. He was getting too close, when he didn't really

know if he could handle things moving forward with Bryce.

"Mom. That's enough. The poor guy doesn't want to hear about Christi."

"No, it's fine." Still, Nick looked at Jamie, quietly trying to thank him. "I better get back to work. I hope you guys have a great meal."

They said their goodbyes and Nick headed back toward the kitchen. He didn't get very far before he heard Jamie calling his name. Nick slowed down to let him catch up, but Jamie didn't speak until they were in a private corner near the kitchen.

"I'm sorry about that. It was a shitty idea for us to come here. I wasn't thinking. I just...hell, if I'm being honest, my first thought was that it would be fun to go to my little brother's boyfriend's restaurant so I could give him shit about it later. I didn't even think about Mom bringing up Christi."

Boyfriend, boyfriend, boyfriend. Jamie had just called him Bryce's boyfriend. Forget that he'd just thought the same thing himself. It was different when someone else said it.

"No, it's okay." Nick shook his head. "Not a big deal at all. I know she thinks they're together. And Bryce and I... it's not serious. I don't even know what it is." Now he was turning into a fucking liar, because in some ways, it was serious. A few days ago he'd told Bryce it was more than sex. They'd shared the same bed every night, sucking and jerking each other off. They were practically living together, even if it was only because of the convenience of living so close.

175

"Oh...okay... I wasn't sure. I just wanted to apologize. If you see Bryce, can you have him give me a call?"

Nick nodded, confused by the sudden change in Jamie. He looked almost standoffish now. Almost frustrated. "Yeah, sure, of course."

"Have a good night." Jamie walked away and Nick tried to pretend there wasn't a hole in his gut over the fact that Georgina was thrilled with her son being in a relationship with Christi, and how much it would pain Bryce to hurt her.

***

Bryce stayed up late waiting for Nick to get home from work. He spent the night in his garage messing around with his Shovelhead even though his thoughts weren't in it.

He fucked up today. He should have told his mom about Christi. The longer it went on, the more unfair it was to everyone involved. He felt like he was letting Nick down, but then if he told his mom, he'd be breaking her heart. This couldn't be easy on Christi, either.

His bike didn't have the power to take away those thoughts, but it still kept him busy until Nick's car pulled into the driveway close to midnight. Bryce stayed where he was, knowing Nick would come to him. He was surprised the man didn't call him earlier to ask how it had gone.

"Hey," Bryce said when Nick walked over. He looked tired tonight. He wore a baseball cap, which Bryce had never seen him wear before. He didn't like the way it hid Nick's eyes.

"Hey. I had company tonight at the restaurant."

Bryce cursed. "Your family or mine?" Both would be awkward. He sure as shit hoped it wasn't Jill. He wanted that woman as far away from Nick as he could keep her.

"Yours. Georgina enjoyed your visit today. She glows when she talks about you and Christi."

"Fuck," Bryce mumbled. He wiped his hands on a towel before tossing it onto the garage floor. "I fucked up. I don't know why I lost my balls when I got there."

Nick didn't move closer, still standing at the edge of the garage. "Maybe," he shrugged. "I don't know, maybe all this should tell us something. Maybe this just isn't the right thing for us. We're straight men. We've always been straight men. Maybe we were just lonely, and we'll get over it. Hell, neither of us even wants anyone to know anyway. What does that say?"

Bryce's jaw hurt he clenched it so tightly. "You know what? Fuck you, Nick. Straight men don't spend every night naked together, blowing and jerking each other off. We said we'd figure it out as we went. Why is there suddenly such a rush?"

"Rush? Are you fucking kidding me? That's not what I'm saying. I'm not ready to announce this any more than you are. I'm just saying that maybe this should fucking tell us something. And Jesus, do you know how I felt tonight? My feelings aren't your fault, I get that, but there was a part of me that was happy they were there. I wanted to cook them a good meal and, hell, to show off, I think. Show them who I am and what I have to offer. I wanted to do something nice for them, because of how I feel about you, and then I had to smile and pretend it didn't fucking hurt to hear your mom talk about how perfect you and Christi are together."

Nick started to pace the garage. Bryce wanted to grab him, pull him close. His words shocked Bryce. Hell, he would have been pissed if the situation were reversed, if he had to hear about Nick and Jill. He hadn't thought about it in that much depth before—none of it. How much this could hurt so many people.

"I understand that things are a little different for me. I run off my heart. Maybe shit like that shouldn't bother me, but it does. I can't help what I feel."

No, he couldn't. Bryce couldn't help it, either, because as much of an asshole as it made him, he wanted Nick angry at the idea of him with someone else. He wanted Nick to want to claim him, even though the thought also scared the living shit out of him.

"Hey," Bryce called, and Nick stopped moving. He walked over to the man. Nick tried to turn but Bryce grabbed his face so he couldn't. "It *should* bother you. You have every right for it to bother you. Fuck, I *want* it to bother you, because I'd lose my fucking mind if I had to hear about you and Jill like that. Don't ever apologize for wanting me to be yours. Whether you realize it or not, Nick, that's what you're saying, so fuck your first statement about today meaning we shouldn't be trying this. I'm not walking away. Tell me you're not, either."

They were at a crossroads, not the first one they'd hit, and he sure as shit knew it wouldn't be the last.

Bryce waited for Nick to jerk away, to pull back, but he didn't. Instead, Nick dropped his head so their foreheads were touching. He grabbed Bryce's waist, his fingers digging into Bryce's flesh. "You're right. I'm not walking away... I just... I didn't expect it to hurt. I should have. I'm a man that likes answers, Bryce, and where you're concerned, I don't have any. Just a lot of questions—what is it about you? Why do we both feel like this? What the hell is going to happen if we keep this up? Why does it feel like my whole fucking life was spent waiting for something, even though I didn't know it until now?"

Bryce's chest expanded, like his insides were parting, making a place for Nick to settle in. "That was awfully sweet. You trying to get into my pants? I'll give you a hint, I already want you there."

Nick laughed, but Bryce could tell it was forced. "I get it. I get it because that's how I feel about you. There's never been a time in my life that I've wanted another person the way I want you. We'll figure this shit out, Nick. We will. Just don't run before we get the chance."

Nick gripped him tighter. And Bryce grabbed him the same way, wanting him close. This was fucking crazy, because they were standing in the middle of his open garage where anyone could see, but right now, he didn't care. "I'm not going anywhere," Nick said, then leaned in closer, his mouth next to Bryce's ear. "I'm not going anywhere," he said again. "I want you. Jesus, I want you. You make me feel fucking wild. Make me feel like I can do anything."

"I'm dirty. Come shower with me."

"I told you I liked you dirty," Nick replied.

Bryce damn near came in his pants. "I know you do, but shower with me anyway."

"You lead and I'll follow, but I might trip up along the way."

Bryce knew he wasn't talking about their shower.

"We both will. Come on, let's go."

CHAPTER TWENTY-FIVE

Nick watched as a naked Bryce leaned into the shower to turn it on. His ass and thighs were muscular, dark hair on his legs. His shoulders and back flexed as he adjusted the water temperature. Nick couldn't stop staring at him.

His whole life, beauty consisted of femininity to him—a woman's curves, her breasts, a smooth body. He liked things soft, and there was nothing soft about Bryce. He was the definition of masculinity, down to the grease beneath his fingernails, yet looking at him now, Nick was pretty sure he didn't even know what sexy was until he'd met the man standing in front of him.

Bryce looked over his shoulder at Nick. "Why are you still dressed? Come get naked and dirty with me."

Nick tried to keep things light the way Bryce did. "You ruin the dirty part with a shower."

"You only say that because you've never taken a shower with me before." Bryce stepped under the spray and closed the shower door. It was detached from the tub, a standing shower with two glass walls, similar to Nick's.

Bryce ducked his head under the spray, running his hands through his hair, and with that visual Nick was suddenly really fucking ready to experience his first shower with Bryce. He pulled off his clothes, his cock already stiff, before opening the door and stepping in. The hot water stung as it beat down on his skin, but it was nothing compared to the heat already coursing through him.

"I'm going to get you dirty," Bryce told him.

"I'm hoping so."

"We have to clean up first, though." He grabbed the soap and a washcloth and started washing up—his hands, chest, legs, his sac and his ass. Bryce didn't shy away from anything.

Nick grabbed the second washcloth and did the same. The second they were finished, Bryce was kissing him. Water ran down between them as they made out under the spray. He couldn't remember kissing Jill this much. Maybe it was because he and Bryce hadn't actually fucked yet, but they sure spent a hell of a lot of time kissing...and he fucking loved it.

He knew the man's taste by now, his distinct smell, soap and motorcycle.

Bryce turned Nick around, and Nick let him. Bryce pushed him so his chest touched the far wall of the shower, keeping Nick out of the spray. Bryce lined his body up behind Nick's—chest to back as he kissed and sucked at Nick's neck and shoulder muscles. "God, I want you all the time," he said against Nick's wet skin, making him shudder.

"Me, too," Nick admitted.

"I've never known anyone like you—your honor and sense of right and wrong. Your kindness. You love so fucking big." Bryce moved to the other side, kissing his neck there. Bryce's dick slid up and down the crack of his ass. Each time he pushed up, Nick's stomach flipped in nerves...and his cock got harder.

"I noticed that about you right away. Your loyalty, when you spoke about your relationship with your ex, or your family. That's a rare fucking gift, Nick."

He shook his head. He didn't do anything special. It's just who he was. "And you're not the same way? Fuck, do that again."

Bryce pushed against him again, his dick cradled between Nick's ass cheeks.

"Nah. Not like you. You make me laugh, too. Most people don't. I love to laugh, but most people aren't as funny as me."

Nick chuckled. "I sure as hell am not the funny one out of the two of us. You're always making me laugh, you cocky son of a bitch."

"Cocky, indeed." He pushed against him harder. Nick's hands fisted against the wall. "I wanna try something they really seem to enjoy on the site. I wanna lick your hole—just my tongue. Need to get it used to being played with... Since you fingered me that first night, I've been playing with my own to get it ready for you. Can I? I want my face between your cheeks and to drive you fucking wild with my tongue."

"Oh fuck." Nick grabbed his balls, keeping himself from coming all over the place. "When?"

Bryce obviously knew exactly what he meant because he answered, "In the shower, mostly—just a finger, sometimes two. It'll be nothing compared to that big cock of yours, when I take it. But right now I wanna hear you tell me how good it feels to have my tongue on your asshole."

Bryce didn't wait for him to reply. Hell, Nick wasn't even sure he *could* speak. When Bryce kneeled behind him, he found himself automatically spreading his legs and sticking his ass out.

The hesitant part of Nick's mind didn't stop spinning—Bryce was spreading his ass cheeks. Bryce was going to lick his asshole. But he still found himself pushing closer as Bryce spread him open.

"It's all pink and waiting."

Nick couldn't stop himself from clenching.

"That's so sexy. Just think, it'll tighten up like that when I fuck you."

And then everything else shut off except the feel of Bryce's wet tongue as he flicked back and forth over his hole. It was hot and humid because of the steam of the water, but Nick felt Bryce's cooler breath where he lapped at him. The shower was big enough to keep them from getting wet, but fuck, Nick would willingly drown if it kept him feeling the sensation of Bryce's tongue on him.

"What does it feel like?" Bryce asked as he briefly replaced his tongue with a finger, rubbing Nick's hole. Then, his face was there again, no shame as he shoved his tongue between Nick's cheeks, licking at him like it was his last meal.

Each time Bryce's tongue touched him, Nick shivered. "I can't...fuck, that feels good." Nick wanted closer, wanted more, so he pushed back into Bryce again. "I can't explain it. It's like everything starts and stops where you're rimming me."

"Can I finger you?" Bryce asked.

"Yes," hissed passed Nick's lips without a second thought.

He figured Bryce wet his finger in the shower and then there was pressure there. Pressure and stretching and a slight stab of pain as Bryce's finger pushed inside him. He fucked Nick with his finger the same way Nick had done to him...the way Bryce apparently did to himself.

It was foreign—something inside him, but each time Bryce pushed in, Nick's cock twitched. His balls got tighter and he pushed back for more. Then, just as he slid his right hand down to jerk his cock, Bryce rubbed a spot inside him and he let loose. Come shot out of him, load after load, hitting the shower wall in front of him. Holy fuck. His whole body tightened up as he had the biggest release of his life.

He leaned against the shower wall, breathing heavy. A million thoughts ran through his head, but he could only steal Bryce's words. "Orgasm fucking heaven."

***

Bryce loved kissing Nick.

It was probably close to an hour after their shower. It had taken Nick a while to recoup, but once they'd dried off, they'd gone straight to bed and were kissing and rubbing off on each other ever since.

Nick laid on top of him, rutting against him, his dick hard again. Bryce held his tight ass; he loved that fucking ass. He'd enjoyed eating it more than he'd thought he would.

"I want...I want to suck you off," Nick said against his lips. "Maybe play with you the way you've been doing with yourself—which I'd like to see sometime, by the way. That sounds fucking hot."

"You pretend to be all innocent, but you're not," Bryce teased. "I wanna try something. Lay on your side with your head at my crotch, so I can blow you, too." Nick's eyes heated. He moved to position himself the way Bryce said and he grabbed the lube.

Bryce felt like shit for fucking things up today. He needed to come clean with his family, because he wasn't sure how much longer he could keep this thing with Nick a secret.

His family loved him. They were a pretty liberal bunch. They believed in human rights. They wouldn't care who he was with as long as he was happy...he didn't think.

Bryce shoved those thoughts away as he rolled over to his side, opening his legs for Nick. Nick did the same thing, and Bryce went right for his balls.

He closed his eyes, sucking and licking, while thrusting into the hot, wet mouth bobbing up and down his erection. He loved Nick's mouth.

He liked everything about him—his loyalty and kindness. The way he looked at the world. The way he trusted Bryce so fucking much. But it was more than that, a connection he felt with the guy almost from the beginning. It was there and he couldn't explain it, and he didn't need to. He just knew he felt it.

Bryce didn't stop sucking as he opened the bottle of lube, squirting some on his finger and Nick's hole before tossing the bottle to Nick. He felt the resistance as he pushed a finger into Nick's body—the cold, wet lube on his own asshole before Nick penetrated him, too. It was like they were learning about sex for the first time with each other—experimenting and seeing what they liked and wanted...and hell, just playing and enjoying it.

The pleasure was intense.

"Gimme another finger, Nick. I want it." Who the fuck knew having something in his ass would feel so good? It wasn't something he'd ever considered before, but he sure as hell enjoyed it.

He felt the burn when Nick pushed another finger in, the pleasure intensifying. He pushed his own finger deeper in Nick, worked a second one in as well, and Nick let out a strangled moan.

The mouth on his dick, the fingers in his ass, and doing the same to Nick was like sensation overload.

The perfect fucking night.

He could tell when Nick was close. Felt it in his movements, in the tightness of his balls when Bryce mouthed his sac. Bryce felt it, too, as the slow tingle started deep inside him, pushing harder and faster to the surface. When Nick jerked and shot a mouthful into Bryce, it set him off, and he let loose and emptied his balls into Nick's mouth.

"Come here," he said, pulling the man close. He wrapped his arms around Nick and buried his face in his neck. "I'm sorry that I didn't tell her."

"You have no need to be."

"I feel like I do."

"We got this. We'll navigate our relationship together... it won't be easy. My family..."

"Shh. Let's not talk about that tonight. I just want to hold you and go to sleep."

Bryce closed his eyes and held his man—the first person he'd ever really wanted to claim as his.

It felt like Bryce had just closed his eyes when his alarm clock went off the next morning. Nick didn't have to get up with him, but he did. They showered and Bryce got dressed for work. Nick didn't have to go in until later.

"You coming over when you get off tonight?" Bryce asked as he shoved his wallet into his back pocket.

"Yeah. I'll be here."

"If I go to bed early, I'll leave the door unlocked for you." The comfortable way they spoke about spending their nights together, Bryce leaving the door open for Nick to come and go as though he belonged there, made a warmth spread through him.

"Okay." Nick twisted the doorknob. He opened the door just a crack when Bryce grabbed for him.

"Come here." Nick came without hesitation. "I'm going to go to Mom's this weekend and talk to her about Christi. I need to tell her. I'm not going to lie and pretend it won't be a big deal for her."

He saw Nick's throat move as he swallowed nervously. "Yeah...yeah, okay. Are you going to tell her about us?"

Fuck. He didn't know. "I'm not sure it's the best time. It's not because I'm embarrassed of you or anything. I just don't know if I should throw all of that at her at once—hey, Mom, I haven't been seeing the girl you love like a daughter in months—oh and Nick's my boyfriend. I'm serious about him. I know you thought I'd marry Christi, but surprise!"

Nick smiled as he shook his head. "You're crazy."

"You like it."

"I do...and you're right. I don't think it's the right time."

Bryce leaned forward and took possession of Nick's mouth. He kissed him deep, wanting to keep Nick's taste on his tongue all day. He grabbed his ass as Nick wrapped his arms around him.

"Bryce, you left the door open—What in the hell?" Bryce jerked away from Nick at the sound of his father's voice. His heart beat so loud, he thought everyone in the room could hear it. He felt the tension rolling off Nick, but he didn't have it in him to look at his lover. He couldn't take his eyes off his dad.

His dad looked down, sort of covered his face like Bryce and Nick were still kissing. "Your mom...she wanted me to drop this off so you could see it before she gave it to Christi, but I can see...Jesus Christ, what is wrong with you?"

His dad didn't hand him the scrapbook as he turned and walked out.

CHAPTER TWENTY-SIX

"Fuck!" Bryce pushed around Nick and went out the door after his father. His pulse got faster and faster as the weight in his chest multiplied. This wasn't how he wanted them to find out. "Dad, wait."

His dad stopped when he reached his car, angry eyes shooting daggers. He didn't think they would care—not really. He thought it would be an adjustment, but the fury on his father's face was more than an adjustment.

"Will you ever take anything seriously? You're thirty-two years old! You're too old for shit like this, Bryce. Christi loves you. She's a good goddamned girl and you're cheating on her with...with a man? I didn't raise you like this, son." The anger in his expression slowly started to melt...into disappointment, which was even worse.

"I'm not cheating on Christi with him, pop." *Him.* It was still something he had to get used to saying. Bryce was with a *him* now.

"It looked like it to me. You can't tell me that you weren't kissing that man. You can't tell me that Christi would be okay with that."

Looking at his father, the guilt began choking him, and it would only get worse. He hadn't even confessed to his mom yet. That would be the most painful blow. "We're not...Christi and I aren't together anymore. We haven't been together for months."

As his normally calm father crossed his arms, he could see the anger was back. "What do you mean?"

"Can we go inside and talk?"

"No, Bryce. I'm not sure that we can. I need to know what the hell is going on here."

Bryce took a deep breath and turned back toward the house. Nick stood there, waiting for him. He'd come over if Bryce wanted him to, would have his back and they'd stand together in this, but Bryce shook his head. Understanding, Nick nodded and went into his own house, disappointment clear in the slouch of his shoulders.

"Christi and I broke up a few months ago. I planned to tell you this weekend. I love her, but I'm not *in* love with her. She's not in love with me, either. We both know we're better as friends. But I didn't want...hell, I didn't want to disappoint you guys—Mom especially, so I haven't said anything yet. And then Nick..."

"Is this something you've done before? Be with men?"

"No." Bryce shook his head. "Just him. It just happened."

"And what does it mean? You're suddenly gay? You're in a relationship with a man? Or is it just a game? An experiment? What is it?"

The questions rained down on him, pummeled him like a

hurricane-strength storm. He wasn't ready to answer all of these questions. He cared about Nick. He wanted to keep doing what he was doing with him. Nick meant something to him, that's all he knew. He couldn't say where it would go or what it meant. "It's just...I don't know. We're figuring it out as we go along. Can't that be good enough for now?" How were they supposed to have all the answers right now? This was new for both of them.

His dad sighed. "Here, take this. Your mother wanted you to look at it, though I'm not sure it really matters anymore."

His dad opened the car door to get in.

"Wait. Can we talk about this inside?" He didn't think his dad would right now, but he really fucking needed that. He needed his family to be on his side about Nick, because the man meant more to him than he could put into words.

"Not right now. I need to sort through this. I don't understand you, Bryce. I don't know what the hell is going on. Right now, I just need to try and work through what the hell I just saw. I'm not telling your mother, but you need to, Bryce, and soon. She deserves to know about Christi."

Without another word, his dad got in his car and drove away. Bryce stood there, watching him go.

***

It wasn't long after Nick had gone into the house that there was a soft knock on his door. He hadn't stopped pacing, his heart in his throat.

Nick pulled the door open. "I'm so fucking sorry. I can't believe I didn't close the door all the way."

Bryce didn't look at him as he walked in. "Nah, I planned on telling them this weekend anyway. This just sped up the process." Bryce walked over, leaned against the back of the couch and dropped his head. "Fuck," he groaned out, which told Nick that it hadn't gone well.

"What happened?" Nick wasn't sure he wanted to know. If Bryce's family didn't take it well, that gave him no hope for his own. The Tanners were much more accepting than Nick's family ever could be.

"He had all these fucking questions that I didn't have answers for. I asked if we could talk more, and he said no and left. That's not my father. He's the levelheaded one. He lets us live our own lives and leaves the rest to Mom."

He'd never seen Bryce so tense before...so down. It didn't fit, didn't compute; it wasn't the Bryce he knew. Nick got it, but it still left a hole in his gut. He wanted to go to Bryce, hug him, kiss him, and tell him it would be okay, but he didn't know if he should. He didn't know if it would help. "I should have gone with you."

"No, you shouldn't have, but thank you for wanting to." Bryce pushed off the couch. "I'm not going to work today. I need...I need to take my bike out, go for a ride; clear my fucking head and try to make sense of all of this."

"I can call off, too. I'll go with you if you—"

"No," Bryce cut him off. "I just...it's better if I go alone. This afternoon when my dad gets off work, I'm going to head over and talk to him and Mom. I have no clue what the fuck I'm going to say, but I need to speak with them. I'll...I'll call you later."

Bryce left, and he didn't try to stop him. When he heard Bryce's motorcycle rev to life, he was still standing in the same spot.

This wasn't just about the fun anymore—wasn't about orgasms and hiding out in their houses together naked. It was all real, and they had to decide how far they were willing to go for each other...what they really wanted. So far, Nick wasn't so sure how it was going.

***

Nick cleaned his already clean house.

Then cooked food he had no plan on eating.

A couple of hours later, when he hadn't heard from Bryce, he got into his car and drove to his mom's house. He had no fucking clue why, or what he planned to say when he got there, but he felt the need to go. Even though his stomach was in knots the whole time.

The ride was quick, and before he knew it, Nick was knocking on her door.

"Nicholas! It's so good to see you. You never surprise me with a visit. My one and only boy and you rarely come and see me." She gave him a tight hug, and Nick returned it, holding on longer than he usually did. She was a good mom, strong, and she loved her family. Maybe loved them a little too much. She'd spoiled both Nick and his dad, expected her girls to do the same with their husbands because that's how she'd been raised. She took what she thought were appropriate gender roles very seriously.

"Things are busy at work. I have to head there in a few minutes, but I wanted to stop by and see you. How's everything going?"

"Good," she led him inside where they sat in the living room. "Your sisters are doing well. Michelle's ready to have the baby. I think she's tired of being pregnant, but she still has a long way to go. I can't imagine a woman feeling that way. I always loved being pregnant. I've been going over and helping her get housework done. Teddy is a little terror, so Ken comes home to a messy house or no dinner, which frustrates him. We need to figure out a better schedule for her."

Maybe Ken should understand... She's carrying a baby and dealing with two kids. She can't do it all.

But then, his mother had done it all, and that's all she saw. She'd butted heads with Jill a lot because she didn't do the things for Nick that his mom thought a wife should do. He hadn't cared. Yeah, Nick had always wanted to be able to take care of Jill, but he also hadn't expected her to sit around cleaning and popping out babies while he worked. She was independent, and he'd liked that about her. She was so different than how he'd been raised.

"That might help, and maybe Ken can pitch in a little, too."

She waved a hand at him as though what he said was silly. "He works so Michelle can stay home. His responsibility is work, hers is the house and kids. I'm thankful you never had kids with Jill. I don't think she would have put her kids first."

"Now wait a minute." Nick's blood pressure skyrocketed. "You can't say that. Jill is a lot of things, but she would have loved any kids we had. We both would have, and we would have taken care of them the way that worked best for us. Are you saying if a mom works, she doesn't love her kids?"

"No. Of course not. Now you're putting words in my mouth. I'm just saying I never liked Jill, and I always knew she wasn't right for you, but I guess you're right. I shouldn't say that about her parenting."

Who would be good enough for me, Mom? Would anyone be right for me? Would Bryce?

"Anyway, I don't want to spend our visit fighting about Jill or your sister. How are things going with you?"

Without thinking about it, Nick answered honestly. "Great, actually. I've been spending a lot of time with my neighbor, Bryce. He's a great guy. He's a motorcycle mechanic. I was thinking of having him come with me the next time we have a family dinner. I'd love for you guys to meet him." This was possibly a huge mistake. His mom would have questions. Hell, he didn't even know where things stood with him and Bryce after today. Maybe he would decide this wasn't worth it. Maybe it would be too hard. Maybe they were only meant to enjoy each other for a short time and then move on. All Nick knew was what he said was true. Bryce was a good man and he wanted his family to meet him. And maybe there was a part of him that was frustrated by the way his mom thought about Jill, and even his sisters and their marriages as well.

It wasn't Michelle's responsibility to take care of the kids alone.

It was a very real possibility that the next person Nick was in a serious relationship with wouldn't be a woman. If things continued as they were, he was already there, and that person was Bryce.

He saw the confusion in his mom's eyes as she watched him. "I'm sure he's a very nice man. I'm not sure why we need to have your neighbor over to a family dinner, though. You've never introduced me to a male friend before, and honestly, it seems like a silly thing to do."

He thought about his afternoon at Bryce's family home. "No, it's not silly. I went to his brother's birthday party with his family and we had a great time. He's...very close to me." *He's more than close to me. I care about him. And I could maybe fall in love with him.*

"That's nice, dear." His mom stood, but didn't look at him. "I'm glad you're meeting new friends. Jill always took up all of your time and you never had time for friends. Friends are important. Your father and I spent a lot of time with other couples and their kids." She started walking toward the kitchen so Nick followed. "I'll let you know the next time we plan a dinner. Maybe Bryce could bring his wife."

"He doesn't have one." *He has a boyfriend and it's me... I hope.*

"Oh, a girlfriend, then. Speaking of, it's about time you started dating again. Find a nice woman. Maybe your sisters know someone. Listen, I'm so glad you came by, but I'm suddenly not feeling well. I'm going to go lie down. Please lock the door on your way out."

She knew. She had to fucking know, but she didn't want to hear it.

Didn't want to believe it.

Nick hadn't expected anything else.

Nick checked his phone. Bryce still hadn't called. Maybe Bryce would end their relationship before it went any further. There was a very real possibility that he'd started outing himself for no reason.

CHAPTER TWENTY-SEVEN

Bryce spent the whole day driving around. Usually riding his bike cleared his head, but his thoughts were still a jumbled mess.

It was around six that evening when he pulled up to his parent's house. He cursed when he saw Mitch and Jamie's cars there.

He didn't want to do this with an audience. Hell, he hadn't wanted to drop both the Nick and Christi bombs on his parents in the same day, but it looked like he wasn't going to get what he wanted. Now that his dad knew, he needed to tell everyone else.

He'd get it all out there at once so there'd be no secrets.

"Having a family gathering without me?" Bryce asked when he opened the door.

"No, your father and I just got lucky that all of our kids decided to come see us on the same day." She kissed Bryce's cheek. "Minus Christi, of course. Where is she?"

Jamie cleared his throat. Hope gave him a shy smile from beside Jamie on the couch. Of course she knew. Bryce ran a hand through his hair. "I don't know where she is. How am I supposed to know?"

"I don't know, because she's your girlfriend?" Mitch said sarcastically. He didn't know about Nick, but he did know about Christi, so of course his brother would have to bust his balls.

"Leave him alone, Mitch." Abbey elbowed him. They sat on the other couch, his mom beside Mitch.

His dad sat in his chair, having yet to say a word.

"Actually, that's what I came here to talk to you guys about. I'm glad everyone is here." Bryce sat in the last chair, because if he didn't, his legs might give out. His dad looked down. Jamie nodded his head, a quiet support. Hope gave him another smile. Mitch rolled his eyes as if to say, *finally*, when he didn't have a clue about everything Bryce was about to say. But Abbey...he could have sworn she gave him a nod of support as well. Maybe for more than just what he had to say about Christi. Had Hope told her?

His mom...she just looked confused as hell. Pretty soon she'd be broken hearted.

Bryce wrung his hands together and his first thought was... *I wish Nick was here.* It wasn't fair to the other man to have him go through this, but Bryce wished he had him here for support. This would be a whole lot easier with Nick by his side. That was another first. He'd never had someone who he looked to for support that way before.

"I've been lying to you all for a while now." Because he wasn't going to throw his brothers and their wives under the bus for knowing. "I'm not proud of that fact, but it came from not wanting to hurt anyone...not wanting to disappoint you."

"What's wrong, Bryce?" His mom's voice was all parental concern.

"Christi and I...we haven't been together for a while now. I think we both realized not long after we got together that it had been more out of fear than real love."

"I don't understand, Bryce." His mom shook her head. Mitch set a hand on her knee.

"I asked her not to tell anyone. I knew..." Knew that he was kind of the oddball when it came to the Tanner kids. Being with Christi would have made his parents happy. Would have made them feel like he wasn't coasting through life like they thought he was. "I knew it would hurt you, Mom—"

"Not nearly as much if you would have told me in the beginning, instead of letting me believe a lie for...how long, Bryce? How long have I thought that you were in love with Christi when you weren't?" Her eyes filled with tears.

Fuck. He knew this would be hard, but nothing compared to the real thing. To the overwhelming feeling of guilt gnawing at his insides. "Too long. It's not Christi's fault, either. She wanted to tell you. I asked her not to." Because it had been a relief not to have his mom on his back about settling down. She'd been happy just knowing he was with Christi. Yeah, there was the kids thing, but she didn't pressure him on that very often. And pretending with Christi had always been easy because they were close. Bryce never expected to fall for someone else and to have that muddy everything up.

"Oh, I'm not blaming her. I'm angry at you, Bryce. You're my son.

You should have told me! I thought…" She buried her face in her hands and started to cry. Bryce's eyes stung as well. He'd really fucked this up.

"I know it's hard, Mom, but cut him a little slack. This hasn't been easy on Bryce. He screwed up, but it came from a place of *not* wanting to hurt you. He's just a bonehead and didn't know what else to do."

"Gee, thanks, Jamie." But really, he appreciated his brother's support.

"What are big brothers for?" he asked.

Bryce ignored him, stood and walked over to his mom. He kneeled on the floor between her legs, gently prying her hands from her face. "I'm sorry. So sorry for hurting you. That wasn't the plan, but I know it's what I did. I love you, Ma. I just didn't want to let you down. I never want to lie to you again, which is why I'm hitting you with the rest of this right now, okay? No secrets. I want to be upfront with all of you."

He saw Mitch stiffen, probably wondering what was going on. His father still had yet to say a word. His mom wiped her eyes and looked up, strong as ever. "Might as well tell me everything so I can kick your ass for all of it at once." Christ, he loved the woman. She was a good parent. Both of them were. He hoped like hell they could accept what else he had to say.

Bryce stood, grabbed the footstool and pushed it to the center of the room. He needed to sit to do this. His right leg was bouncing up and down like crazy. "I…" He needed to spit it out. It's not that big a deal. They wanted him to get serious about someone and now he was.

There was a shifting sound and he looked up to see Jamie stand, walk toward him and put a hand on his shoulder. He'd never loved his brother more than he did in that moment. It gave him the strength he needed to continue. "I've met someone else. We've been seeing each other for a while now. I can't promise where it'll go for sure...well, once I tell you who it is, you'll understand why, but this person means a lot to me. He means more to me than I ever thought someone could."

The room was deathly quiet.

Mitch didn't take his eyes off Bryce. Abbey studied him as though he'd confirmed something to her, but she still wasn't totally sure what to think about it. His mom...well, she looked confused as hell—red eyed and dragged through the ringer.

"He?" she finally asked. "You're gay? Is that why you've never been serious about anyone?"

"No," Bryce shook his head vehemently. "I mean, I'm with a man, with Nick, so I guess that means I'm gay...? Or bisexual at least, but it isn't something that's ever happened to me before. I've never been attracted to another man or anything. I didn't settle down before because..." Well, he guessed because he hadn't met the right person. "I've just never felt the need. But yeah, I'm with Nick. Christi knows, and she's happy for me. I just..." *Need you to be happy for me, too.*

Bryce's mom pushed to her feet. "When are you going to grow up, Bryce? You're thirty-two years old. Don't you think it's time you grew up by now?"

Jamie spoke before Bryce could say anything. "Mom, he's happy.

Hell, I could see what Nick meant to him before Bryce did. I know it's a shock, but—"

"Yes. It is a shock, but that's not what pisses me off. If Bryce was gay, I wouldn't have a problem with it. He just can't make up his mind about anything! How many school programs did you start before settling on motorcycle mechanics?" she asked Bryce.

"That has nothing to do with this."

"It has everything to do with this. Too many, and that doesn't count working with Dad. Every time you started one, you'd tell us you finally found *it*. What you were meant to do. You'd get excited and then we'd get excited, only for you to change your mind. You dated like crazy because you couldn't settle on one woman, either. Then you decided your best friend was the woman for you and I didn't dare let myself hope. I knew you'd change your mind about her as well, but after a while...I believed. I hoped. You fell in love with motorcycles and you stuck with that. Then I thought you fell in love with Christi and were sticking with her as well, but obviously that was a lie. Now I'm supposed to believe you've suddenly realized you're into men and that you're serious about Nick, when you've never honestly been serious about anything in your life. None of it has really lasted, Bryce... I just thought... I thought you would have grown out of it by now, but I guess I was wrong."

Each of her words stabbed another nail into his chest. Is that really how she saw him? Is that really how he was? He'd never told her he was in love with Christi, or that they were serious, she'd just assumed. With

Nick, he was telling them. He needed them to know.

"You jump into things full speed ahead only to later realize it's not what you want, and now you're taking Nick along for the ride. Are you his first, too?"

Bryce couldn't answer because the truth scared him. She couldn't be right. That couldn't be what he was doing. He would know something like that.

"That's not how it is. It's different with Nick."

Mitch laughed humorlessly. "I love you, little brother, but wake up. It was different with Christi in the beginning, too. Working with Dad would make you happy. Then business school was different. After that it was bartending that you loved, or going into computers. They were all different. How the hell is this any different?"

"I never fucking said those things were different. I tried them, yes, but I never said they were it for me." And he'd settled down now—both in his career and with Nick.

"Mitch, I'm not sure you're being fair," Abbey interrupted. "If I'm being honest, I'm not surprised by this in the least. I thought something was different the day Nick came over here."

"Me, too," Hope added. "And when Nick came to talk to us at dinner the other night, I could see it. Bryce obviously means a lot to him."

Bryce appreciated Hope's support, but that wasn't his mother's worry. She didn't believe Nick didn't care about Bryce. She thought

Bryce would hurt Nick. That he'd jumped into this with his eyes closed and would soon realize it wasn't what he wanted.

And he *had* jumped. Hell, he'd kissed Nick before knowing how Nick felt. He'd pushed the sex stuff, been the one to initiate everything. What if they were right?

"I love you, Bryce. I do. And I don't have any issues with someone being gay. If you fall in love with Nick, that's fine. I'll support you and welcome him into the family, but I'd be lying if I didn't admit that I'm worried. You don't think about the consequences of your actions. You react. I have no doubt that you really feel like Nick is important to you. But I'm scared to death that he'll get attached and we will, too, only for you to realize it's not really what you want. That's the reason I can't support this."

Bryce couldn't move. Couldn't speak. All he could do was close his eyes and hope like hell his mom wasn't right. He would never forgive himself if he hurt Nick or his family.

CHAPTER TWENTY-EIGHT

Nick struggled through his whole night at work. He couldn't stop thinking about his conversation with Bryce, Bryce's conversation with his father, Nick's own conversation with his mother, and the fact that he hadn't heard from Bryce since he said he had to go on a drive.

Logically, he knew Bryce had a lot on his mind. He was hoping the reason Bryce hadn't called was that he didn't want to discuss things while Nick was working, but that didn't stop him from thinking the worst.

He would just go to Bryce's house when he got home. That's all there was to it. Regardless of what happened, Nick needed to know the truth. They could tackle whatever happened head on, or they'd walk away, but at least Nick wouldn't be in the dark.

A few minutes later he pulled into his driveway. As his lights moved across the garage, he saw Bryce leaning against it. He looked up when Nick parked and their eyes met.

Bryce looked a mess. Nick had never seen him like that before, and just like that, he fucking knew things were about to change. That whatever this was between them could be ending before they even had the chance to really see what it was.

Maybe that was for the better. Though, the weight on his chest didn't feel like it would be better, and Nick couldn't make himself move. Not until Bryce nodded toward the house, as if to tell Nick to come here.

He went.

"Hey," Nick shoved his hands into his pockets.

"Hey," Bryce pushed a hand through his hair. Great. They were both doing nervous gestures. That didn't bode well. "Why are you standing out here?" Nick almost reached for him, but didn't. He couldn't read Bryce right now and wasn't sure it was the right thing to do. They were skating a thin line together. In the bedroom, everything was great. Friendship-wise, it was fantastic. It was everything else they still had to figure out.

Bryce shrugged. "I just got home and figured I'd wait for you."

Fuck it. If it was the wrong thing to do, so be it. Nick stepped forward, right up against Bryce, in the darkness of his driveway. The moon was bright, giving him enough light to make out some of Bryce's features—the stubble on his face, the curve of his jaw. The frown on his lips and confusion in his eyes. "This okay?" he asked as he leaned close, one of his legs between Bryce's and the other on the outside. Their bodies touched. Nick cupped his face.

"This is better."

"Good, because it was driving me fucking crazy not to touch you."

"You think this is real, Nick?" There was nothing except honest hunger in Bryce's voice. "What we're doing, I mean. Can it really fucking work? Is it real? I feel like it is, but what the fuck do I know?"

This wasn't like Bryce, to question himself this way. He was the one who jumped in head first, asked questions later. Or asked questions, ignored the answers and still jumped anyway. "Is this over?" Nick asked plainly. Then, he fucking held his breath while waiting for an answer. He couldn't even think about that next breath until he knew.

"I don't know. Come on, let's go inside and talk." Bryce slipped out from around Nick and walked away. Nick had no choice except to follow. He was surprised when Bryce went for Nick's house instead of his own…and then he was kind of pissed about it. Most of the time, unless it was a day off and Nick was cooking, they were at Bryce's. Was he looking for an easy escape? He'd say what he had to say and then walk away? The Bryce he'd come to know wasn't a coward like that. Nick would kick his ass if he tried to turn into one now.

Once he had the door closed behind them, Nick hit the lights, tossed his keys on the table. "What happened? Just fucking tell me, Bryce. The way I see it is, we either figure this shit out by being honest and talking about it, or call it off."

His insides convulsed at the last part, broke apart, ached. The thought of losing Bryce left an empty space in his chest, a space he hadn't known was there until Bryce and it belonged to him.

***

Even though Bryce was in a shitty mood, he couldn't stop the half-grin from pulling at his lips. "You're getting bossy, aren't you?"

"Not now, Bry. It's not the time to joke."

Nick tried to walk toward the couch, but Bryce grabbed his arm. "You called me Bry." He didn't know why he liked that so fucking much. It wasn't as though it wasn't a name half the people he knew called him. Nick had never used it, though.

"I did. Now tell me what the fuck happened. I've been thinking about you all day."

He liked that, too, liked Nick having him on his mind. But then his mom and his brothers' words bled in again. He knew they hadn't said them to hurt him, but because his family was big on honesty. They told Bryce their worries, and now he was scared they were right. "Let's sit down." He nodded toward the couch, and they sat.

"I drove around all day. It's fucking gorgeous out there. I want you to go on my bike with me sometime."

Nick shook his head, and Bryce realized he'd gotten off track.

"I went to my parents' house when I knew they'd be home. Just so happened that Mitch, Abbey, Hope and Jamie were also there. I admitted to my mom about Christi. She was understandably hurt, felt betrayed and lied to. It..." broke his fucking heart to hurt his mom that way.

"You didn't mean to hurt her," Nick said, reading his mind.

"Doesn't change the fact that I did." And that she worried Bryce would hurt Nick as well. "I told them all about you. Didn't want to keep any more secrets from them." And there was a part of him that just wanted them to know about Nick. To know that he had found someone he really cared about. It might not be Christi, but he had Nick.

Nick leaned away from him on the couch, his leg bouncing, reminding Bryce of when his own had done the same thing at his parents' house. "And?" Nick asked.

"And in some ways, it went better than I thought it would. It doesn't bother them that you're a man. It'll take some getting used to, but they can accept that. I might have lied to my parents, but I know that they really do only want me happy." They just didn't think Bryce knew how to be serious about anything. "So you aren't the problem. I am."

"What do you mean?" Nick's eyebrows pulled together.

Nick reached for him, but Bryce shook him off. His body was jittery, so he pushed to his feet, pacing Nick's living room. "I've fucked up a lot, Nick. I've never taken life too seriously. I told you about the career thing. I've fucked my way through too many women to count. They've had to bail me out of shit they shouldn't have had to bail me out of. When I first got sick, I didn't take that seriously, either, and could have cost me my life. I'm fucking lucky I'm still here. They thought that was my wake-up call, and why I got serious with Christi. Now they find out we weren't serious, I lied about still being with her, *oh, and by the way, I have a boyfriend now, and I'm serious about him.* You can see why they don't believe me."

When Nick didn't reply, Bryce stopped pacing. A quiet voice was in his head, praying for Nick not to agree with his family. Praying that they weren't right. He looked at the man who turned his whole life upside down. "They think I'm playing a game—or not that, I guess, but they think it's just another way for me to not be serious about my own life. They think it's a way to keep myself from settling down and growing up. They think we're going to get involved and it'll change our whole fucking lives and then I'll just move on." *I'm scared that they're right...*

It felt like a whole fucking lifetime passed by before Nick spoke. "You told them you're serious about me?"

Damned if the man didn't make him smile again. "That's what you focus on out of everything I just said?"

"Did you ever tell them you were serious about Christi, or did they just assume?"

Bryce shrugged. "I never used the words, no." He'd never technically said he was serious about anything before bikes, and now Nick.

"Do you think this is just a way for you to avoid settling down?"

"Fuck no." The answer came quickly and easily.

"Do you want this?" Nick asked more quietly, "Want me?"

This answer was even easier. "So fucking much I can't think clearly most of the time. It's like you filled this place in my world that I didn't know needed to be filled. Hell, I didn't even know it was there before you came and claimed it. Wanting you is the only thing I'm sure of. I don't know how it happened or why, but I know it's there."

Nick felt right in a way nothing in his life ever had. It was natural and automatic, and he couldn't imagine his life without the other man. "This is when you tell me you want me, too, Nick."

He smiled, his green eyes deep, full of meaning, and firmly locked on Bryce. "I want you, too, you crazy son-of-a-bitch. If I've learned anything in life, it's that nothing is a guarantee. I thought Jill and I were, and we weren't. Anytime you date someone there's a possibility of getting hurt. I want you. I trust you. I'm willing to take the risk."

Jesus Christ, he fucking loved this man. Loved? Yeah, he thought he did, and it didn't scare him or make him want to run. It made Bryce want to hold tighter. "You're the only risk I've ever taken, Nick. Nothing else could hurt me except you." That still didn't mean this would be easy. They still had a lot of shit to work through, but they both wanted it, and that's all that mattered.

Bryce walked over and dropped to his knees in front of Nick. They met in the middle as their mouths devoured each other's. He loved Nick's taste—peppermint. The way he felt, hungry and urgent. The way he smelled, man and spice. He wanted it all, every fucking piece of the man...and he wanted Nick to have him, too.

Bryce pulled away to tell him just that as a grumble sounded between them. Nick laughed and asked, "Did you eat?"

"I haven't eaten all day."

"Me, either. Let me cook for you."

He tried to stand but Bryce didn't let him. Fuck food. He wanted Nick to have him instead. "I don't want to eat. I want you to take me into your bedroom, take my clothes off and then fuck me."

No, that was a lie. Bryce didn't *want* that, he *needed* it. Needed Nick to claim him, and show him that everything would be okay.

CHAPTER TWENTY-NINE

They still had a shitload of things to talk about, but logical thought fled Nick's mind when Bryce said that to him. They'd kissed, rubbed and sucked each other like crazy, but this? The thought of fucking Bryce, the hole that hugged his fingers so tightly, made Nick go out of his mind. "Are you sure?" Because he knew he was big...he knew it would hurt. Hell, he didn't even know if people enjoyed anal sex the first few times.

"Jesus Christ, don't ask me that. It's fucking. Yes, I'm sure."

They both pushed to their feet at the same time. They kissed as they stumbled down the hallway toward Nick's bedroom. He hadn't made love since before his divorce. Hell, he hadn't made love to anyone except his ex; and soon, Bryce. He wanted that more than he could put into words. His dick dripped pre-come as his heart thudded in both excitement and nerves.

He'd felt it before, but after this, Bryce would be his.

As soon as they got into his room, they both kicked out of their shoes, lips still attached. He could kiss Bryce all night. He loved the passion and hunger behind it. The roughness, in both the way Bryce touched him and of the hair on his face and cut of his jaw.

He pulled away, kissed Bryce's neck as he started working the button on Bryce's jeans. "I can't believe we're doing this. Are you...?" Yeah, he needed to spit out what the fuck he was trying to say.

"We're good. Don't worry. But I think you're going too slow."

Nick laughed against Bryce's mouth as he pushed his zipper down and shoved his hands down the back of Bryce's jeans, gripping his muscular ass and pulling Bryce closer to him. "I can't wait to sink my dick inside you." He ran a finger up and down the seam of Bryce's ass, making him shudder.

"With that thick cock of yours, you're going to fucking kill me. I'll take it, though. Want to. I've never wanted anything more than you and that cock of yours inside me."

Nick pulled Bryce's shirt over his head. He felt like he would burst out of his skin he was so fucking needy.

Nick kissed his chest. Rubbed his cheek on the hair there, licked Bryce's left nipple. "I know...I know you're going to want me eventually, too. We'll get there. I promise. It might take me a little while, but—" he did want it, even though it made him nervous at the same time.

"Shut up and finish taking my clothes off, Nick. I need this."

It was those words that made Nick drop to his knees. Bryce had said he'd wanted him to kneel, but Nick had yet to go down on him this way. He pushed Bryce's jeans and underwear down and buried his face in the rough hair at Bryce's crotch. "Nothing about you is soft. Nothing is feminine. And it drives me fucking wild. I love everything about you."

And then he sucked Bryce's dick into his mouth. Tasted the salt on his skin. Sucked him as deep as he could, wishing he could go all the way down to the base, make his lips touch Bryce's pubic hair as he sucked him.

"Fuck," Bryce hissed. "Not yet. I don't want to come till your dick is inside me."

He pulled Nick to his feet. "You can suck my cock all night afterward if you want, but I really want to feel you inside me."

Nick had never wanted anything more.

***

They lay on their sides, naked on the bed. Nick lubed his fingers as Bryce hooked his top leg over Nick's waist. They pulled close, Nick's dick against him. When Bryce felt the cold, wet finger pushing at his hole, he leaned forward and took Nick's mouth. He'd never loved kissing so much in his fucking life.

He moaned into Nick's mouth at the sensation of a finger easing inside him. He fucked Bryce with his finger as Bryce's tongue did the same to Nick's mouth. He groaned again when Nick added another. Pleasure pulsed through him.

"It's so fucking hot and tight in there. I'm going to bust my load as soon as I get in."

"I'll kick your ass if you do. It's my first time. You better make it good for me," Bryce teased, and then they were kissing again. Nick was driving him insane. His skilled mouth, his hard body rubbing against him, Nick's finger in his ass.

He needed to be fucked. Needed to give himself to Nick that way. "Another...give me another one, baby. You're going to have to stretch me good if I'm going to take your cock." Which Bryce knew wasn't going to be easy.

Nick rolled over, lay on top of Bryce as he kissed down his chest. "You need to keep doing that. Talk dirty to me all the time. Makes my dick hard."

"That the only thing here that's making you hard?" Bryce asked.

"So cocky." Nick kissed each flat nipple. Ran his tongue down Bryce's chest; he wanted Nick to lick him all over. He loved the feel of Nick's tongue on him.

"Three fingers, Nick."

Nick eased down between his legs, pushing them open farther. Without pulling his two fingers out, he used his other hand to add more lube, then tried to work a third finger in. Bryce's hole protested while the rest of him screamed, *yes!* Nick kept working for it until he could get the third finger in, but it was a struggle. His asshole burned as Nick twisted his fingers inside. "Fuck...we should have gotten a toy or something to help loosen me up." The three fingers didn't have Nick's girth and Bryce already felt the pain spread through him, waiting for the pleasure.

"You have such a sexy hole. I love watching it stretch to take my fingers. It's perfect." Nick kissed the tip of his cock and then sucked the head into his mouth.

Bryce loved it. Thought maybe he could live with his cock in Nick's mouth. Keep Nick with him all the time so he could suck Bryce's dick whenever he wanted him to; like he'd told Nick earlier—his own cocksucker. But Bryce really wanted Nick to fuck him. Wanted to prove that he could give himself to Nick.

"I want your cock in me, Nick. Let me give myself to you."

Nick sat up, grabbed a condom and rolled it onto his thick erection. He pressed a quick kiss to his lips and leaned his forehead against Bryce's. "I... Fuck, I want you so goddamned much. I'm going to hurt you."

"And you're also going to fuck me and make me come, so do it." He kissed Nick this time. "Do it."

Nick sat up. "Is this the best way for you, Mr. Research?"

Bryce laughed. "Don't know. I only looked at the pictures," he teased. He'd read up, just not on that part of it.

Nick coated them both with lube. Bryce pulled his legs up as far as he could because...fuck, another man was about to put his dick in his ass. How in the hell did he get here?

And then Nick was there, his head at Bryce's hole as he tried to push in. When he was met with nothing except resistance, he pulled back before trying a second time. Bryce pushed down the way he'd read might help, trying to open himself up for Nick, but Nick couldn't slide in.

There was nothing but pressure.

Nick pushed forward again and pain shot through Bryce, causing him to hiss, which made Nick jerk away. "Come back."

"Fuck that. You just yelled."

"It's going to hurt Nick, we both know that. It'll be okay." Bryce rolled over, got on all fours with his ass in the air, presenting it to his lover. Christ, he didn't know why he needed this so badly, needed to give himself to Nick, but he did. "Fuck me, Nick. Take me."

Fire sparked in Nick's green eyes. He lubed himself up again, worked his fingers inside Bryce. Bryce pushed back, trying to get more of him as Nick stretched him farther than he'd been stretched before. He pulled his fingers out, replacing it with his cock again, trying to breach Bryce's virgin hole.

"You're tense. You need to try and relax," Nick told him.

No shit he was tense. Someone was about to fuck him for the first time. No matter how much he wanted it, that didn't mean there were no nerves. "I am trying to relax." How did he relax his asshole?

Nick tried again, pushed against Bryce's tight ring of muscles.

It felt like...hell, he didn't want to say what it felt like. It was more than just the burning, the stretching, as Nick tried to work himself in. He couldn't even get the whole head in before Bryce's body tried to reject him, fight against him. His brain told him to pull back as his libido begged for more, but then Nick was making the choice for him. He kissed Bryce's back, rubbed his ass. "You're not used to it... You have to prepare the muscles. It's too soon. Maybe toys, like you said…something smaller than me but bigger than my fingers."

Bryce closed his eyes. His dick went soft. There was a loud rumble in his head before the word *failure* broke through the clatter. He really fucking needed Nick to claim him. "Try it again."

"Bryce."

"Nick."

"I won't. Not yet. You're too tight, too tense. It'll hurt you, and I can't do that. I can still make you come." He kissed Bryce's back again, soothing him with his touch. "You said I can suck your cock all night. Let me practice and see how deep I can take you."

"I don't want a blowjob. I want to fuck." Bryce fell onto the bed, the word *failure* getting louder in his head. He went to his back, slung an arm over his eyes. There was no sound in the room except his deep breaths, and the thoughts running through his head. He was being a dickhead. He knew that. Nick didn't deserve him acting like a spoiled asshole. It was just… "I want this with you. I've fucked people I don't give a shit about."

Nick had *only* slept with people he cared about. One person he'd cared about. Bryce hadn't cared much about anyone he'd fucked, except Christi, and that was different. "I want to know what it's like to be with someone I care about. That's it. I just want to be with you. Want to feel your cock inside me. Is that too fucking much to ask?"

There was a long pause and Bryce felt the silence in his bones.

Suddenly the quiet was much worse than the noise in his head had been.

And then Nick's hand was there...on his arm, pulling it off Bryce's face. "Then take me. Have me. I want to be with you, too. You can fuck me."

CHAPTER THIRTY

Nick almost couldn't believe his own words. From the beginning, he'd always just assumed he'd start out fucking Bryce, and then eventually he'd let Bryce have him. Bryce wanted Nick to fuck him, and Nick sure as hell wanted to. He just figured that's how it would go down, but Bryce's words hit something inside him, changed something. He didn't care how they did it; he just knew he wanted Bryce. Wanted them connected in that way, to know each other like that.

"You don't want to be fucked," Bryce told him.

"Don't tell me what I want. I want you. That's all that matters." Nick fought to push his fears away. He wrapped a hand around Bryce's dick and stroked, trying to get him hard again.

"I didn't want it to be that way. I needed to give myself to you first."

"I know." Though he didn't know why. "This is what we have, though." Because Nick wouldn't hurt him. There was real damage he could cause, and the truth was, it would be easier for Nick to take Bryce than the other way around.

"Are you sure?"

"What did you just tell me? Don't ask me that. Fuck me, Bryce. That's what I want." Nick pulled his condom off and tossed it into the trash. When he turned back around, Bryce was kneeling on the bed in front of him.

"Come here so I can kiss you."

Nick went up on his knees too, as their mouths moved together, their tongues tangled roughly. Bryce's hard-on pushed against Nick's. It hadn't taken much to get him stiff again.

Bryce eased Nick down to his back, and Nick let him. He covered Nick's body with his own and Nick let him do that, too—every hard, muscular inch of him. They thrust their cocks together, rutting against each other. And then Bryce's finger was at his ring, somehow wet with lube, when Nick hadn't even realized he'd done it.

He probed Nick's hole, slowly pushing a finger inside.

"It's going to fucking kill me to get in there. I might want to stay there all night."

"Yes…" Nick hissed, tensing slightly when Bryce added a second finger. The burn was there, the stretching, and then, "Fuck!" more girth, as Bryce used three fingers on him. Each time he fingered Nick, he scissored his fingers, stretching Nick's hole. The burn was there, but then…this was Bryce inside him. Bryce getting ready to take him. It somehow made things easier, made the pleasure overcome the pain. That didn't mean he didn't have any worries though.

Nick wrapped a hand around his own erection, needing some friction, but Bryce swatted it away. "Leave your cock alone. I might not be able to take it in my ass yet, but it's still mine."

"Then do something with it. I'm fucking dying here." He needed something to ease his nerves with what was about to happen—that Bryce was about to fuck him. "I want you."

He didn't have to tell Bryce twice. The man grabbed a rubber from the drawer, sheathed himself, and then poured lube in his hand as he jacked his condom-covered dick. They'd talked about being clean, but since they were still on unsteady ground, he was glad they both thought condoms were the best choice. Still, Nick had gone to get checked again since the night they watched porn, just to be safe.

"Such a tight hole. I'm going to fucking lose it in there, baby. Turnover. Put your ass in the air so I can play with your dick better while I take you."

Nick rolled over and...fuck, he was shaking, both from pleasure and nerves.

"It's okay. I'll take care of you. Orgasm fucking heaven, Nick. Let me give it to you. I want to give it to you."

He turned Nick's head to the side, leaned over and kissed him. Bryce's tongue plunged into his mouth. His hands roamed Nick's body, touching him, relaxing him. And then he felt pressure on his asshole...stretching...burning. Bryce moved against him, still kissing him, and slowly pushing at his ring. He felt Bryce's hand there, guiding his dick into Nick's ass.

"Fuck...fuck, fuck, fuck." But then...he started pushing backward, too. The burning was there, the stretching, and then Bryce slipped an inch inside. The head of his cock was *inside* Nick's ass. "Don't move. Not yet."

Bryce kissed him between his shoulder blades. "I'm not. You tell me when. I don't move till you give the word."

Nick moaned, let himself adjust to the new sensation.

"Jesus, you're so fucking tight. I can't wait to push all the way inside. Feel my balls slap against yours. That's what they'll do, and you'll like it, Nick. We both know how much you like your sac played with."

"Oh, fuck." Nick's whole body lit on fire and he shoved backward. Pain instantly shot through him. Bryce cursed, but then...then the pain eased and Bryce was buried balls deep in Nick's ass. "Oh fuck, you're inside me, Bryce." It was different...good, but different. He felt full in the best possible way. But it wasn't enough. Now he wanted more. "Fuck me. Give it to me like you said."

Bryce's blunt nails dug into Nick's hips as he pulled almost all the way out before slamming forward again—hard and fast. Over and over without stopping. Their bodies collided together. Their balls slapped with each thrust...and he fucking loved it. Loved the sting of pain, and the reward of pleasure.

"Jesus Christ, this is fucking perfect."

Bryce wrapped a hand around Nick's erection, jerking him in time with each thrust. His body surged forward every time Bryce pounded into him.

His balls were already full, tight against his body. Bryce increased the pressure as he fisted Nick's cock. With each pump of Bryce's hips, the pleasure built stronger and stronger. Nick could hardly hold it back. He worked him in time with each of his thrusts, and before Nick knew it, he let go. He felt his asshole tighten as his cock shot all over the place. His spunk coated Bryce's hand, creating lube as he kept jacking him off.

Bryce shoved into him deeper, harder. He stiffened behind Nick, holding his ass flush to his body as he groaned and filled the condom inside him.

They fell to the bed, a mass of sweaty, hairy bodies. "I can't move. Can't even take care of the condom. I'm leaking jizz all over your bed," Bryce breathed behind him.

"Then it'll be there with mine, too." He thought that was fucking perfect, their bodies tangled, their sweat mixed, and now their come, too. The man behind him had Nick thinking all sorts of thoughts he'd never considered before. Made him want to be dirty, but also love Bryce in a way he'd never done with anyone.

"How are you?" Bryce's hand softly rubbed his ass cheek.

"Perfect." Sore, but good.

"Well, I'm pretty good."

Nick chuckled, then answered honestly. "The connection…knowing you were inside me…it's like nothing I've ever known. I've never felt as connected to someone as I did with you inside me."

"Good," Bryce whispered, but he almost sounded sad. "You sore?"

"Yeah, but it's worth it."

"I'm sorry that you couldn't have me. I hate that I couldn't give myself to you first, the way I thought I would. I'll fix it. I'll make it so I can take you."

"There's nothing to fix." It would happen eventually, but Nick wouldn't hurt him. He rolled over to face him. "That was pretty fucking sexy, though. I loved it."

He grabbed the condom that had slipped off, tossed it into the trash and then wrapped an arm around Bryce. He looked him in the eye. "I'm falling in love with you. I don't know what it means for us, or how you feel about it, but I thought you should know."

Bryce rubbed a hand though Nick's short hair. "I think I'm falling in love with you, too."

Nick's chest puffed out, making him feel fucking invincible. How could he make this man fall in love with him?

In a perfect world, that would be all that mattered. Nick wasn't stupid, though. He knew love didn't always fix everything.

***

Bryce was in a shitty mood. He shouldn't be. It was Monday, the only day off they both shared, and he'd had his dick in Nick's ass twice over the past few days. He'd had the best orgasms of his life, and slept beside Nick every night. They laughed, kissed, and hung out. He was in his first real relationship, and it was with an incredible man who he enjoyed spending time with, even when he wasn't fucking him.

But none of that could wipe out the fact that he hadn't spoken to his mom and dad since the day he left their house. And Nick had told his mom that he wanted her to meet him. She'd had a mild coronary and she didn't even know they were together yet.

Oh, and apparently he suddenly sucked at sex, because he couldn't give himself to Nick. If he was going to be gay, he wanted to be gay all the way. He wanted Nick to have him, the way he had Nick. Hell, Bryce needed it. He'd asked Nick more than once a day to try again, but every time Nick told him no.

"What's wrong? Why are you in such a bad mood?" Nick asked from the driver's seat of his car.

"Do I really have to answer that? We're on our way to an adult store to buy a dildo to train my ass to take your cock." Apparently he not only didn't take life seriously and had the potential to hurt those he cared about, but he couldn't even be a gay man correctly.

"Aww. Don't feel bad, baby. It's not your fault I have a monster cock," Nick teased, obviously trying to lighten the mood. That was Bryce's job. It annoyed him that he wasn't doing that, either.

He crossed his arms and didn't reply. Nick didn't get it. Bryce himself didn't get it, but this sex thing was a big fucking deal to him.

"Hey, what's wrong? Why are you taking this so seriously? It's toys. It'll be fun. I've never played with sex toys before."

That made Bryce turn Nick's way. "Never?" And the toys weren't the point; the fact that Nick wouldn't fuck him was.

He shook his head. "Nope. And don't look at me like that."

"You're sheltered. And yeah, toys are fun if you don't need them. I do, which means I'm not doing something right. I don't like that."

Nick sighed as he pulled off the freeway. They'd gone an hour away from home because they were both pussies and didn't want to run into anyone they knew. "I have a big dick and you have a small hole. Those are both good things. You're not doing anything wrong. What else is it?"

The second Nick said it, Bryce realized he was right. That definitely wasn't the only thing bothering him, but he wasn't sure how to express what was.

Bryce dropped his head back against the seat, turning to watch Nick as he drove. Christ, the man really was sexy. "I just...I want something to go easy. To go right. So far we've had to deal with freaked out family members, and sexual problems. Can't just one fucking piece of it go exactly the way it's supposed to? I just want to give myself to you. That's fucking it. I want to show you that I'm really in this with you. One hundred percent in it."

And there was Bryce's truth. Nick must have realized it, because he pulled into the first parking lot he found and killed the engine. "You have nothing to prove to me, Bryce. I told you the other night. I get it. Nothing is a guarantee, but I trust you. I know you're not playing games with me. I know you want me just as much as I want you. Whether or not I'm able to fuck you right away doesn't matter. We're in this together. There's no doubt in my mind about that, no matter what

231

happens."

And just like that...some of the worry disappeared. Bryce's chest felt lighter, his head not quite as full. "So, you don't think you're better at being gay than I am?" Bryce winked at Nick.

"Maybe a little." Nick grinned.

"Come here and kiss me." It would be their first kiss outside in broad daylight, where anyone could see them. "You're about to go into a sex store with me to buy a butt plug, or a dildo or something. You can fucking kiss me. Come here."

Nick smiled and leaned in. "A butt plug, huh?" he asked against Bryce's lips before kissing him.

When they pulled apart, Bryce said, "Well, obviously I'd rather have your dick, but that thing is too fucking big for your own good. It's going to hurt, regardless. We both know that. It's a rite of passage, I think."

Nick ignored the second part of what Bryce said. "You'll like it when we can get it in."

"Don't brag."

"I'm not."

He totally fucking was. Nick started the car and they got back on the road. When they pulled into the parking lot of the adult store, Nick turned to him. "It'll be okay, Bryce. Your parents are just confused. They'll come around when they see we're both serious. My family...fuck, we'll make them get it somehow. Pretty soon, we'll be the best fucking

232

gay men around."

"The best gay men, or the best *fucking* gay men?" he teased.

"Both."

Bryce smiled. He really fucking hoped Nick was right.

CHAPTER THIRTY-ONE

Holy shit, he was shopping for dildos with another man.

In public.

Where anyone could see him.

Dildos.

Or, according to Bryce, butt plugs.

They definitely should have done this online.

"Can I help you gentlemen find something?" Nick froze at the male voice behind him. He knew he needed to turn around and respond to the employee who spoke to them, but he couldn't make himself do it. *Turn around, Nick. It's not a big deal. I'm sure he's seen so many crazy things working in here that this is nothing.*

"I'm trying to find something that'll help train me to take him." That was enough to make Nick whip around and face his lover. Leave it to Bryce to lay it all out there.

"Jesus, Bryce. What the fuck?"

"What?" Bryce looked at him innocently. "It's true. I'm pretty sure it'll be obvious something's going on when we make our purchase."

For the first time, Nick eyed the employee who'd spoken to them. He was younger, probably in his early twenties. He had brown hair, wore eyeliner, had tattoos and a sticker on his shirt that said, "Ask me to recommend my favorite products!"

"What are your favorite products?" Bryce asked him, and Nick rolled his eyes. Only Bryce would get them into this situation.

"Follow me. My favorite products might be of some help to you guys." Okay, so it was safe to assume he might be gay, or at least bisexual.

The man started to walk and then stopped. "I'm Rod."

Oh fuck. Of course he had to say something like that. He waited for Bryce to say something, and he didn't disappoint. "Rod? No shit? I—"

"Bryce," Nick cut him off before he could say anything else.

"No, it's okay. I mean, a gay guy named Rod? Perfect, right? It's a great ice- breaker. My name's gotten me laid more times than I can count."

Bryce laughed, and then looked at Nick. "I like him."

Nick rolled his eyes as Rod gave a soft chuckle and then started walking again, Bryce by his side, Nick trailing behind them.

"We're new to this... Well, not sex, but neither of us has been with a man before. I didn't expect this to be a problem," Bryce told him, because obviously Rod needed to know all the details. Fucking Bryce.

"Really?" Rod asked Bryce. "You're just coming out?"

"No. We'd just never been into men before we met each other.
Threw us both for a fucking loop, didn't it, Nick?" He glanced back at
Nick and winked. Something told him Bryce knew exactly what he was
doing. He enjoyed embarrassing Nick, the bastard. Nick was going to kill
him.

"Yes, but I'm sure Rod doesn't want all the details."

"I'm sure Rod wouldn't mind at all. I'm all ears. Please continue."
Rod grinned. Nick threw his arms up. Great. Just what he needed, two
funny men giving him hell while they shopped for dildos.

He knew Bryce well enough to see that it was just his way of trying
to deal with everything. The fact that he couldn't take Nick bothered
him a lot. Add his argument with his family the other day, and he knew
Bryce just wanted to forget and try to make things as natural as he
could.

Nick sped up, wrapped an arm around Bryce's shoulders and pulled
his...boyfriend closer. "Sorry to disappoint you, Rod, but I'm going to
have to make him keep his mouth shut on this one. Obviously, I'm the
boring one in the relationship."

Nick stumbled, making Bryce do the same thing. What he'd just
said had been the easiest thing in the world.

"No, not boring. There's nothing about you that's boring," Bryce
said, and Nick realized he'd just given Bryce something he needed. He'd
been comfortable enough with him to say they're in a relationship, and

to touch in public. With his fears over what his family said, maybe he needed that more than Nick had realized.

"Well, if you change your mind..." Rod nudged Nick. "I'm kidding. Come on. They're right over here," he said, prompting them to walk again. He led them to an aisle filled with every shape, size and color of fake cocks ever made.

"I'm not going to lie to you, it hurts. Especially your first few times. I was lucky. I met a man who really knew what he was doing. He showed me how to enjoy being fucked." Rod crossed his arms.

"I have no doubts I'll enjoy it, if I can ever get him in," Bryce replied, and Nick wanted nothing more than for this conversation to be over. Did Bryce really have to share all of this with the guy who worked in the sex store?

"I'm sure Rod has to get back to work."

"I'm sure Rod is fine." Rod winked at Nick, clearly enjoying embarrassing him.

"So, it took a while for you?" Bryce asked him. "Because Nick seemed to enjoy it the first time." Bryce smiled, obviously happy with himself.

"Yes, Bryce, we get it. You have a magic dick. Can we please stop talking about our sex life?" Nick had to admit, he held himself back from chuckling. Bryce always found a way to make everything more fun.

Bryce and Rod laughed, and Nick wanted to kick both their asses. Finally, Rod got back on the topic of their purchase. "I probably should get back to work. So, how big are we looking for here? And do you want just a dildo? Something that vibrates? Double-ended, for both your pleasure? Whatever you want, we have it."

Nick's eyes went wide.

"Um....Double-ended?" Bryce asked exactly what Nick wondered, and Rod just laughed.

"You guys have so much fun to look forward to!"

Just like that, Nick was embarrassed again. But not Bryce; he grabbed Nick's hand and pulled him closer. "Come on, baby. Let's see what we can find."

***

Bryce bought two dildos, a plug and more lube. He had no idea if he'd need all of it, but he wasn't taking any chances. They were going to get this problem fixed, and get it fixed as soon as possible.

And have a whole lot of fun in the process.

A few hours later, they were home and in Nick's kitchen while he cooked dinner.

"Come help me for a second," Nick called to him. "Stir this." He handed Bryce a bowl. "Don't stop until I tell you to. It'll fuck with the consistency."

Bryce took over stirring the white mixture. "How'd you realize you love cooking?" he asked. He knew Nick went to culinary school right after high school, so it seemed as though he always knew. Bryce had never been as set in a decision as Nick had been, with both Jill and his career.

He envied Nick for that. Envied Jill that she'd had him for so long, even though she hadn't realized the good thing she had.

"I've loved it for as long as I can remember. I used to help my mom when I was young. The girls were all older, and Mom wanted them in the kitchen with her. She's got these very traditional ideas about gender roles. She'd want the girls with her, but then she'd let me sit around after school, not doing anything. I helped Dad with outside chores sometimes, and I enjoyed it. I like being outdoors, too, but while my sisters would complain about helping cook dinner, I'd ask her to help. Mom was funny about it at first, but then it became our thing. It made us close in a lot of ways."

Nick shrugged it off, but Bryce saw how big a deal it was to him. He may not agree with his mom on a lot of things, but they were close. It would kill him if she wasn't on board with their relationship.

"Pretty soon you were probably taking over and showing everyone how it's done, I'd guess." Bryce winked at him.

"Eh. I don't know about that. I enjoy it, though—providing for people I love. That's how I feel about cooking. I'm giving people something they need. It makes me feel good."

Nick made Bryce feel good. Everything about him did. "So, then it was automatic? There was never another possibility for you other than culinary school?"

"Nope. Not really. I guess maybe I pretended there was when I was young...like I didn't really know for sure, but I did." Nick mixed ingredients into another bowl. Bryce had no clue with he was making, but he didn't ask, either. He'd be surprised.

"Same with Jill?" Bryce felt a stab in his chest at the mention of Nick's ex-wife.

Another shrug. "I loved her, so yeah, I guess. It wasn't always the way it had been in the end. We were happy at some point. Now, when I look back, I realize we might not have been happy in the right ways. I think we got married because we were all each other knew. We loved each other, but I think maybe we hadn't been in love with each other for a long time. I didn't realize it then, though. Hell, I don't think I realized it until I met you. Mom was never fond of her, but she accepted her. She was good to Jill, even though to me, she never hid the fact that she didn't think Jill was good enough for me. She didn't think she, and I quote, *'possessed the right qualities in a wife.'*" Nick laughed. Bryce didn't. He sure as hell didn't possess any of those qualities either, the biggest one being that he wasn't and would never be a wife. Boyfriend, yes, but he wasn't a woman.

"But she accepted her because she loved you?" Bryce asked, still stirring.

Nick looked at him, and Bryce thought he heard the question in his voice. "Yes, she did. It might take her a little while, but she'll accept us for the same reason."

He didn't sound as sure about that as Bryce needed him to sound.

"When do you think things started to go downhill with Jill?" he asked.

Nick moved to the cabinet and grabbed a few spices, mixing them. "You know, I can't totally blame her. I can blame her for cheating, but not everything. That's something else I hadn't realized until recently. Jill's parents were like mine, in some ways. They never cared for me, only they didn't hide it as well as my mom did. After I got my degree, I worked as a chef, and then continued on for my Masters. I always knew I'd want my own restaurant, and I wanted every skill I could learn, so I worked my ass off. Still paying that shit off, by the way; that and the restaurant." Nick laughed and then continued.

"I think I partly did it because I wanted to prove to her parents I was worthy of her... Jill's from a very wealthy, rather stuck-up family. But really, I loved it. I wanted it, but I think Jill started to feel neglected. That was the first time she cheated. She didn't tell me until later, but she had asked to spend more time with me, which I now see was out of guilt." He glanced in Bryce's bowl.

"Stir a little faster, please. Anyway, so we tried reconnecting, when I didn't even know what had happened. I realized we'd drifted apart, though, and I didn't want that. I didn't want my marriage to fail. Soon, she was the one with longer and longer hours. I never even considered that she would cheat on me until the day I came home and she gave me divorce papers. She told me she was moving in with her boyfriend, who I found out was her second affair."

"Christ." Bryce couldn't imagine going through that. It made him thankful he'd never gotten serious with anyone before.

"Everything happens for a reason, Bryce. I didn't see it then, but I do now. Two more minutes with that bowl and then I need it back. What about you? Tell me more about you and Christi."

Bryce leaned against the counter. "We met in ninth grade. She was new. Started dating this guy who then decided he didn't want to date her and told the whole school she gave him head under the bleachers."

"In ninth grade!"

Bryce winked at him. "Not all of us are as innocent as you. So yeah, they gave her shit. Typical girl stuff. Called her a slut. I told them Devin was a lying sack of shit, that I was hiding under the bleachers skipping school and heard him ask her for a blowjob and she said no. He got embarrassed and made up the rumor, then everyone gave him shit instead of her."

"Was it true?" Nick cocked a brow at him.

"Hell no. She blew him, but she thought he liked her, and he was an asshole for calling her out like that, so he deserved what he got. We've been best friends ever since."

Nick walked over to him. "I love that story. It's things like that that I love about you. You're a good man, Bryce Tanner." He gave Bryce a quick kiss and grabbed the bowl out of his hands before walking away to finish the meal. Bryce just stood there wondering how in the hell he got so lucky, because he was in love with the man standing in the kitchen with him, too.

CHAPTER THIRTY-TWO

They ate dinner together and talked about everything. Afterward, they showered separately. Nick made sure to take care of everything he needed to for their night, and he knew Bryce had done the same.

Before he knew it, they were naked in Nick's room, their purchases from the day laid out on the bed. "I was re-tested," Nick admitted.

"No shit? Me, too."

"I didn't want to assume, and I'm not saying we should go raw, but here, so you know." Nick pulled the results out of his drawer and showed them to Bryce.

Bryce pulled his wallet out and grinned.

"You carry them with you?"

"I wanted to have it in case you needed to see and we weren't home." He unfolded the paper and handed it to Nick. "So, now we know."

Nick nodded. "We do. There's no one else for me, Bryce. You're the one for me."

"I already told you, you're it for me, too."

Nick loved hearing that. "There's four dicks and a butt plug in the bed with us. This is another first for me," he teased.

Bryce didn't reply to that, just laid back and said, "Use the smaller one on me first. We'll move up to the bigger one, and then hopefully I can take the real fucking thing."

Nick had something else in mind. He leaned down and kissed Bryce, probing the other man's mouth with his tongue before retreating to say, "You once told me you played with your own hole to get yourself ready for me. I told you I wanted to see, but you never showed me. I want to see tonight, Bryce."

A big grin stretched across Bryce's face. "I'm corrupting you, and I think I like it."

"I like it, too."

"You have to jack off, though. You want me to fuck myself for you, you at least have to jerk off while I do it. I want to see how much it turns you on."

"Okay." Nick grabbed the lube, coated his hand and started to work his cock. He didn't take his eyes off Bryce as the man laid back and grabbed the dildo and lube. "Wait. Let me go to the other end of the bed. I want to watch it go in."

He saw Bryce's erection flex against his stomach. Obviously he liked that idea as much as Nick did.

Nick moved to the foot of the bed. Watched as Bryce opened his legs, rubbing his hole with a finger. "Oh, fuck, that's sexy." He stroked his cock faster.

"You ain't seen nothing yet, baby." Bryce pushed two fingers inside his pink hole. Stretched them and fucked himself as he watched Nick stroke.

Pre-come ran down Nick's shaft as he jerked. "You're so fucking sexy. I don't think I knew what sexy was before you." Bryce was the sexiest person he'd ever seen. He couldn't take his eyes off the man.

"You, too."

Nick made an O with his fingers around the base of his cock, cutting himself off before he started to jerk again. Bryce kept fucking, kept fingering his asshole for Nick, because he wanted Nick inside him. Nick couldn't fucking wait to be there, to feel Bryce from the inside, but he wouldn't do it until Bryce was ready.

They kept masturbating, watching each other before Bryce said, "I'm ready for more." He grabbed the smaller of the two dildos, lubed it, and then slowly stretched his hole while putting it in.

"Oh, fuck. That's sexy. Pull it out. Let me see you work yourself with it."

Bryce did as he said, pushing the dick inside himself before pulling it out again. It was the most erotic sight Nick had ever seen. He had to grab his balls again to keep himself from coming.

"Christ, Nick. I'm so full, stretched, and I want more. I want this to be you so fucking much. I want to be completely yours." He worked the dildo in and out.

As much as Nick wanted that, he spoke the truth. "You are mine. You so fucking are."

Bryce fucked faster. Nick's balls felt like they would burst.

"Don't come. Not yet. Want you." Bryce pulled the dildo out, grabbed the plug, lubed it and pushed it inside himself.

"Sweet Jesus. Goddamn, that's hot." Nick almost came from the sight.

"It's about to get even hotter. I'm going to fuck you while I keep this in my ass, and you'll know even though it's my dick in your ass, I'm doing everything I fucking can to get ready to take yours."

***

It was strange...the feeling of something lodged inside him. A part of him wondered if he should be embarrassed, but he wasn't. Not with Nick.

Bryce grabbed Nick's legs and pulled. He went down to his back easily. Bryce lay between his legs, pushing his tongue in Nick's mouth. He rubbed his cock against Nick's hot, full sac. "You want it, don't you?" he asked.

"Yeah, so much," Nick moaned.

"Not as much as I want you. I'd beg you to fuck me right now, but I know you'd say no." If he were being honest, he'd admit that the knowledge kind of killed him. He'd never had to beg for it, but he would for Nick.

"Not because I don't want you."

Bryce ignored that.

He grabbed the lube, went to coat himself before he remembered a rubber. Even though they'd seen each other's test results, he didn't know if they should go there yet. It felt like going raw was a big fucking step, and even though Bryce knew Nick was the only one he wanted, he didn't need to push it. Nick's wife had cheated on him. As much as Bryce hated the thought, he might worry that Bryce would do the same thing.

"I need to grab a rubber." He turned toward the bedside table, but Nick grabbed his arm.

"You're clean. I'm clean. I don't want anyone but you. Just do it."

Bryce's heart nearly stopped beating. "I've never fucked anyone bare before."

He fucking hated that Nick couldn't say the same thing. Of course he couldn't; he'd been married.

Bryce wanted it. Wanted it so fucking much. "You know I won't touch anyone else while we're together. I won't cheat," he confirmed.

"And I told you I trust you. Fuck me, Bryce, before I have to use one of your dildos on myself."

Bryce couldn't find it in himself to laugh. He was too fucking needy. He lubed up his cock and Nick's hole before he pushed in, burying himself inside Nick. He pushed Nick's legs up and open farther as he started to thrust. The plug moved in his ass each time he pumped his hips.

"Oh, Christ. The feel of you around my dick, with nothing between us, and the plug in my ass...I'm not going to last long, baby." He already felt the tingle forming. Felt his balls getting ready to unload. This was Nick...nothing between them as they made love. As Nick felt the connection of being filled that he longed for himself. Every day he wanted Nick inside him even more.

Bryce pumped his hips as fast and hard as he could. He used his arms to hold Nick's legs out of the way. "Jack yourself off. I'm a little busy here," he teased. Nick groaned, wrapped a hand around his erection and started to jerk. Within seconds, thick, white come pulsed out of his dick with each of Bryce's thrusts. Seeing him pushed Bryce over the edge. He let go, emptying his balls into Nick's ass, filling him.

Slowly, he pulled out, watching his come leak out of Nick's hole and run down his leg, and damned if his cock didn't jerk again.

He lay down on Nick's chest, taking his mouth, knowing that he would never want anyone other than this man. It was time to make that clear to everyone in their lives. He didn't give a shit how hard it was for everyone, they'd need to accept it. Because Bryce wasn't letting Nick go.

CHAPTER THIRTY-THREE

Despite the fact that Karrie was the oldest Fuller child, and Nick the youngest, he'd always been the closest with her. Growing up, she was the one he'd always go to. She'd helped when his Mom had been so angry that he was proposing to Jill at such a young age. She'd confronted her on the fact that she treated Nick like he was helpless while also putting him on a pedestal because he was the only boy.

And he wanted to talk to her about Bryce.

Nick told her he wanted to meet up in private, so they picked a day her husband's parents would have the kids, and Nick went over.

His goddamned hands wouldn't stop shaking. This would be the first time he actually told someone in his personal life that he was in a relationship with another man. He wasn't sure how she would take it.

"You look like you're going to vomit all over the place, Nick. What's wrong?" Karrie asked as she opened the door.

He walked into the house. "Nothing. I'm fine. I'm—"

"A liar," she interrupted.

He shrugged, because she was pretty close to being correct. "I am a liar. I'm not fine. Not in some ways, but in others, I'm more fine than I've ever been, if that makes any sense." It was such a confusing cluster in his head. He knew how he felt and what he wanted, even though he didn't understand it.

Karrie frowned, pushing her brown hair behind her ear. "You're scaring me, Nick-o. What's wrong?"

She hadn't called him that since he was a kid. "Come on. Let's go sit down. Do you have any coffee?"

"I'm a mom, Nick. I live on coffee."

The two of them walked into the kitchen, made a cup of coffee, before sitting down at the table. Nick blew on it. Took a drink. Blew on it again. Stalled.

He was being a fucking pussy.

He leaned back in the antique, wood chair and eyed his sister. "I'm in a relationship with my neighbor."

Another frown. "Okay...I'm not sure why that's a big deal. I know Mom gets funny about who's good enough for her boy, but you're a grown man. You're single. You have every right to be in a relationship if that's what you want."

Nick's grip on his cup got stronger, but he didn't turn away from his sister when he said, "My neighbor is a man, Karrie. I'm in a relationship with another man."

If this wasn't such a serious moment, he'd laugh at her expression.

Karrie's mouth dropped open, her eyes wide. He'd never shocked his sister in his life. Leave it to Bryce to be the thing that did it for him. He was always giving Nick new experiences, even when he wasn't around.

"Oh… You're gay? I never guessed. Is that what caused problems between you and Jill?" Her voice sounded far away, as though she was drifting as she spoke. Nick didn't think she realized it, though, didn't think she did it on purpose.

"I guess gay is what you have to call it. I'm in love with another man, but it wasn't what caused problems between Jill and I. I've never so much as looked at another man before him. I don't…I don't know what it is about him. It's just…right." There was no other word for it than that. For the first time since Nick told her, he looked away. He leaned forward with his elbows on the table and his face in his hands. It was minutes later before he spoke again. "I'm scared to death, Karrie. I'm scared of what this means. I'm scared of the changes in my life. I'm scared because I'm not sure how my family will react…but none of that is enough for me to want to walk away from him. The thought is unimaginable. It doesn't matter if I understand any of it. It's just the way I feel."

When the silence stretched on, Nick pulled his hands away from his face to look at his sister again. Karrie was always strong. In a lot of ways, the strongest Fuller child. She was a realist, and she didn't let her emotions run her; but now, when he looked at her, he saw her chin quiver and tears run down her face. She was sad…hurt, making his stomach drop. He didn't expect this from her. He didn't think he would lose Karrie. Maybe it was a possibility with the rest of them, but not her.

"Karrie…" *Don't do this, Karrie. I need you.*

"It won't be easy." Her voice was nothing more than a soft whisper.

"I know. We both do." Everything about this was a learning experience for both Nick and Bryce.

"Mom's going to have a hard time with it. I've never been anything other than honest with you, and I'm not going to change that now. I'm not sure she's going to be able to accept this. She struggled to accept your wife, and this is… this is a man. I know it shouldn't matter. Love is love; but it'll matter to her."

It was completely the wrong time for this, but Nick smiled. It wasn't just any man, either. It was Bryce. Bryce, who laughed all the time and had no filter. He said inappropriate things, and didn't take life seriously. His mom would hate those qualities in anyone…but they're what grabbed ahold of Nick and held him. They're what made him laugh every fucking day of his life since he met the man. "It'll be even worse when she meets him."

"So you want her to, then. This is serious. You want to introduce him to Mom. You're sure?"

It wasn't even a question for him. "Yes. I'm not stupid. I know this isn't what she'll want or expect. I know she's going to struggle with it. I'm sure she's not the only one, but I've never been more sure about anything in my life."

Nick didn't realize he needed his sister's smile so much until she finally gave it to him. "Then I guess we need to make her understand, Nick-o. You're in love with him. I can see it in your eyes. We'll make it work. No matter what, we want you to be happy. Sounds like this man does that for you. That's all that matters to me."

"He does." Nick stood, moved to his sister, and pulled her up and into his arms. "Thank you, Karrie. I need you by my side on this."

She started to cry again as she squeezed him tightly. "I'm always by your side. You're my little brother. The prodigal boy. Our family wouldn't be complete without you."

Nick's chest vibrated with laughter.

"I love you, Nick-o."

"I love you, Karrie."

***

Bryce sat in his office on his lunch break. Nick was with his sister today, and Bryce was nervous as hell for him. If Nick's family wasn't on board with them...what if Nick couldn't be, either? What if it was too much, and Nick decided to walk away?

"Jesus Christ, I'm turning into a sap." Bryce picked up his phone and called Christi.

She answered the phone saying, "You know, I heard women all want a gay guy for their best friend. I'm still not sure what's so special about it. So far, it's the same as having anyone for a best friend. Aren't you supposed to do something cool?"

Bryce rolled his eyes. Of course Christi would have something like that to say. "Ha ha. You're funny. Is that true? Women want a gay best friend?"

"I don't know. I've heard things like that. You could be my shiny new toy."

"You suck."

"Ha! You do, too, now!"

Bryce's mood lifted as he laughed at her. "You're an asshole, Chris."

"Ooh! We get to talk about assholes next?"

He knew she was joking, but sex was the last thing he wanted to talk about. Even if it was with his female ex-wingman. Bryce rubbed a hand over his face. "Please, no sex talk. I don't have it in me to go there today."

Christi paused for a second before saying, "Wow. That's a first. So, the sex isn't good, huh? Who would have thought hot neighbor Nick wouldn't be good in the sack."

Jesus, he was going to kill the woman. Bryce groaned. "First of all, please stop calling my boyfriend hot. He is, but it pisses me off when you say it. Second, Nick has no problems in bed. He makes me come so hard my head spins. He's not the problem, I am." Fuck. He hadn't meant to say that. He knew Christi would never let it go.

"First of all, don't go all Neanderthal on me. Nick's hot. You're my best friend. Calling him hot doesn't mean anything. Second, awww, you called him your boyfriend! And third, what's wrong, Bry? There's a big percentage of the population who can vouch for the fact that you don't have problems in bed, and I'm one of them. Which is another reason you shouldn't care if I call him hot. He has to live with the fact that we've slept together and were in a relationship. That can't be easy on Nick."

Fuck. She was right about that. He hated it when Christi was right. And yeah, this sex thing was really bothering him. He tried not to let Nick know it was a big deal to him, but it was.

As much as he didn't want to get into his sex life with Christi, she was the only person he had. "I haven't been able to take him. It feels like the bastard is trying to split me in two, and now he refuses to try." He rubbed a hand over his face. "Ugh. I want him, Chris. I do. I fucking hate that I'm not able to give myself to him. I mean, Jesus, I pushed this on him. I kissed him first and now he can't even fuck me. I don't...I don't want him to think I don't want this, that I don't want us. I want him to know I'm in this relationship just as much as he is."

Christi breathed heavily through the phone. "Holy shit, Bry. You shouldn't hide that big heart of yours behind laughs and the pretense of not taking things seriously. You're human like the rest of us."

"What the hell are you talking about?"

"You act like things don't matter to you, but they do. Nick does. You're just as insecure as the rest of us are. Nick knows how you feel. I know you've never seen it this way before, but sex isn't everything. It's not what matters. How you treat him is what's important. You treat him right and be fair to him, and he'll know you're in this just as much as he is. And it won't be like this forever. You guys will figure it out. In the meantime...if he needs..."

Bryce heard the humor in her voice and laughed. "Hands off! Nick is mine. And thanks. Don't know what I'd do without you."

"I *am* pretty good. Have you talked to the family since you told them?"

That quickly, the weight in his chest was back. "Just Jamie and Hope. Well, Abbey called once, but mostly just Jamie and Hope. Jamie called this morning. He wants Nick and I to go to Mom and Dad's for dinner this Saturday. He said he knows she misses me, but she's just as stubborn as I am and won't make the first step."

"Which you know he's likely right about."

Yeah, he did. At least with the stubborn part. "He said she's just hurt because of you, and the lies. And she's confused. She still doesn't believe I'm serious. She apparently told Jamie that she doesn't think even I realize what I'm doing, that I don't realize this is just another fun experiment for me..." Bryce paused. Thought. Felt the ache in his chest and the anger at himself. "You don't think she's right, do you? You don't think I'm subconsciously using Nick as an excuse not to settle down, and to just...I don't know...play." Because the truth was, Bryce had always liked to play around. That truth never bothered him until now.

"I don't think so, but only you can answer that."

The answer was no. He was more serious about Nick than he'd ever been about anything in his life.

"Are you going to dinner on Saturday?" he asked.

"No. I think it's better that I sit this one out."

He knew that Christi was right. He hadn't expected this to be so hard, the fallout that trickled down; not just between Nick and him, but with the people they cared about as well.

CHAPTER THIRTY-FOUR

He and Bryce were out of their fucking minds.

It was Saturday. Bryce was working most of the day at the shop, and then they were going to Bryce's parents' house for dinner. Nick would be lying if he didn't admit he was nervous as hell. This was the first time he was meeting Bryce's family as his...partner? He guessed that was as good a word as any, and knowing how confused his family was about them didn't help.

Not only that, but Monday they were going to see his mom—together. Mona Fuller wasn't aware of that fact, though. That probably made Nick a bastard—that he was taking Bryce—but the truth was, he needed Bryce there. And he wanted his mom to meet the man without a house full of people. He hoped like hell she could see all the great things in Bryce that he did. That's all he wanted.

To say the next few days would be stress-inducing was an understatement.

So Nick cooked a big ass lunch that he had no business cooking, since he had no one home to eat it.

He showered.

Dressed.

Cleaned.

Ate.

Looked at the clock.

Twelve thirty. Fuck. Why did he get up early with Bryce?

He was too damn restless to sit around the house all afternoon, so he packed some food into a container, jumped in his car and drove down to Bryce's shop.

Bryce had to eat. Nick knew he didn't usually eat until around one, so he hoped he'd make it before that. If not, oh well, it wasn't a big deal since it got him out of the house before he went fucking insane.

The garage doors were open when Nick pulled in. He saw Bryce right away, sitting next to a bike on a ramp with his hands under it.

Unlike the other time he was here, there were at least five other people around—some workers—and it looked like a customer was here to check on his bike.

Shit, now he felt like an idiot for bringing Bryce his lunch. No one outside of family and Christi knew about them. Would it be obvious when Nick brought him a home-cooked lunch?

Yes.

What the hell was he doing here?

Maybe he could pull out and no one would notice.

He glanced up at Bryce again, only this time Bryce was looking at his car. He hadn't moved from the bike, but he smiled and nodded Nick over. Obviously there was no chickening out now, so he got out of the car, leaving the lunch on the seat, and walked over.

"Hey."

Bryce stood, oil and grease stains all over his hands and pants, before walking over. "Hey. What are you doing here?" They spoke softly, not loud enough for anyone in the garage to hear.

"I was going fucking crazy at home. I brought you lunch."

"Great. I'm starved." Bryce looked down at Nick's hands. "Where is it?"

Oh yeah. Back to feeling like an idiot. "I left it in the car. I wasn't sure if you'd want me to bring it out to you in front of everyone. I know we've talked a little bit about..." Fuck. Why was this so hard? "Making our relationship more obvious, but I wasn't sure if people here should know, or if we wanted to wait a little while before we went public or not. I—"

"Nick?"

"What?"

"Fair warning so you don't punch me this time. I'm going to kiss you and tell them you brought me lunch. We'll go eat it in my office and then everyone here will know. Okay?"

Nick liked the sound of that more than he should. "Yeah, okay. I wasn't sure how you felt about it."

"Until right now, I wasn't sure, either." And then Bryce did exactly as he said. He leaned in and pressed his lips to Nick's mouth—just a few soft kisses and then he pulled away.

Every pair of eyes in the garage was on them when they turned around. Every one. Nick felt naked, cut open, exposed; but he didn't turn away.

"Nick brought me lunch. Be fucking jealous, because he's an incredible cook. We're going to go eat in my office. I'll be back in a little while."

There were a few nods, a few mumbled *okays,* but Nick could see they were all in shock. Welcome to the fucking club.

"I'm going to go clean up. Meet me in the office." Bryce went inside without another word, so Nick didn't have a choice except to go back to the car, grab the food and head to Bryce's office.

Nick stepped inside and set the container on Bryce's desk before sitting in one of the chairs.

They'd just kissed in front of people at his work. That meant this was getting more real.

"Hey." Bryce closed the door behind him and sat at his desk. "What is it?"

"Smoked apple pork chops with garlic roasted potatoes and grilled red wine brussel sprouts."

"You're going to make me fat," Bryce teased, as though they hadn't just kissed in front of his shop. "Thanks for this. I wish you would have brought yours and eaten with me, though."

"How do you do that? You just go for it, just react, and not think of the consequences?" Nick asked, envious of Bryce's ability to be so carefree.

Bryce opened the container of food and then sat back. "I guess because I don't take anything seriously. That's what my mom thinks, at least." His voice was filled with sharp irritation.

"That's not what I meant, and you know it."

"Well, it sounded like it."

"Fuck you, Bryce. Don't twist the meaning of my words. I've dealt with that shit from Jill, and even my family. I won't deal with it from you."

"Shit." Bryce shook his head, scratched the back of his neck. "You're right. I'm sorry. I'm nervous about tonight, so I'm on edge. I didn't mean to take it out on you. As for the other thing, I don't know. Maybe my mom's right and I do just react and not take things seriously enough. Was that bad? What I did out there? I was trying to show you that we're moving forward and that I'm okay with it. I want our relationship. To do that, people need to know. Overthinking it won't change anything, but if you don't want that, tell me now."

"No." Nick shook his head. "That's not it. I envy that about you, that you're full speed ahead. You don't worry about shit the way I do." Nick wished he could be more like that. He was trying to be.

"It's not always a good thing, and it gets me into trouble

sometimes. I don't want to get myself into trouble with you, Nick." Bryce's insecurity briefly showed.

"You won't," Nick said, meaning it. Fuck, he loved this man. His reaction today was a reminder why. "I'm nervous, too."

"We'll be okay. You'll win them over. They'll be surprised I landed you."

Nick laughed, shaking his head. Somehow he didn't think things would go down that way. It didn't matter how nice Nick was, he knew how much Bryce's mom loved Christi, and how much she wanted her son to love Christi as well.

***

The conversation was light as Bryce ate his lunch. That was to be expected, he figured. They had a lot of shit on their minds. After he ate, he walked Nick out to his car, thanked him and told him that he'd see him in a few hours.

Bryce watched as Nick drove away, stood in the parking lot for a few minutes before he got the balls to go inside. Nick was wrong about him. Yeah, Bryce often just reacted, but he thought about things; it was usually just after the fact.

He hoped like hell the men in his garage didn't give him shit.

It wouldn't change things, but he really needed some parts of his relationship with Nick to be a smooth transition. He didn't want to lose people over something that shouldn't fucking matter. Why the hell did anyone give a shit about who he or anyone else loved?

Everyone was quiet when he got back into the shop. Everyone worked on their bikes, and Bryce went back to work on his. Every so often he'd feel eyes on him. He'd turn to look, but whoever had looked at him would've turned away.

After about an hour of silence, Bryce couldn't take it anymore. He shoved to his feet. "Alright, let's hear it. If anyone has a problem, a) fuck you, and b) I want to hear about it right now. We'll get this shit out on the table, and then it's over with. Nick is mine, he's my boyfriend. End of story."

"I don't have a problem with it. I don't give a shit who is or isn't yours. Didn't expect it, but don't care. Do you have my Allen Wrench?" Tim asked.

"I have my own Allen Wrench, fucker. I don't need yours." Bryce smiled at him, appreciating the fact that Tim wasn't making this into more than it should be.

"Then shut the hell up and let me get back to work."

"Not a problem for me, either," Chuck, one of the part-time employees said. "Hell, it looks like you have yourself a nice girlfriend there. He cooks for you, brings it to work for you. See? I always knew it was bullshit when they said one person in a gay relationship wasn't a woman and the other a man. Bet he never has a headache when you want to fuck him, either." Chuck laughed, and everything inside Bryce went rigid.

"What the fuck did you just say?" His throat was so tight he could hardly get the words out.

"Ah shit, Chuck," he heard Tim say in the background.

"What?" Chuck replied. "You can't tell me the rest of you weren't thinking it. And you," he looked at Bryce, "can't tell me that's not the way it is. I wish I could get my girl to bring me lunch at work."

Bryce didn't realize he'd even moved until he had Chuck held against the wall, his forearm against Chuck's throat.

"Bryce," Tim called.

"Back the fuck off, Tim. This is between us." He pushed tighter against Chuck's throat. "You don't know shit about him. Don't ever fucking talk about him like that again, do you hear me? It takes more of a man to take it than to give it, and let me tell you, I go fucking crazy for his dick. Nick is all man. More than you, asshole."

Bryce pushed off of him, then grabbed for this neck. "What the fuck? I was just giving you shit. I didn't mean anything by it," Chuck said.

Bryce's chest hurt from breathing so heavily. Part of him knew Chuck was just a fucking idiot who hadn't meant anything by it, but it didn't change the way he felt. He'd beat the son-of-a-bitch's ass if he ever said something about Nick again.

Still, deep down he knew this was more about him and his hang-up. He wasn't half the man Nick was.

CHAPTER THIRTY-FIVE

Something wasn't right with Bryce. Nick knew it the second he'd come home after work, and it became more and more obvious as they drove to his parents' house.

"I wish we could have taken my bike. I really fucking need to be on my bike," Bryce said from the passenger seat as they pulled up to the house.

That was definitely directed at him, because he knew Nick didn't want to ride the damn thing. "I could have driven my car and you could have taken your bike."

"Yeah, because that would have looked great. We're trying to make a good impression on my family. Taking separate vehicles when we live next door to each other would help our case tremendously. We couldn't agree on the ride to take, Ma, so we rode separately."

Nick didn't turn the car off. He silently counted backward from five to calm his frustration. "I didn't realize this night was about making a good impression. I thought it was just about us spending time with your family and showing them we care about each other."

"By showing them we couldn't agree on what vehicle to take?"

"So is the whole night going to be about the picture we're painting for your family? Let me know ahead of time if I'm supposed to pretend to like certain things you do, or agree with everything you say. I like to be aware of things up front."

"Don't pretend you wouldn't be the same way if we were going to your house. My parents know, Nick. Your Mom doesn't."

Nick dropped his head back against the seat. He got it. They were both on edge. They'd made things public at Bryce's work, were going to see Bryce's family tonight, Nick's on Monday. They had a lot on their plate, but the fighting was driving him crazy.

"I just got out of a marriage where I fought a lot with my wife in the end, Bryce. I don't want to fight with you. If you have something to say, say it. If I did something wrong, tell me. If we're moving too fast, tell me. Maybe I should just go. It's probably too soon for this."

Nick held in his groan when two women appeared at the passenger window, waiting for Bryce. "Your sisters-in-law are waiting for you. What do you want me to do?"

"Get out of the car, Nick. You can't leave now." Bryce pushed open the door and pasted on what Nick could plainly see was a fake smile. "Miss me that much, huh?" he asked Hope and Abbey, who both hugged him, but then looked into the car as though they were waiting for Nick.

He turned off the engine, took a deep breath, and gave them a fake smile to rival Bryce's. When he got out of the car, both women came around, hugging him one at a time. "It's great to see you again, Nick," Abbey said.

Hope spoke in his ear. "They're all great people. They'll come around. Jamie and I support you both."

He appreciated that, he really did. But if he was being honest, it made Nick want to climb back into the car and drive away. All they wanted to do was be in a relationship with each other. Why did they have to wait for people to come around, or need other people to support them? The only thing that should matter was the fact that they cared about each other. End of story.

The thing was, he knew it would be even worse with his own family. "Thank you. I appreciate that."

"Okay, ladies, I know he's sexy, but give him some space. You're worse than Christi is with him. If one of you starts calling him hot neighbor Nick, I'm going to lose my shit."

The women laughed. Nick tried not to groan. Bryce didn't look at him.

Hope and Abbey led the way inside, followed by Bryce and then Nick.

Jamie met them in the foyer, because obviously they needed, what? A back-up squad? That's what it felt like.

"Hey, Bryce." Jamie hugged his brother, slapping him on the back as he looked at Nick. "Damn. He is good-looking. I didn't notice before. I think he could turn me gay, too."

Nick actually saw Bryce tense up. Jamie had nothing but support in his eyes. Nick could tell he was similar to Bryce in that he tried to make people laugh to take the tension away. Unfortunately, it had the opposite effect this time.

"Jamie!" Hope tugged on him. "Not, now," she said out of the side of her mouth, as though they couldn't all hear. Obviously, she sensed the tension between him and Bryce.

"Shit. I'm sorry. Apparently I suck at breaking the ice. That's supposed to be Bryce's job."

Before anyone could reply to Jamie, Bryce's parents and Mitch appeared in the doorway, the three of them standing there awkwardly.

Bryce did just as Jamie had said: he took over the job he usually had. "We might have a problem, guys. Looks like Jamie might switch to the other team, as well. Sorry about that, Hope. All I know is, I'm not sharing Nick."

No one laughed.

Nick was going to fucking kill him.

***

The whole evening was a disaster. Bryce knew he had been an asshole to Nick. He should have told him what was on his mind, but it was too late now. So instead, he practically ignored the man all night. Not completely. He'd reintroduced Nick to his parents as his boyfriend, even though they obviously knew that part. He made sure Nick had a drink when he needed one, and that he felt comfortable in that respect, but that was it. His sisters-in-law had taken to keeping Nick company. Bryce hadn't held his hand, or so much as touched him all evening, which was something he knew he really should be doing. He wanted to show his family who Nick was to him, what this man meant to him, but he was doing a really shitty job of it.

"What's your problem?" Jamie pulled him aside and asked.

"Nothing. What do you mean?"

"Don't bullshit me, Bryce. I'm not stupid. Don't tell me you're already having second thoughts about the guy."

Huh? Absolutely not. "Hell no."

"You've hardly spoken a word to him all night. You're letting Hope and Abbey fawn all over him like you don't give a shit."

Bryce shook his head. "I had a bad day. We're all entitled to bad days, Jamie. Nick and I are fine."

"Dinner's ready!" his mom called, breaking up their conversation. Bryce would prove to them that everything was okay. He went straight to Nick, tried to smile at him, and then held out his hand. It took Nick a minute, but he latched on and let Bryce help him up.

"Come on, let's go eat." He hated that he'd been a miserable bastard all day.

They all made their way to the table.

"I hope you like it, Nick. It's nerve-racking to cook for a chef." Bryce appreciated the hell out of his mom for trying. That's the way she was.

She might be unsure and angry at Bryce, but she wouldn't take it out on Nick.

"Thank you. I'm sure it's fantastic. It's nice to have a night off," Nick replied, and they all began to dig into their lasagna.

It was a few minutes later when his mom spoke again. "I was disappointed that Christi couldn't make it tonight."

So much for her being polite to Nick. "Mom."

"What?" she asked.

"It's fine," Nick replied.

"No, it's not," Bryce countered. "As much as we all love Christi, she's not a staple to our family dinners. I don't appreciate you bringing her up like that. Nick's here. He's who I want here. Hell, Christi's a whole lot happier seeing me with Nick than she was when we were together. If you're not going to respect Nick, then we're leaving."

His dad started, "Bryce—"

"No. We don't need to discuss it further. That's how I feel."

He could feel Nick tense beside him, but it was his mother who spoke. "You're right. I'm sorry, Nick. I didn't mean to disrespect you. You're a very nice man, and I like you a lot. I just... Please excuse me." She got up and walked out of the room. They were all silent for a minute. Bryce knew he should say something to Nick, but he wasn't sure what.

"It's not that we have a problem with Bryce being gay, or with you, Nick. You just have to understand that Christi has been a part of this family for years, and we thought she and Bryce were in a relationship for longer than they actually were. We found out in one swoop that they'd been broken up for months, and that he's suddenly with you. We're just trying to make sense of it all."

Which was Bryce's screw-up. Bryce's fault and he knew it. "That's on me. Take it out on me, not Nick. He doesn't deserve it."

For the first time since he saw him at work, Bryce turned and really looked at Nick. At his dark green eyes, which were pretty fucking lost right now. At the hair Bryce often had his hands in, and the lips he often kissed. The man he wanted. The man he loved. He pulled Nick forward and pressed a kiss to his forehead. "I've been an asshole tonight, and I'm sorry. Come on, let's go."

Nick smiled at him. "Go talk to your mom first. It'll kill you if you don't."

They were the exact words he needed to hear. Bryce kissed him again, this time on the mouth, where Nick could kiss him back. "Thanks."

"So, Nick, how long have you had your restaurant?" They all looked up at the sound of Mitch's voice, and Bryce knew exactly what it was. That was Mitch's way of showing he accepted Nick as Bryce's. He believed in Bryce and was supporting him.

He remembered when his brother told him he'd find a woman who would make him fall. Bryce hadn't believed him, and he was right not to. It wouldn't be a woman at all. It was Nick.

Bryce gave his brother a quick nod and then walked out. He found his mom on the back porch, her arms wrapped around herself. "That's not me, Bryce. I didn't mean to purposely hurt Nick. I don't know what came over me."

"I know." He stood beside her.

"I'm sorry."

"I know that, too."

"That doesn't change how I feel, though. I'm still angry and confused. I'm afraid to get attached. I don't want to fall in love with the idea of you settling down with Nick and then he's out of your life. I know there are no guarantees in life—nothing that says Jamie and Hope or Mitch and Abbey will be together forever—but I worry so much more when it comes to you. I worry that nothing will be forever with you, Bryce, and then tonight...I wanted you to prove me wrong, but you hardly spoke a word to Nick all night. Are you pulling away from him already?"

Bryce cursed silently, threaded his fingers together behind his head and looked up at the dark sky. This was all on him. He'd let his day screw things up. "No, I'm not. It's different with him. I'm serious about him. I know today didn't show that very well, but it's true. I also know I can't prove it to you. You'll believe me, or you won't. But none of that will change how I feel about him."

It took her a couple of minutes to reply. "And I'm trying to believe in that, Bryce. All I can tell you right now is that I'm trying, and I love you."

Bryce turned to the door and stopped. "I love you, too, Ma. And just so you know, I love him as well. He's the only person in my life I can tell you I've ever been in love with."

CHAPTER THIRTY-SIX

They were silent the whole drive home. Nick wasn't sure what to expect when they pulled into his driveway. Would they sleep in their separate homes tonight? They hadn't slept apart in months. But more importantly, he wondered what in the hell had happened today. All he knew was, he was tired—mentally and physically. He didn't have it in him to argue, or even to question Bryce's behavior.

But when he turned off the car, Bryce spoke, answering one of his silent questions. "Your house or mine?"

A relieved breath deflated his lungs. He hadn't known he needed them to stay together tonight as much as he obviously did. "Is mine okay?"

"Yeah."

They got out of the car and went into the house. Both men went straight for Nick's bedroom, Nick into the bathroom there. What the fuck had happened today? Something was going on with Bryce. It drove him crazy not knowing how things had gone with Bryce's mom...but they had to be okay. They were both here, together, which meant they had to be good.

Nick splashed some water on his face to wake up, took a piss, washed his hands and then brushed his teeth. When he stepped out of the bathroom, Bryce lay on his bed, head on the pillows, arms behind his head, looking at him. "I'm sorry."

"I know," Nick replied, and he did.

"It's hard. I didn't expect it all to be so fucking hard."

"I know that, too." They were both in foreign territory, both trying to make their way through the landmines to find their way out. "Did something happen at work when I left?"

"Nothing important. I was just being an ass. If there's one thing my family is right about, it's that I've had it easy. Besides the aneurysm and surgery, there's nothing I really had to fight for. If something didn't go my way, I quit. I'm not proud to admit that, but it's true. When I fell in love with motorcycles...that was easy. It came naturally. I think when I fell in love with you I expected it to be the same."

It still made his chest feel full to hear those words from Bryce— that he loved him.

Nick lingered in the bathroom door, knowing he should go over. "If we're going to work, we have to be honest with each other. We have to talk about the bad days, knowing we're going to have them. This is new for us. We don't know what the fuck we're doing."

"I know I want you. That's what matters. Take off your clothes and come here, Nick."

His dick instantly went hard. They should probably talk more. He needed to know what happened at work with Bryce today, but, fuck, he just needed to feel close to him, as well. In some ways, he worried they were just screwing up each other's lives. Bryce and his family were close, yet they were at odds because of Nick.

Who the hell knew how bad things would go with Nick's family, but like Bryce, Nick knew he wanted him. Every part of him. So, despite the fact that they'd figured nothing out, that Bryce lay on the bed fully clothed, Nick took off his shirt. His shoes, pants and underwear followed. His cock bobbed against his stomach as he walked over.

Bryce scooted down the bed a foot or so, taking the pillows with him. "Kneel on the bed. Straddle my neck. I wanna try something I saw on Sexy Man Lovin'."

"Ah, fuck." Nick stroked his dick a couple of times as he climbed onto the bed, getting into position.

"You know you're going to have to try and fuck me again. It's something you just have to do, Nick. I'll be okay."

Nick nodded, stroking his erection. "I know." Even with Bryce using the dildos, he was reluctant to try again. It wasn't that he didn't want Bryce. He wanted him so fucking bad he couldn't see straight. He just didn't want to hurt him. Maybe he was afraid it wouldn't work again, and what that would mean for them.

"I might not be able to take your dick in my ass yet, but I can take it in my mouth." Bryce squeezed his ass. "Feed it to me."

A shiver ran down Nick's spine. Pre-come leaked from the head of his dick that was begging to do exactly what Bryce said.

Bryce opened his mouth, and Nick wanted to fill it with come right then and there. He was so fucking sexy, so masculine. To see Bryce below him, waiting with his mouth open to take Nick's cock, made his balls ache.

It made his chest swell, too.

He guided his dick with his hand, angling it down before pushing it in. Jesus, he'd never done something like this before. Get head, yeah, but shove his dick into someone's mouth from above, no. Slowly, he thrust his hips forward. Not all the way, not wanting to give Bryce too much. When he pulled out, his erection was wet, shining with Bryce's saliva. Bryce leaned forward to take him again.

He tightened his hold on Nick's ass when Nick tried to pull out again, holding him in place as he took him deep. All the fucking way to the back of his throat. He felt Bryce swallow as he sucked, felt this throat move around the head of his cock, and it took everything inside him to hold off from exploding in his mouth.

He groaned when Bryce pulled off, fought not to grab him by the hair and put him back into place. All he did was slide lower, sucking Nick's balls into his mouth. He road Bryce's face, pumping his cock as Bryce licked his sac.

"I've been practicing…trying to ease my gag reflex."

"Ah, fuck. You're going to fucking kill me. Take my dick again. I want in your mouth, Bryce." He loved the feel of Bryce's mouth.

Bryce propped himself on the pillows so Nick could slide into his mouth. Bryce sucked, licked and swallowed him down, hollowing his cheeks at one point, driving Nick insane.

Nick grabbed his hair, and fuck if he didn't see Bryce smile around his dick. He kept thrusting as his balls tightened. A few more thrusts, and the orgasm barreled through him as his come ran down the back of Bryce's throat. He took it all, swallowed him down, licked him clean before pulling Nick down for a searing kiss.

He knew what this was about, Bryce trying to make up for the fact that Nick hadn't fucked him. What Bryce didn't know was that he had nothing to make up for. Nick was happy.

"Who knew I'd be such a good cocksucker?" he said lightly, obviously trying to steer them out of the heavy conversation from earlier.

"My cocksucker." Nick fell down on top of him, his hand tangled in Bryce's hair as his eyes fell closed. "Sorry if I shouldn't have stopped by the shop today."

"Yes, you should have. I want you there. Fuck everyone else."

Those words breathed life into him again. "Give me a minute. When I can open my eyes again, it's your turn. Not that I can rival your cocksucking abilities."

Bryce laughed. "You can suck me off in the morning. Let's get some sleep. Roll over, so I can get the light." He pulled out from under Nick, and Nick let him. He heard rustling, then the bed dipped and a muscular, naked body was against his.

"I love you," Nick mumbled. "Fuck everyone else." He just wished it were that easy.

***

Bryce woke up early Sunday morning and told Nick he needed to go for a ride, and that he wasn't sure he would be back before Nick went to work. He could see the confusion on Nick's face, and he wanted to reassure him, so Bryce leaned in and kissed him. "We're good. We're okay. I just need the open road."

"Okay. I'll see you tonight."

Bryce drove around all day. Every little while he had to stop because his hand or arms would fall asleep, but then he'd just get back on and ride again.

It had been hard enough seeing his family yesterday. Tomorrow they were going to Nick's mom's house. Bryce knew how much pressure she put on Nick, how much she wanted her son to have a traditional life, with a wife at home, and kids. Even if they did settle down and try to adopt one day (which, honestly, he wasn't even sure he wanted kids), their life would still never be what she had envisioned for her son.

Bryce spent his whole life laid back, relaxed, and just trying to live an easy, happy life. This thing with Nick wasn't easy. It should be, and maybe eventually it would be, but dealing with the fallout of...loving each other, was more than he expected.

He rode until he couldn't ride anymore, then he went home to wait for Nick. It was close to midnight when there was a knock on his door. Bryce called for him to come in. "Come here," he said after Nick closed the door.

Nick walked to the edge of the couch, and Bryce pulled him down to lay on top of him. His head rested on Bryce's chest as he lay between Bryce's legs. It wasn't the most comfortable position, trying to fit the both of them on the couch, but he didn't care. It got them close.

"How was work?" he asked. It felt like they didn't get to do this enough—just talk without worrying about sex or family or what the hell they were doing.

Bryce ran his hand over Nick's short hair, touched his jaw, rubbed his neck, just feeling him.

"Good. We were busy. It feels like I can almost say that every day now, which is good. I was scared to death when I opened the restaurant. Jill hated the idea. She said I would be too busy, and threw out statistics on how many new restaurants failed. And I get it. This was our lives. If it failed, it affected us both. I guess I probably didn't give her as much say in it as I should, but I can't regret opening it. It feels good, seeing how well it's doing."

Bryce shook his head. "You're always fair, Nick."

"No," he said softly. "I'm not sure I always was. I'd like to think so, but I probably wasn't. No one's perfect."

"Except me," Bryce teased.

281

"Obviously. I didn't think I even had to say it. It's just something everyone knows."

"You're smart. That's why I like you so damned much. You know a good thing when you see one." Bryce felt Nick's laugh rumble through his chest, and it settled in Bryce's.

There was a moment's pause between them before Nick spoke. "Were you scared when you found out about the aneurysm? I guess that's a stupid question, in some ways. Of course you were, but...did you just know you'd beat it? That's you, push fucking through and conquer whatever is in your way."

Bryce thought for a second. He liked the way Nick saw him. Unfortunately, it wasn't really who he was. "I'm going to tell you a secret—something I've never told anyone else."

Bryce had his right arm around Nick, holding him close, and Nick held him back.

"I was scared out of my fucking mind... I almost didn't even have the surgery, I was so scared. I played it off like that wasn't the case, but it was."

Bryce paused, let out a deep breath, and then continued. "I don't know why, but I just knew I was going to fucking die. I hid it, laughed about it and pretended it wasn't a big deal...but part of me just fucking knew that was it for me. I'd decided that was how I would go, and I just wanted to enjoy my life until the time-bomb in my head exploded. I wanted to ride my bike, fuck women and enjoy my family. It sounded a hell of a lot better than a surgery that could make me stroke, have seizures and a whole list of other things. I'd just fucking go one day and not know it."

"What changed your mind?" Nick asked.

"You'll laugh if I tell you." Hell, Bryce wanted to laugh at it himself. He couldn't fucking believe it. Not really. And he hadn't even thought about what it was that had changed his mind until right this minute, lying here, telling Nick.

Nick lifted his head, still chest-to-chest with Bryce, looking down at him. "Holy shit. You're embarrassed. You're never embarrassed."

"You'd get it if I told you."

Nick nodded once at him, and smiled. "So tell me."

Bryce ran a hand through his hair. "Fuck, Nick. I think it was you."

Nick's brows pulled together, but he didn't respond, just waited for Bryce to continue.

"I only had a few days to decide. I had all the preparations, still not sure what I would do. Then, I had this dream. I was riding my bike. I don't even know where I was, but it was beautiful. There was someone on the back, their legs squeezing me, arms around me. We were just fucking going. Flying. I thought about how free I felt out there. Like the whole fucking world was waiting for me to explore it. I could go anywhere or do anything. I had someone I loved riding with me, willing to go wherever the fuck I took them, and all I could think about was the fact that if I didn't fight, I couldn't have this. Yeah, maybe I could for a while, but the aneurysm would grow, get thinner, it's walls would get weaker, and one day something in my head would burst and I'd die. With surgery I had a shot at a normal life. There's an extremely low risk of regrowth after clipping and that dream made me want that fucking chance. I was a fighter. I could come out of surgery. I had to believe that if I wanted my dream."

He touched Nick's hair again before continuing. "I thought it was Christi. I told myself it was her riding with me in that dream. Besides my family, she's the only person I love like that. I had to know it wasn't her, though—I just didn't want to believe it. Or think about what it meant. Or, hell, fucking admit it to myself."

Nick cocked his head slightly. "Why?"

He really couldn't fucking believe he was saying this. That he might believe it, or hell, that he hadn't really thought about it before this moment; but he hadn't.

"I was driving forever in the dream, when suddenly I was at a dead-end. I sat there, knowing I had to go left or right. I didn't know which way to go. I assumed it was to get surgery or not...left or right, and I couldn't fucking decide. Then the person on the back of the bike said, *it's a crossroads, Bryce. Which way are you going to go?* I didn't let myself think about what the voice sounded like. I didn't let myself remember what I knew the second I heard it... It wasn't Christi's voice, Nick. It wasn't a female voice at all. It was a guy. I think it was you."

Neither of them spoke. Nick just stared at him, right in the eyes, like he was searching for something. Bryce let him, as he ran a hand over Nick's short hair. Finally, Bryce said, "See? I told you it's fucked up.

Look what you've done to me. You turned me into a sap."

Nick didn't respond the way Bryce thought he would, though. He didn't laugh or give him shit for being really fucking over the top. He just said, "I think it was me, too," before he set his head down on Bryce's chest, and let Bryce hold him.

CHAPTER THIRTY-SEVEN

Nick hadn't been able to get what Bryce said to him last night out of his head. He thought about it all day and night. It was still distracting him now, as they drove to his mom's house.

"How's this going to go down, Nick? We go right in and tell her? After dinner? Do you have a plan at all? And you look like you're going to rip the steering wheel out." Bryce touched his hand. "Loosen your grip. Do you want me to drive? I sure as hell hope you're the one cooking dinner over there, so it'll help calm you down."

At that, Nick couldn't help but to turn Bryce's way. He loved that Bryce knew how much cooking settled him. Unfortunately, that wouldn't be happening. "No way. I told you it took a while before she'd even let me help her in the kitchen as a kid. I was the son. Men don't do kitchen duty. It doesn't matter that I'm a chef. It's different at my place, but if we're at her house, she'll be cooking. She thinks it's what she should do to take care of me."

"What year is this?" Bryce teased.

"Funny." But Nick smirked.

"I made you laugh. That's all I wanted."

Jesus, this man made him all sorts of crazy. "And she knows you're coming. Karrie said she's been weird about you, and after the way she acted when I told her I wanted her to meet you, I assume she knows something's up. We're here." Nick pulled over to the side of the road. He dropped his head against the steering wheel. Fuck, why did this have him tied in knots? His mother was meeting the man he was in love with. Nothing else should matter. Just how they felt about each other.

"Nick. Relax." Bryce touched his leg. "Otherwise I'm going to have to give you head in the car to release some tension. Your mom will come out, and then she'll really fucking hate me."

Nick turned his way. "I'm almost willing to take you up on that. Not the part where we're caught, but the part where I get to come and release some pent-up energy."

"Hand job?" Bryce asked, and Nick laughed, feeling better.

"Let's go in before you get me into trouble."

"I like getting you into trouble." Bryce went to open the car door but Nick stopped him.

"There's not a part of me that thinks this is going to go well, Bryce. I want you to know that. It's important to me that we do it, though. Just don't expect her to understand. I know that, and I'm still here."

There was a split second where he almost asked Bryce to be on his best behavior, but Nick held back. He wanted Bryce to be himself. There was nothing wrong with the man he was.

"I'm here, too," Bryce replied, and they got out of the car together. Bryce stood beside him, a gentle hand on Nick's back as he knocked on the door. When the doorknob twisted, he gave Nick a reassuring pat and then dropped his hand.

"Nick. How's my son?" His mom pulled him into a hug.

"I'm good, Mom." This was...strange. He hadn't expected a hug first thing. When they pulled apart, he said, "This is my friend Bryce, who I was telling you about. Bryce, this is my mom, Mona."

"Hello. It's nice to meet you." Bryce held out a hand for his mom. She looked at it, gave a tight smile.

"You, as well," she replied, but she didn't shake it. She stood back for Nick and Bryce to come in.

"Your home is beautiful," Bryce tried again. "Nick grew up here, right? This is the kitchen that the master chef learned to cook in?"

Bryce peeked around the corner into the kitchen, while Nick waited for his mother to reply. She talked about Nick all the time, so much so that it drove him crazy, yet she couldn't speak to Bryce about him now?

"If you don't mind, I'd like to go sit in the living room, where we can be more comfortable."

Bryce turned toward them, and he could see his boyfriend realize that Nick's mom wanted nothing to do with him. That she didn't even want to speak to him if she could keep from doing it. Nick's chest felt like the weight of the world was on it.

"Mom—"

"It's fine. Let's go sit down," Bryce cut him off, and damn if Nick didn't take the lifeline.

The whole afternoon Nick tried to talk to his mom about Bryce—his family, his shop. It was on the tip of his tongue to bring up the fact that he'd had an aneurysm, looking for *something* to make her feel for the man. But he knew it would upset Bryce if he did. So, Nick kept trying, and she continued to cut him off at every point. If he said something about him and Bryce, she would reply with something about Karrie, Erin or Michelle. She'd make comments about the grandkids, and that maybe Nick would give her some soon, even though she'd never pushed him on that topic before.

They ate dinner with Bryce trying to bring up Nick's childhood, or ask questions, but she kept her responses short, or just changed the subject. With each passing minute, the weight on Nick's chest got heavier…and the more upset he became.

After they finished eating, Nick offered to wash the dishes. "No, that's fine. You know how I feel about that. You're my son. You don't need to be in my kitchen washing dishes."

Nick didn't plan the words that came out. He didn't even know what he would say when he opened his mouth and spoke. He just knew he couldn't do this with her. Not anymore. "Why not? I'm gay now, so your traditional gender roles are a little blurred, aren't they?"

His mom gasped.

"Jesus Christ, Nick," Bryce cursed.

"Don't take the Lord's name in vain at my table," his mom scolded Bryce.

"Don't do that. Even now you're taking your anger at me out on him. It's not fair, and I won't accept it. Bryce is my...boyfriend now, and—"

"Your boyfriend? Do you hear yourself, Nicholas? You don't have boyfriends. That's not you. You were married to Jill for years. You loved her. I know that. I'm not sure what's going on with you right now, but you're not gay. *I* won't accept *that*."

She pushed to her feet but didn't move as Nick spoke. "You don't have a choice. Whether you accept it or not, this is the way it is. I'm with him. That's not going to change. I know it's confusing, but you're going to have to deal with it, Mom. I love you, but I love him, too, and I won't have you treating Bryce as though he doesn't matter."

Nick had never spoken to her like that in his life. Even when she made it obvious she wasn't fond of Jill (though not quite as boldly as she did with Bryce), Nick tried to keep the peace. He wouldn't do that anymore.

"I'm with him, no matter how you feel about it. I'd like your support, but if you can't respect Bryce, I won't come back over until you can."

Bryce started, "Nick—"

"No. That's how I feel about it." He looked at his mom. Her eyes filled with tears as her hand shook while holding the back of the chair.

"Your father would be turning over in his grave if he heard you speak to me like this. If he knew you were…doing whatever it is you're doing with that man. This would kill your father, and I refuse to accept what I know he wouldn't have been able to."

Nick's stomach dropped. He'd hoped that she would surprise him, that she would accept this, but he saw now that she wouldn't.

"You're my only son, and I love you. I know you'll come to your senses. I know you'll see this isn't you. I will never stop loving you, Nicholas, but I can't accept this, either."

She looked at Bryce. "I'm asking you nicely not to come back with him. He's my son, and this is my home. I deserve that. You two can continue to do whatever you're doing, but I don't want to see it. I don't want to hear about it. I don't want to know you even exist in my son's life." She turned to Nick. "You're my son. My baby. I won't lose you. I won't walk away from you, but I'm still your mother, and I deserve your respect. If you love me at all, pretend he's not in your life when you're in my house, or your sister's houses. I want my son, my Nick, but I don't want to know anything about him." And then she added, more softly, "I don't want to lose my boy."

Nick closed his eyes, pain ricocheting around in his chest. She sounded broken. Lost and broken. He knew she loved him. But he couldn't do that to Bryce, either. It wasn't right. Nick opened his mouth to tell her no, that he couldn't accept that, but Bryce's hand squeezing his leg stopped him. It was Bryce who spoke. "Yes, ma'am. We can respect that."

His mom turned and walked away.

"Bryce—"

"It's what she needs. She has a right to make that request. I don't have a right to push myself into her life. You want me in yours, I'm here. She's your mom, Nick. I know you. It'll fucking kill you to lose her. It'll kill us. We can do this. It's not a big deal. It's no different than the way we've been living, anyway."

For the second time in the last minute, someone Nick loved walked away from him.

CHAPTER THIRTY-EIGHT

Nick was pissed off.

He was beyond pissed—at his mom, at Bryce, at himself. What was the big deal? He didn't fucking get it. Why did everyone act like he and Bryce were committing this huge fucking crime by being together?

And why the hell had Bryce accepted what his mother had said? That wasn't the Bryce he knew.

Nick didn't think he could do what his mom asked, and what Bryce seemed to be okay with. He was one hundred percent in, or one hundred percent out. That's the way he worked, and he thought that was the way Bryce worked as well.

"Maybe we should take the night to be by ourselves," Bryce said when they pulled into Nick's driveway.

"Excuse me?"

"We've been through a lot. Don't tell me you don't have a lot of shit on your mind, Nick. If we're not working, we're together. We've basically been living with each other since the start of our relationship— a relationship that's a big fucking deal for both of us, for a number of reasons. It's only been a couple of months, and..." he shook his head. "I'm just saying that it's a lot. Maybe we need some breathing room."

He guessed there was his answer. Bryce was ready to throw in the towel. He'd just fucking told his mom that he was in a relationship with a man, and now Bryce was asking for space. "Yeah, sure. Whatever you say."

"Nick, I don't—"

Bryce reached for him, but Nick pulled his arm away. What the hell was Bryce's problem? He couldn't believe they'd spent the weekend dealing with their families only for him to ask for space now. "You want space, you got it. You say this is too much, I agree. My last relationship was a hell of a lot of work. Jumping into another one was a bad idea."

Nick shoved the door open and got out.

The tears in his mom's eyes...the sadness in her voice, for fucking nothing. He'd wrecked her. For the first time in his life, he fucking wrecked her.

"Nick," Bryce called from behind him. "I'm not...it's just. I'm not saying I'm done with you."

Nick turned and looked at him. "Maybe you should be. Maybe this is all too fucking much."

* * *

Bryce didn't know what to think, or what the hell to do. Life was a whole lot easier when the only things he cared about where his family, his shop and Christi. Everything was different with Nick, everything was *more*, yet he didn't say a word as Nick walked away.

He didn't go to Nick's house, instead making his way into his own.

Bryce wasn't sure how he felt about anything right now. No, that wasn't true. He knew how he felt about Nick; but then there was that voice in his head telling him there was no fucking way this could work. Not when Nick's mom would never accept him and Bryce's own family couldn't trust him.

Even knowing all that...he hadn't been ready to walk away. Fuck that. Bryce didn't want to throw in the towel. He only thought they needed a night to clear their heads, but it seemed pretty fucking easy for Nick to walk away.

The pictures on the walls rattled when Bryce slammed his door. He went to the kitchen and drained a bottle of beer before going straight into the bathroom.

He turned on the shower, stripped out of his clothes and got in.

Bryce washed his body, as though cleaning the day off his skin would mean it didn't happen. Soap ran down his back, down the crack of his ass, as he washed every inch of himself.

Hot water pelted his skin. There was a knot in his gut, an ache in his chest. With his hands flat against the wall, Bryce leaned forward, letting the stinging hot water run over his head and down his body.

A hundred different reasons as to why this couldn't work spun around inside his head—they'd both considered themselves straight before this, their families, turning their whole worlds upside down for each other, and yeah, even the sex. Nick got him harder than anyone ever had, yet every time they were together, Bryce thought about the fact that Nick had yet to fuck him. He knew it would happen eventually, but couldn't one fucking thing just be easy between them?

Even if it couldn't, it didn't change a damn thing. He didn't want to fucking walk away, didn't want to lose Nick. He'd do anything to keep him.

Bryce didn't turn when he heard a noise behind him. He didn't turn when he felt strong arms wrap around him from behind, a body flush against his back. He kept his hands against the wall, but pulled his head out from under the spray. "What took you so long?"

"It's been fifteen minutes."

"Fifteen minutes too long."

Nick squeezed him tighter. He dropped his head back on Nick's shoulder. "I'm sorry," Nick said softly.

"I'm sorry, too. I feel like we're on this fucking rollercoaster. We keep going over the same loops, the same dips, over and over."

"The same highs, too." Nick leaned in, his mouth right next to Bryce's ear. "I'm not getting off the ride without you."

Bryce moaned in response. "That right there. That's what I want to hear."

"You know part of it is nerves, right...?" Nick's words hung in the air. Bryce knew exactly what he meant. Yes, part of the reason he couldn't take Nick, had to be fear. Even though he wanted Nick, his body tensed, freaked out.

"Yeah...I know." He was stressing himself out over it so much, that his body froze up. "I just need you."

He heard Nick gasp. "I need you, too. I want you." Nick ran his hand down Bryce's body, wrapping a fist around his cock. "I want inside you. Want to fuck you all night, maybe even all day tomorrow, too. I want your ass hugging my dick, and to know I'm the only one who's ever going to be there, the same way you own mine. I want to wake up at night and know I can roll over, push my cock inside you and have you any time I want. To know that you can do the same thing to me. Fuck, I want you so goddamn much, it's like a part of me. Something I can't live without, like my heart or lungs."

Bryce's legs nearly gave out. He thrust forward, letting his dick slide through Nick's fist. "You're getting better at the dirty talk."

"I learned from the best."

"Fuck me, Nick."

Nick spun him, shoved Bryce's back against the shower wall before their mouths collided together. It was a hard kiss, urgent and fucking needy. He bit Nick's lip as Nick thrust his cock against Bryce's. Bryce used both his hands to wrap around their erections as Nick thrust powerfully, pushing Bryce into the wall over and over.

He grabbed the sides of Bryce's face as he pushed his tongue deep into his mouth—stroking, probing, licking.

All Bryce could think was that he fucking wanted more. He didn't

297

care what happened, he needed Nick inside him, buried balls fucking deep, living there until Bryce could take him easily.

Suddenly Nick's hands were gone from his face. He grabbed Bryce's sides, lifting so Bryce could wrap his legs around Nick's waist.

"It's so fucking incredible to feel you like this—the hardness of your body, your muscles, the hair on your chest, legs and face. To have you in my arms. All fucking man, and all fucking mine."

"Jesus Christ, what the fuck happened to you? Keep talking to me like that and we're never leaving the bed." Bryce bit into Nick's neck. "I'm all fucking yours, but you're mine, too."

"Let's go. Damn, I feel like there's enough come in my balls to shoot out of me for twenty-four hours straight."

Nick put him down and Bryce turned off the shower. "I want your tongue in my ass, Nick. You're going to have to eat it, get it real fucking ready for me to take your cock."

Bryce moved to walk into the bedroom but Nick grabbed him, turned him around and shoved him so he was bent over the bathroom counter. His shaving cream and toothbrush container hit the floor as Bryce's arms slid across the counter.

"I can't wait. I want to taste every part of you."

Nick dropped to his knees behind Bryce. His dick twitched, pre-come leaking out and dripping onto the floor.

Strong hands spread Bryce's ass cheeks. Nick's hot touch seared him, and then he dove in. It was...fuck, he couldn't explain it, the feel of a tongue running back and forth over his rim. Like every sensation in his body originated from that one spot. It was everything, made even more powerful because it was Nick doing it.

"It's so tight. I don't know how I'm ever going to fit in there."

"You will." Bryce pushed backward, shoving his ass into Nick's face. Nick got the message and licked him again—soft, hard, fast, slow, alternating the pressure and movements.

"Fingers, Nick. Gimme some fingers. You need to stretch me." Nick gave a deep groan that vibrated through him. Bryce wanted to feel it over and over. Feel Nick. This time there was no going back. He'd take Nick, because he wanted nothing more than Nick inside him.

He heard Nick spit, and then there was pressure at his hole, Nick's finger pushing in, fucking, twisting, and then more pressure as he added another finger.

Bryce shoved backward again, needing more. He wanted all of Nick. "Three. Give me three." Nick was pleasure, and passion, and Bryce wanted Nick to devour him.

He closed his eyes at the pressure, the stretching, but then three fingers were deep in his ass, turning left and right. Shoving in, and pulling out.

"I see you in the mirror, Bryce. Open your eyes and watch me."

Bryce fucking trembled at Nick's words. He opened his eyes, saw Nick's reflection through the slightly foggy glass as he kneeled behind Bryce, watching his own fingers work in and out of Bryce's ass.

And it was...incredible. Fucking beautiful, seeing this man on his knees worshiping him. It was unlike anything Bryce had ever seen before. "I want your face there, between my cheeks. Give me your tongue again."

Bryce bent over more, spreading his legs, before Nick's face was right where he wanted it. He tongued Bryce's opening around his own hand. Licked and tongue-fucked Bryce's hole. Bryce squeezed the base of his cock, keeping himself from blowing all over the place. He wanted to save that for when Nick's cock was buried in his ass.

He felt empty when Nick pulled back. He stood, leaned in with his mouth close to Bryce's ear. "I want inside you. Go to the bedroom and let me love you. Let me bury my cock inside you and make you mine."

Bryce was already fucking his, but he knew this time, nothing would stop them from Nick physically claiming him.

CHAPTER THIRTY-NINE

Bryce's dick was leaking. His heart pounded in anticipation, hunger and need, a violent storm inside him. He wanted to take all of Nick for the first time. But when they made it to the bed, everything slowed.

Nick lay him down, slid on top of Bryce and kissed him. They rubbed their dicks together as they thrust against each other—kissing, touching and needing.

"I don't want to hurt you too much."

"You won't," Bryce replied. "Some pain is a rite of passage. My cock's not nearly as thick as yours, but it was still uncomfortable for you at first. I'll get used to it. I fucking want it. I've been fucking myself with those dildos every spare minute I have. It's time for the real thing. Real men take it up the ass, Nick," Bryce teased, and got the smile he wanted.

Nick reached over and grabbed lube out of the drawer. He kneeled between Bryce's spread legs, pushed his knees up to his chest and dripped lube onto his asshole. He used a lot, fingering Bryce again to stretch him. Each time he thrust, Bryce let out a groan. He liked the sting, the burn. Liked having any part of Nick inside him.

"I need to use a lot of lube. It'll help." He kept working Bryce until he thought he'd go out of his mind.

"I'm ready for you, Nick. Make love to me."

Nick leaned in and kissed him before lying on his back. He squirted more lube onto his hand and ran it up and down his thick erection. "Get on top, so you can control how much of me you take."

"I want you balls deep."

"Then do it."

"I fucking love this side of you. Talk like that to me all the time from now on."

Bryce sat up, threw a leg over Nick and straddled him. Nick's cock leaked onto his stomach, shiny and wet from the lube, and so goddamn big. "Of course I had to go gay for the guy with the biggest cock in Virginia."

"Funny. Now let me make love to you, Bryce. "

Yeah, he so fucking wanted that.

"Clench. Tighten as much as you can," Nick said.

Bryce stared down at him, confused. "Huh?"

"You're not the only one doing research. Just do it. Clench your hole as tight as you can for as long as you can. Tell me when you can't do it anymore."

He did as Nick said, clenched, held it as long as he could and then his hole automatically started to relax...to loosen. "I can't...not anymore."

"Do it now. Let me in," Nick whispered. "Let me inside of you."

Bryce went up on his knees, grabbed Nick's cock and angled it toward his hole. And then Nick's hand was there, helping guide him. Both men holding his erection as Bryce lowered himself and Nick slowly began pushing inside.

He was stretched, pulled open to what felt like was as far as he could go. Pain shot through him. "Fuck..." he groaned out.

"We can wait—"

"Fuck that. Just give me a minute." Bryce took a couple of deep breaths and then tried again, lowering himself onto Nick's rock-hard dick—more stretching, more burning, more pressure; *fuck*, the pressure he felt...but then, it wasn't as bad as it had been when they tried before. He was looser, more relaxed, but not relaxed enough.

And then...Nick's thumb brushed his thigh. "You're so fucking gorgeous. Giving yourself to me like this...I'm never going to want out of you."

Nick's words made Bryce lower more. There was pain, sharp pain, and a burning sensation, like he was being ripped open...and then the head of Nick's dick was all the way inside him.

"Oh, fuck. Jesus, it's so goddamn hot and tight inside you. I'm going to come the second I get fully inside."

"I'll kick your ass if you do. After all of this, the ride better be worth it," Bryce teased...then lowered more, and more, ignoring the pain, slowly taking inch by inch, until Nick was all fucking in there, balls deep the way Bryce wanted him.

It was...different, and yeah, it was fucking uncomfortable being full and stretched like that, but when he pulled up and lowered himself again, pleasure shot through him. Nick's erection rubbed all the right places, making Bryce move faster. He rode Nick's cock. Nick let him run the show, let Bryce fuck himself on him.

"You feel so good, Bryce. So fucking hot, and tight. I love this. Love being inside of you. I'm so close to filling you up."

Bryce looked down at the man beneath him. His man, at his green eyes and brown hair. At the curve of his jaw and the stubble there. He was fucking beautiful. He was fucking everything.

Nick had been right—the connection, there was nothing like it, nothing like letting someone inside of you, giving them that honor. Nick was a part of Bryce in even more ways than he'd been before.

"Flip me over. Take me. I want you fucking me, Nick."

Nick growled, grabbed him and flipped them. Bryce kept his legs wide, while Nick shoved them close to his chest. He pumped into Bryce fast and hard. It still fucking hurt...but it felt so good at the same time. It felt right, Nick being a part of him like this.

"You know we're never going to be able to stop doing this now," Nick said.

"I'm counting on it." Bryce hardly got the words out before Nick's mouth covered his. He pushed his tongue in deep as he fucked hard—loved hard.

Bryce squeezed a hand between their bodies, wrapping it around his dick and stroking. His balls were already pulled tight against his body.

"I'm going to come. Fuck, I don't think I can hold back much longer." As soon as the words left Nick's lips, he covered Bryce's mouth again.

Their tongues tangled. Their bodies were slick with sweat, rubbing against each other. He savored Nick's firm body, loved the feel of it against his own.

Nick changed his angle, moved slower, but deeper. Bryce kept his hand going, kept stroking himself as the intense pressure built stronger inside him. It was all too much. His orgasm slammed into him, an explosion of pleasure. Like he felt every fucking good thing in his life in that one moment as he tensed, come shooting up his chest and hitting his neck.

"Fuck, I feel you clenching around me," Nick moaned, the veins in his neck popping out. Then the muscles in his arms tensed as Bryce felt hot seed shoot into him. Fill him. Nick kept thrusting through his orgasm, his semen giving them more lube, until he shot one last time before dropping down on top of him. Bryce felt Nick pull out, felt his come drip out of him.

"Every fucking day. We're doing that every day from now on."

Nick ran his finger through the come on Bryce's chest. "So, it was good for you?" He sounded unsure, and as crazy as it was, Bryce loved that.

"Hell yeah. Were you nervous?" He looked down at Bryce, then watched as he stuck his tongue out and licked the come off his chest.

"I just wanted it to be right. I knew this was important to you. Not that it wasn't to me, but I like having you make love to me. I was okay with that, but I knew you needed me to make love to you."

"You needed it just as much as I did, and that's okay. But yeah, it was fucking amazing...and the rest of it...like you said, I'm not getting off the ride unless you are, and I really want you to stay on it with me, Nick. No more back and forth. No more worrying about everyone else. We're happy, you and me. But you have to talk to your mom, though. That's one thing I need from you, baby. Don't walk away from your family because of me. It'll eat me alive if you do."

It took Nick a long time to answer, but finally he whispered, "Okay. Whatever you need. Now come on, let's go to sleep. I just want to lay here and feel you."

Bryce wrapped his arms around Nick, closed his eyes, and went to sleep.

CHAPTER FORTY

"We waited until the end of summer to buy lawn furniture. We're not going to get to use it much. I like this one." Nick pointed to a long table, chairs and umbrella, all in Earth tones. It sat six people, with a brown, green and beige square pattern on the top.

"I do, too. We should get two of them, though. We both have big families, and we might want to throw parties or something. Since we have a big yard, we should take advantage of it."

Nick looked over at his lover. It had been two weeks since the day at his mom's. They hadn't had any more incidents with family or friends, but that was probably because they'd mostly kept to themselves. Nick went to the shop a couple times, and Bryce had been to the restaurant. All his employees knew he had a boyfriend now, and it had basically been like telling them he had green eyes. No one cared. He spoke with Karrie a few times over the phone. She wanted him to know she still supported him, and that she'd work on their mom. Other than that, they'd just lived their lives, and Nick was fucking happy.

"We might not always, though." Nick knew what his words meant. He hadn't planned to say it this way, but the meaning behind them was sincere.

"What do you mean?"

"We're in the same bed every night. We're paying for rent on two places." He shrugged. "It just seems useless."

Bryce grinned. "If we moved into one place, we'd have to share the yard with someone else."

"Or we could look for a new place."

"With a big yard to fit two tables?" Bryce asked, like a ten-year-old begging for a toy. Nick laughed.

"Sure. A big yard is nice. We don't have to rush. It's the end of August. The holidays are coming, and this time of year is always crazy. We can plan for the beginning of the new year."

"A large yard and a live-in chef? Sold. We should start looking soon. And by the way, we're getting two tables now."

Nick rolled his eyes. Damn, he loved his man. Just being around Bryce made him happy. Things weren't perfect. They were still stumbling around in their relationship. But it was worth it. Bryce was worth it.

"Yes, sir. We need to hurry, though. I have to head to work."

"You can go. If we want this one, I can take care of the rest." They'd taken Bryce's truck and Nick's car so he could head to the restaurant afterward. "Oh, will you bring me home some of those potatoes I like? The ones with all the stuff in them?"

Nick let out a loud laugh. "All the stuff, huh? Yeah, I'll bring them home." He didn't think about what he was doing. Just let himself feel as he leaned in, pressing a quick kiss to Bryce's lips. "I'll see you tonight—"

"Nick?"

Nick tensed at the female voice he would know anywhere. He'd ignored a few phone calls from her in the past month or so, not wanting another episode like they'd had the last time they'd spoken. He knew there wasn't a chance at avoiding Jill this time.

He turned toward her. "Jill. Hey." His eyes darted to the man at her side, the one she'd had an affair with during their marriage. Nick and Jill's eyes locked, neither of them turning away.

It was her fiancé who spoke first. "Hi, I'm Shelton." He held a hand out to Bryce.

"Bryce." They shook hands.

"It's nice to meet you," Shelton replied.

"This is my..." he stumbled on the word for just a moment, before saying, "boyfriend. Bryce, this is my ex-wife, Jill."

It took Jill a moment, but then she grabbed Bryce's extended hand and shook it. "Shopping for lawn furniture?" There was a soft unease in Jill's voice. Bryce wouldn't know her well enough to hear it. Maybe Shelton did or didn't, but Nick did.

"Yeah. He thinks we need two."

"We do need two," Bryce responded.

"How's your mom?" Jill asked.

Nick felt Bryce tense beside him. "She's my mom."

He could have sworn Jill looked sad at that. Not because of how things had been with her and his mom, but maybe because she knew how things must be going with Bryce and his mom.

"She loves you. That's the most important thing."

"It is," Nick responded. He couldn't believe he was standing here talking to Jill and her fiancé while he was with Bryce—the man he loved.

Jill paused a moment, still watching him, and Nick knew she had something to say. He waited it out, until finally she spoke. "I'm sorry, Nick. For everything. I know I was wrong. I know I didn't speak to you the way I should have to explain what I was feeling. My therapist and I have been discussing that a lot. I didn't treat you the way you deserved to be treated, and I know that now."

No, she hadn't, but then, he thought maybe he hadn't always been as perfect as he used to think. He didn't cheat, no, but feeling what he felt for Bryce, and remembering what he felt for Jill, there was no comparison. Maybe things just went the way they were meant to go. "It's okay. We were young when we got married. We hadn't really lived yet."

"That's not an excuse."

"No, it's not, but it's still okay."

She smiled and her chin began to quiver, as though she might cry. He was proud of her. She looked good, looked like she was really trying to make some changes.

"We should let you guys get back to it." Jill took Shelton's hand. "Good luck, and…" she paused, and then added, "You look happy, Nick. Maybe happier than I've ever seen you." Jill looked at Bryce. "We were standing back there for a few minutes before you guys heard us. Good luck on the house hunt. And I agree, if your family is as large as Nick's, I'd buy two."

Jill and Shelton took a few steps before she turned around. "We didn't take the easy road, but I think things turned out the way they were supposed to." And then she walked away.

"You okay?" Bryce asked when they were gone.

Nick nodded. "I am. And she's right. We're both where we're supposed to be. Come on, I'll buy these with you, and then we'll get them in your truck before I go to work."

They bought the furniture and were on their way out when Nick's phone vibrated. He pulled it out of his pocket, saw *Mom* on the screen, and hit ignore.

"Who was that?" Bryce asked.

"My mom. I'll call her when I get to work." They said their goodbyes and Nick was on his way. They were busy at the restaurant all afternoon and evening. It was later than usual when he got out. He almost forgot Bryce's potatoes, but made sure to grab them before he got some paperwork out of his office, and then headed home.

They'd started staying at Nick's most of the time just because he had all his kitchen supplies there.

Nick closed the door to the house right as a naked Bryce stopped in the bedroom doorway. "Oh, hey. I just got out of the shower. You're late. Were you guys busy? Oh, did you get my potatoes? Hell, I can't believe I used to think those potato skins at the bar were good. I could live off yours."

Two things happened at once: Nick's cock went stiff behind the fly of his jeans, which happened any time Bryce was naked, and his pulse sped up while a smile stretched across his face; so he guessed that was three things, not two.

That's what Bryce did to him, though, made him feel everything a hundred times more than anyone else could. Something as easy as asking about potatoes made him want to curl up with the man and never let him go.

"I did bring your potatoes. You can't have them right away, though. You only get to eat when I get to fuck."

Bryce raised his brow. "I get you hard that quick, huh?"

"You do." Nick turned and set the to-go container on the table. When he looked back, Bryce was heading his way, bottle of lube in hand. There was nothing sexier than Bryce coming at him, naked, cock long and bobbing against his stomach, balls plump, no-holds-barred desire in his steely eyes.

"Since you brought me food, I'll feed you, too," Bryce said as he stroked his cock.

It was incredible how a few months before, sucking Bryce's dick, sucking any man's dick, wouldn't have seemed in Nick's realm of possibility. But now? Now his mouth fucking watered, and he wanted nothing more than the taste of Bryce's salty skin on his tongue. The taste and scent of his man invading his senses.

"Out here?" Nick asked, and Bryce rolled his eyes.

"Yes, out here. You're lucky I don't make you do it in your precious kitchen. Afterward, you can take me over the back of the couch."

Right where he stood, Nick went down to his knees. Bryce moved in front of him, angling his dick to trace Nick's lips with the head. He stuck his tongue out, let Bryce run the tip back and forth over it, while Nick tasted the pre-come leaking out.

Bryce nudged Nick's lips open with his erection. He took the mushroom head into his mouth, sucking just the tip the way Bryce liked.

Bryce ran a hand over Nick's head, guiding him, petting him, like Nick was a fucking treasure.

"Take me deep, baby," Bryce whispered, and Nick did, opening his mouth and sucking as much of Bryce as he could. He smelled Bryce's— their—soap on Bryce's skin. Tasted salt and smelled the intimate scent of his crotch.

He fucking loved it.

Nick palmed his tight balls, rolled them, sucked deep and then pulled off before taking Bryce's sac into his mouth. He nudged Bryce's legs open, stuck his finger in his mouth full of Bryce's nuts before tracing a path up his taint and to his hole that Nick couldn't wait to bury his cock inside of.

"Christ, that's enough. I want you inside me." Bryce pulled Nick off, pulled him to his feet and took his mouth. They kissed as Bryce worked the button and zipper on Nick's pants. Once it was undone, Nick pulled back and stripped. He looked up to see Bryce bent over the back of the couch, just like he'd said, his tight ass there waiting for him.

They'd made love enough in the past two weeks that it was easier for Nick to get inside him now, right where he couldn't wait to be.

Nick grabbed the lube off the table, squirted some in his hand and then rubbed it up and down his erection as he walked over to Bryce.

"You're so fucking beautiful," he said as he ran a hand down Bryce's back. He squirted more lube onto his hand, then slipped his finger between Bryce's spread legs, rubbing his finger there, before working two into Bryce's asshole.

"Jesus." Bryce pushed backward, taking Nick's fingers deeper. "Who would have thought it would feel so good? That I'd go fucking wild to have something in my ass?"

"Not just something," Nick replied. "Me." He stretched Bryce, twisting and parting his fingers before he couldn't take it anymore. He rubbed more lube on his dick, parted Bryce's muscular cheeks, and then eased into his tight hole.

"You and that big, fucking dick of yours," Bryce hissed out as Nick thrust into him.

"You love it." He grabbed Bryce's hips, pulling out and then thrusting again, pumping his hips into Bryce's tight channel. He felt Bryce's nuts each time he pounded into him. His body got slick with sweat, mixing with Bryce's as they made love.

"Ah, fuck. Right there. Go harder right there," Bryce choked out.

Nick did as Bryce said, hitting that magical spot that Bryce seemed to ache for. His own orgasm bore down on him, making his balls pull up. "Fuck, Bryce. I'm close. I need to come so fucking bad."

"Do it," Bryce moaned, shoving back into him. "Need to feel you."

Nick exploded, his cock jerking in Bryce's tight ass. He spilled everything he had in him, wrung himself dry. Bryce pulled away and shoved Nick back onto his knees. Before Nick realized what was happening, Bryce's dick was in his mouth again, fucking it, once, twice, and then spilling into Nick's mouth and down his throat.

"I said I was going to feed you," Bryce said breathlessly. "I keep my promises."

Nick leaned forward, kissing Bryce's softening cock, before looking up at him. "I love you." He heard the awe in his own voice.

"You act like you just realized that." Bryce smiled.

"No...but I still feel fucking lucky every time I say it."

Bryce pulled Nick to his feet. "I love you, too, baby. Now, can you get my potatoes and meet me in the room? I have your jizz running down my leg. After I clean up, we can eat them naked in bed."

It sounded like the perfect night to Nick.

CHAPTER FORTY-ONE

It was the middle of September when Bryce lay on the bed, watching Nick get ready for work. "How's your mom doing?" Bryce asked him.

He stuck his head out of the bathroom, toothbrush hanging out of his mouth, and shrugged. "Fine."

He knew this whole thing had to be a bigger deal to Nick than he was letting on. It was his family. Even though Bryce's parents were still a little iffy on them, it didn't come from homophobia or even Nick. It came from their worry about Bryce not taking his life as seriously as he should. "How does she sound when you talk to her? Is she…" He hated asking, because he didn't really want the answer. Bryce didn't want to cause problems for Nick and his family. "Is she coming around at all?"

He heard Nick spit, rinse his mouth, and then he walked out in a pair of jeans and nothing else. Bryce still couldn't get over how sexy he found the man. He wanted to lick every inch of his bare chest. "Yeah…yeah, I think so. It'll be okay. She's my mom. When she sees what you mean to me, she's got to come around."

Bryce really fucking hoped so. Nick bent and kissed him. "I need to get going. I'll see you tonight."

Bryce watched as Nick finished getting dressed and then they said their goodbyes.

After getting ready himself, Bryce went for a ride on his bike. The whole time he couldn't get Nick's words out of his head...the fact that he thought she was coming around. That she had to accept it eventually because of what Bryce meant to Nick.

Bryce wasn't sure when he made the decision, but he drove straight to his mom's house. He wasn't even sure what the hell he planned to do here, but Bryce got off his bike, removed his helmet and then went to the door. "Ma?" He knocked while opening the door enough to stick his head in. "You around?" They talked often, but he hadn't seen her since the day he and Nick came to dinner.

"I'm in the kitchen!" she called back, and Bryce walked into the room. He sat at the bar while his mom stood at the sink, washing dishes. "Hey. What are you up to?" There was a slight distance in her voice. Before the past couple of months, his mom never would have sounded that way when she spoke to him.

"Coming to see you... I miss you, Ma."

She turned to look at him with the same brown eyes that Bryce had. Only this time they were filled with something he didn't often see from his mom: Guilt. "I'm right here, Bryce. Always. I know things have been tense between us, but you're my son. My baby. I'll always love you, and I'll always be right here."

He knew that. He did, but he still needed to hear it.

Bryce leaned forward, resting his elbows on the counter. "We went to see Nick's mom about six weeks ago. It was right after we had dinner here. She...she said she couldn't accept me. She loves Nick, and she won't turn her back on him, but she can't accept me. She told him he has to pretend I don't exist when she talks to him. She wants to know nothing about me, because she'll never be okay with Nick and me together."

Bryce slid his hand to the back of his head, rubbing it, before sliding it to rest on the back of his neck.

"She said what? That woman better watch whose son she's talking about that way!"

There was the mom he knew, the one who stuck up for her boys and believed in them no matter what.

"Is that...you don't think I feel the same way, do you? I never meant to hurt you. If you're serious about Nick, he'll be a part of this family. I didn't..." she shook her head. "I've been terrible. I was hurt. Angry. Maybe even pouting a little bit because I really wanted you to give me grandbabies with Christi. But Bryce, I would have come around. I already have. It wasn't your father you got your stubbornness from."

"I know, Ma." And he did. "I lied to you. Not for a day, or a week, either. For a long time. I get it. This is different. Nick wanted to walk away from her. He was so pissed, but I couldn't let him do that. How could I take him away from his family? It would have killed us. It would have killed him. I just..." Bryce shrugged. "I want him happy. His birthday is at the end of this month, and I just keep thinking about how it'll go. How he's going to take having to spend time with me and his family separately. But he has to go. They're his family. He said he thinks she's coming around; maybe he's right."

"This is where you would have given up before...where you would have walked away."

"There's no walking away from him, Ma. He's it for me."

When he looked up again, he saw that his mom was crying. She had a shaky hand over her mouth as she looked at him, a broken heart in her eyes. "You really do love him, don't you?" Her voice trembled as much as her hand.

Bryce gave her a sad smile. "So much it hurts. Hell, we never really do much of anything, except work and spend time together; still, I don't think I knew what living was until I met him. Just looking at him makes me happy. Nick was an automatic with me, just like when I fell in love with bikes. I waited to find my passion, what I wanted for the rest of my life, and it's the same with him. I knew it was right when I met him."

His mom rounded the counter and threw her arms around him. She buried her face in his neck and cried. "I'm sorry. I'm so sorry, Bryce. I've been a terrible mother. I should have believed in you. Don't you dare think there is anything wrong with your love for Nick. If his mom can't see it..." She combination cried/laughed now. "Well, being honest, fuck her."

Bryce squeezed her tighter. "Don't say that in front of Nick. And I love you. You're a great mom. I get it. I understand why you were leery."

He held her while she continued to cry. A few minutes later, she pulled back and Bryce asked, "What do I do, Ma? I love him. I want him happy. I want them to see what he means to me... if they see, they have to understand, don't they?"

"I would hope so. Unfortunately, the world doesn't always work that way. If Nick said he thinks she's coming around, maybe she is. All you can do is show her how much you love him. If she can't see how incredible you are, how incredible you both are, then it's her loss."

Bryce couldn't accept the fact that she might not come around. He would do everything in his power to change her mind.

An hour later, Bryce's motorcycle sat in front of Nick's mom's house. This was probably a big fucking mistake, but then, Bryce never let anything hold him back before, and he didn't plan to start now. He wanted Nick to have his family. He'd do whatever it took to make that happen.

He knocked three times before the door opened. "You have some nerve coming here," Mona started in on him the second she saw him. "Not only did you put crazy thoughts into my son's head, but you turned him against me!"

Huh? What was she talking about? Bryce's stomach rolled with uncertainty but he ignored it. "I'm not sure what you mean, ma'am. I'm not trying to turn Nick against you. I...I love him. That's why I'm here. His birthday is coming and—"

"And he hasn't spoken to me once since the two of you left this house! He ignores all of my phone calls, and he hasn't called me once."

Bryce squeezed his eyes closed. He was going to fucking kill Nick. This whole time he'd let Bryce believe that they were still talking, but he'd turned his back on his family...for Bryce. Bryce wouldn't let Nick take the blame for it, though, even if that meant she hated him more.

"I'm sorry about that. It was wrong of me, but I love him. I love him so much, and I was afraid to lose him. I promise you, I see more clearly now. What I did was wrong, but please don't take it out on Nick. He misses you. He loves you. We're going to have a get together at the house for his birthday. My family will all be there. It would mean the world to us if you, your daughters and their families could come. It'll be at three o'clock, on the day of his birthday. We're lucky it landed on a Sunday," he laughed, hoping to keep the mood light.

"Don't try to play me, son. I see you for who you are. You try to take my son away from me, and then come here pretending to be the good guy. I don't believe a word of it. What you've done to him...that's not the boy my husband and I raised. You took him away from us!"

Bryce felt his heart start to crumble. Maybe they saw it that way, but he couldn't. Part of him did blame himself for what was going on now, but when he looked at what he and Nick had, he knew it wasn't a mistake.

"I'm sorry you feel that way. If you change your mind, you're welcome to come. And if you think there's something wrong with the man your son is, then you don't know him. He's the best man I know."

With that, Bryce turned and walked away. He couldn't believe Nick had lied to him about this...couldn't believe Nick would risk losing his family for Bryce. And Bryce couldn't even tell him he knew. Not yet. Because if he did, Nick would know he came here today.

CHAPTER FORTY-TWO

Nick lay beneath a sweaty Bryce in their bed. He called it theirs now. It didn't matter that Bryce had one next door.

"It's after midnight. Happy birthday. That was your birthday fuck. That'll be our new tradition. I'll fuck you senseless on every one of your birthdays."

Nick shook his head with a smile on his lips. "Is that the only time you're going to fuck me? On my birthday? And is that all I get?"

"What? My magic dick isn't enough for you?" Bryce teased.

Nick cupped his ass. "It's more than enough. Your dick, your ass. I want it all."

"Good. Then I'll fuck you with it every day if you want. By the way, you're taking the day off work tomorrow."

Nick looked at him even though it was too dark to really see him. "I can't take off at the last minute."

"You're not. Everyone knew but you. I'm a fucking perfect boyfriend. I went and talked to them. That Henry guy is going in for you.

There's a shit ton of meat marinating at Christi's. She'll bring it over. My mom is making her famous potato salad—it's not as good as your potatoes, but they're a close second."

Nick cupped the back of Bryce's head, threading his fingers through his hair. "You did all that for me?" Bryce had planned a party for him. Bryce's family was coming. Georgina had called him a couple of weeks back to apologize for her behavior, and to let Nick know that it was never about him. She was happy to have Nick as a part of their family. It meant the world to him, almost made him pick up the phone and call his own mom, but he couldn't. Not if she wouldn't accept Bryce.

"I did. I want you to have everything."

"I do," Nick replied easily. Still...there was a part of him who wished, who hoped, that he could have just a little bit more. He wanted his family.

Karrie would come, if he asked. He knew that. He'd confided in her often lately. She enjoyed hearing how happy Nick was with Bryce. Erin and Michelle would probably come, too. Nick had never spent a birthday away from his family.

"Well, yeah, you have me."

Nick chuckled, but didn't really feel it. He missed them, missed them so fucking much he could hardly stand it. But he wouldn't give in, either. As much as he wanted to, he knew he couldn't invite his sisters. The last thing he wanted was to cause a rift between them and his mom. And it would, too.

"You okay, baby?" Bryce ran a hand through the hair on his chest.

"A little sad, but I'm okay. Thank you...for tomorrow. It's perfect."

"It hasn't happened yet."

"It's still perfect."

***

"You're not supposed to be the one to come out and help me, hot neighbor Nick. It's your birthday!" Christi said to him when Nick came out to help her get things out of the car.

"Stop calling my boyfriend that."

"You're right. I'm sorry. I don't know what I was thinking! You're not supposed to help, hot live-in boyfriend, Nick. It's your birthday."

Bryce ruffled her hair like she was a kid and Christi yelled at him. Nick loved watching the two of them together. They were about as close as two people could be, he thought. But it wasn't romantic. Anyone could see that.

"I can't believe you're not going to let me cook!" Nick said to Bryce when they got inside. They had their new tables out back, and the grill ready to get going. The weather would change soon, so it was nice to take advantage while they could.

"It's your birthday."

"So? I'm a chef. It's what I do."

"Yes, but all I can do is barbeque. This way, I cook for you at least once in a while."

The three of them had a beer, and a few minutes later there was a knock on the door. "Come in!" Bryce called out.

Mitch, Abbey, Jamie, and Hope came in. "Hey, you guys. Thanks for having us," Abbey said before hugging Nick.

"Of course. We're glad you could come."

Hope hugged him next. "Happy birthday."

"Thank you."

Nick shook Mitch's, then Jamie's, hands, who both wished him a happy birthday. They all grabbed drinks before there was another knock.

"Come in!" Bryce called again, leaning against the counter in the kitchen.

The door opened, and Georgina and William came in. Nervous, Nick pushed off the counter and walked over to them. Bryce was right behind him. "Thank you for coming."

Nick hugged Georgina, who squeezed him as tightly as his own mom used to. "Happy birthday, Nick. We're so honored to be a part of your day."

Her words made his heart both ache and soar at the same time. They accepted him and Bryce, and while that meant so fucking much to him, it made him miss his own family even more.

"We're honored to have you here."

He shook William's hand, and then they realized there definitely wasn't enough room in the house for the whole Tanner family plus Nick and Christi. They made their way into the backyard.

Bryce put on some music and got everyone drinks. Nick watched Christi and Bryce tease everyone. Watched Jamie give them shit every once in a while as well, while Mitch shook his head like his family was crazy. Hope and Abbey spent a lot of time chatting with Georgina and Christi. Bryce started the grill a little while later, adding the meat when the charcoal was ready. At least Bryce didn't cook on propane. The chef in him would go crazy at that. If Nick grilled, he did it right. What was the point without the smoky, charcoal taste?

There were a lot of laughs, conversation…and love.

These were wonderful people. He felt lucky to be a part of them.

Nick turned and went into the kitchen. He checked on the beans Hope brought over in the slow cooker. When the door opened, he expected it to be Bryce, but he turned to see Georgina.

"They smell good," she said.

"They do," Nick replied.

She walked over and stood beside him. "I didn't see it at first… Bryce is good at looking happy. Maybe he always thought he was, but when I see him now, the way he walks, talks, smiles, and looks at you…he wasn't happy before. He is now. You gave my son something no one else could. I thought you should know that."

"Thank you." Nick reached out and gave her hand a gentle squeeze. "He gives me the same thing. I don't know what I would do without him." He had to remind himself it wasn't his or Bryce's fault if his family couldn't see that.

"What are you guys doing in here?" Bryce walked inside.

"Talking about how big a handful you are. Now, excuse me. I need to go get something from the car." Georgina walked out the front door just as Bryce's arms slid around Nick's shoulders. Nick wrapped his arm around Bryce's waist.

"Thank you," Nick said.

"Nothing to thank me for. Are you okay?"

He nodded. "It hurts. I miss them, but I'm okay." Maybe he should have tried. Maybe he should have invited them.

"They love you, Nick. They'll come around."

Nick should have invited his sisters, at least. Maybe that would have helped. But he'd tried Karrie once and hadn't gotten ahold of her, and he hadn't tried again.

Bryce pulled him close, pressing a soft kiss to his lips. As he did, the front door opened again and Georgina said, "There's someone here for you, Nick."

He turned to the door to see his mom walk in...followed by Karrie, her husband and their kids, then Erin, her husband and their kids. He looked, waiting for Michelle, but Erin closed the door.

"I'm sorry we're late," Karrie said. "Happy birthday, Nick-o."

Nick couldn't think. Couldn't move. Couldn't fucking breathe. Bryce had done this. He knew it. He needed to say something, yet nothing would come out. Bryce had done this for him, and they'd come.

"Here, let me take your things." Bryce moved toward them. "Thanks for coming. And we're really kick-back, so the timing is just fine."

Move! Nick told himself, then he finally did. He walked into the living room where Bryce stood with his family.

"Aren't you going to introduce us?" Karrie asked.

"Oh, yeah." Nick shook his head. He was fucking losing it. "This is Bryce. Bryce, this is my oldest sister, Karrie, and her husband Eric. Behind her is Erin and Dave. You've met my mom, and all these little rugrats are—"

"Uncle Nick! Uncle Nick!" The kids bulldozed him before he could introduce them. He heard Bryce welcoming them all as a little voice asked, "Who's Bryce? Is he your friend?"

Nick shot his gaze up to Erin. He didn't know how to answer that. What they'd told the kids, or if they'd want him to keep the truth hidden.

"Remember what we talked about?" Erin said. "Uncle Nick loves Bryce the way I love Daddy."

In that moment, everything was okay. It was more than that. Just like Bryce said, it was perfect—or as close to as he could get.

"Cool," was the only reply the kids gave.

"Do you all want to go out and play? There's a ball and a few things out back. You need toys. We should get you some toys here, Bryce," Georgina said, and even Nick could tell she was in heaven with little kids running around. She led them all out back.

"Michelle?" Nick asked Karrie when he stood.

"She wanted to come. It's not that she didn't. She's okay with it all, but Ken…he wouldn't let her. He's worried about the kids. He thinks… well, you know how he is." Karrie wrapped her arms around him and hugged him.

Nick nodded. He did know. He loved her and would miss her, but he did know how Ken was. That's the way life went sometimes. It took some people longer to come around—if they came around at all. He had to be happy with what he had, and he was.

"Thank you, for being here for me, Karrie. For the phone calls and everything else. I appreciate it," he whispered into her ear.

"You're my brother. I'll always be here for you."

Nick pulled away and eyed his mom. She hung toward the back, looking obviously uncomfortable. "Can you show everyone out back, Bryce?" Nick asked him.

"Yeah, yeah I can." He squeezed Nick's bicep and then led everyone except his mom from the house.

"I still don't understand," she said.

He thought of how he and Bryce bonded so quickly. How close they got, how fast they fell and how real it was. He thought about the connection he felt. Hell, he even thought about Bryce's dream. "You don't have to. Maybe none of us do. Why does everything have to be so black and white? Boy or girl? Gay or straight? Why does everything have to have a reason? Maybe some things don't have reasons. Maybe they're destined to be for no other reason than the fact that they *are.*"

She nodded, looking down. "I won't pretend this will be easy for me. It's not going to happen overnight, Nick, but I'm trying. I love you, and I'm going to try."

"That's all I ask."

Finally, she looked at him again. "He really loves you. I was so angry at him when he came to see me. I was so hurt that he turned you against me, that you'd stopped calling. He apologized, but it didn't matter…then I talked to Karrie. She said you told her that you hadn't told Bryce we weren't speaking. That you felt guilty lying to him, but you felt strongly about it. That boy took the blame, risked me hating him even more because he loves you. That's what got me here today."

Nick smiled. He loved the man so damned much. He'd taken the blame for Nick. He'd gone to Nick's mom for him, too. "That's who he is. He's a good guy. The best. You'll see…and I love him. That's never going to change."

She gave him a single nod.

Nick led her outside. They all ate and chatted. He watched Bryce play football with the kids and pretend to trip or get tackled. They had a blast with him. Georgina spoke with his mom a lot, and Mitch and Eric seemed to get along well.

This was his family, his and Bryce's. None of them were perfect, but they were his, and he was happy.

"You ever lie to me again and I'll kick your ass," Bryce sat down beside Nick, where he sat away from everyone else, watching them.

"I'm sorry."

"I know."

"I love you."

"I know that, too."

They all had a long way to go. He had no doubts that Michelle loved him and supported him; she just went along with what Ken said. Maybe Ken would eventually come around, too. His mom still had to adjust, as they all did in some ways. Regardless of how he and Bryce felt, they were still new, and still had things to figure out. Loving someone and being in a relationship was never easy, but they'd do it, they'd figure it out, together.

Nick couldn't wait to keep on living his life with Bryce at his side.

EPILOGUE

There was nothing like the feel of cruising down an empty road, with nothing but the wind and the world around you. It was like flying. It was freedom.

Bryce drove. He had no idea where, but that didn't matter. The destination wasn't the point, the journey was. He took turns and explored and let his bike lead the way.

It was the perfect fucking day.

He kept going, surrounded by nothing but trees, open road and the future, until he saw something ahead of him that looked familiar.

No...it couldn't be.

He sped up, his bike heading straight for the spot he somehow knew, even though he'd never been here.

He slowed down, and stopped the bike at the crossroads. Left or right, he couldn't go straight.

"Holy shit," Nick said behind him, squeezing him tighter. He loved having Nick on his Shovelhead with him. It took a while, but he finally managed to get Nick to ride with him. Nick had said when the Shovelhead was ready, he would be, too. Bryce worked on it more often after that, and Nick helped him sometimes. When she was done, Nick kept his promise, and now here they were.

Bryce smiled. "That's not what you're supposed to say here."

"This is your dream, Bryce. This is it, isn't it?"

Yeah, it totally fucking was. He should be surprised. It wasn't every day one of your dreams came true. Somehow he wasn't surprised, though. It just fit...made everything even more right. "Yep. It's my dream. That's still not what you're supposed to say here."

Nick chuckled. "You got us lost, didn't you? I told you to ask for directions. We're fucking lost."

Bryce shook his head and smiled. Damn, he loved this man. "Think you're a funny guy, do you? Say it, Nick. You have to say it."

Nick squeezed him tighter. "It's a crossroads, Bryce. Which way are you going to go?" Nick finally repeated the lines from his dream.

"Whichever way you are," he replied. He'd do anything for his man. Go anywhere. Being with Nick was where he was supposed to be.

"You lead and I'll follow. I'm right here with you, Bryce. Always."

"Nah, I don't need to lead, we'll go together." Together, the way they'd done everything since they met. They'd changed their lives together, were happy together, fell in love with each other.

The direction they went in didn't matter. The only thing that did was the fact that they'd travel the bumpy roads, twists and turns, rises and falls by each other's sides.

"Let's go, Bryce. I want to keep riding with you. You show me the world in ways I've never seen it. Show me more." Nick's hand fisted in Bryce's jacket.

His pulse sped up. He smiled, squeezed Nick's hand, and then they rode.

THE END

Acknowledgment

I cannot thank my readers enough. I'm not quite sure how I got so blessed, but thank you for your support. Thank you for reading my books and loving my guys. It means more to me than words can ever say. I owe a huge thanks to the members of Riley's Rebels. I love our group and I look forward to chatting with you all every day! Chris and Evette, thank you for answering my questions about aneurysms. Any mistakes are my own. As always thank you to Jamie for your eyes. You are amazing. I couldn't do this without my awesome beta readers, editors and proofers. Thank you, thank you, thank you.

About the Author

Riley Hart is the girl who wears her heart on her sleeve. She's a hopeless romantic. A lover of sexy stories, passionate men, and writing about all the trouble they can get into together. If she's not writing, you'll probably find her reading.

Riley lives in California with her awesome family, who she is thankful for every day.

You can find her online at:

Twitter
@RileyHart5

Facebook
Blog
Amazon
Barnes and Noble

Other books by Riley Hart

Rock Solid Construction series:

Rock Solid

Broken Pieces series:

Broken Pieces

Full Circle

Losing Control

Blackcreek series:

Collide

Stay

Pretend

CPSIA information can be obtained
at www.ICGtesting.com
Printed in the USA
FFOW01n1406301115
19137FF

9 781515 196730